POST CARDS FROM PERIL

"Had splendid weather today—howling wind and flashes of lightning!"

"What a delightful view from my balcony—twenty-two hundred assorted gravestones!"

"Spent the morning in the sun reading—how juicy the local obituaries are!"

"Met a fascinating woman on the beach—she's been widowed five times and is on a honeymoon with her sixth victim!"

"Busy, busy, busy—the slaying just never stops!"

HAVING A WONDERFUL CRIME

(*signed*)
Alfred Hitchcock

P.S. Wish you were here!
   (And if you're one of my fans, I know you
   will be.)

HAVING A
WONDERFUL CRIME

Alfred Hitchcock

A DELL BOOK

Published by
Dell Publishing Co., Inc.
1 Dag Hammarskjold Plaza
New York, New York 10017

Dell ® TM 681510, Dell Publishing Co., Inc.

ISBN: 0-440-10677-X

Printed in the United States of America
First printing—November 1977

CONTENTS

INTRODUCTION

Arriving at a film studio one day recently for conferences with some of the executives, I came upon an old friend, an actor, who was there to read for a part. To conceal his true identity—and possibly his reputation—I shall refer to him as Fred and say that the part he was reading for was that of the Empire State Building in a remake of *King Kong*.

Be that as it may, Fred was in towering spirits. He had not worked in months, he told me, but he was supremely confident of getting the part he was to audition for. His certainty stemmed from what his horoscope had told him that morning. According to the stars, he was to "find joy and success in every aspect of life today." Being a true believer in the power of the heavenly bodies to determine the course of human affairs, he was absolutely positive that this was to be his luckiest of lucky days.

A skeptic myself, I attempted to bring Fred a little closer to earth, hoping to spare him a devastating plunge into depression if he did not get the part. I pointed out to him that with only the normal complement of eyes, two, he might have some difficulty portraying all the windows in the Empire State Building.

He was not in the least daunted. So convinced was he of the infallibility of his horoscope that he believed he could get the role even if he read for it blindfolded.

As I made my rounds, I'm afraid the talk was taken up more with chitchat about astrology than business. The executive with whom I first met—the man in charge of choosing the type face for the words "The End" at the end of the studio's films—was also a believer in the power of the stars. He showed me a chart on which he had been given instructions for every day of the year by his astrologer. On that particular day, he was to avoid contact with persons who had been anywhere near Columbus, Ohio, on August 6, 1945, the day of the bombing of Hiroshima. Not thinking, I revealed that I was one of those persons. That, of course, ended our conference. The executive dived beneath his desk, crying out "The End" and refusing to have anything further to do with me.

When I left his office, I was of the mind that astrology was merely silly. Soon, though, I was persuaded that it could be dangerous. For I learned from a friend of his that Fred had suffered a terrible personal tragedy. It seemed that his wife, whom he adored, while disposing of the morning garbage, had slipped on a soggy cornflake and fallen into the trash compacter and been reduced to the size and density of a hockey puck. I could imagine what this could do to Fred, who had been expecting the best of days. With that on his mind, he might very likely forget that his head and neck were an observation tower and fail in his portrayal of the Empire State Building.

As usually happens in such situations, coincidence followed on coincidence. The next executive with whom I met, the gentleman in charge of stampeding cattle for Westerns, was also a believer in the omnipotence of the stars. His horoscope had cautioned him to beware of mysterious strangers. Aware of my connection with mysteries and considering some of them rather strange, he decided to take no chances. He insisted on conducting our meeting from the safety of his private water closet, with the door closed between us.

The barrier made conversation almost impossible. While I tried to explain to him that I had asked for the conference in order to request that he keep his stampeding cattle off my set, a reproduction of Catherine de Medici's boudoir, he kept promising me more bulls and fewer heifers in my herd. We finally postponed the meeting until the next day, when the stars promised that mysterious strangers would be no threat to him.

Upon leaving the executive's office, I received further distressing news concerning Fred. While his wife was away at the chiropractor's, being stretched back into shape after her unfortunate encounter with the trash compacter, the house caught fire, and the firemen, in a fit of zeal, had chopped it down to the foundation. What's more, he had received a telephone call from his only daughter informing him that she had eloped with a bongo player in a rock band.

Shortly after that, I came upon Fred himself. His eyes were glazed over; he appeared to be in a state of shock. I'm afraid I acted the Dutch uncle. Instead of offering solace, I remonstrated with him for trusting his fate to the stars, pointing out to him that rather than finding joy and success in every aspect of his life that day, as his horoscope had promised, he had suffered tragedy after tragedy.

I was in error about his state, however. It was not shock I saw but euphoria. "What do you mean, tragedy?" he replied to me. "I got the part!" He was the happiest of men.

For the true believers, evidently, fortune, like beauty, is in the eye of the beholder. As Fred saw it, the stars had foretold his fate for that day with consummate accuracy. I now invite all true believers and skeptics alike to behold the spine-tingling chillers that follow, confident that both will find them to be rare beauties.

—ALFRED HITCHCOCK

A LOOK AT MOTHER NATURE

by Frank Sisk

There was not a thing about this deputy sheriff that Waxy Lustig liked. He didn't like the dirty Panama hat the old schmo was wearing, and he didn't like the klutzy way he wore it—set square on his head. A real hick, this fuzz, strictly from Lower Slobbovia.

"Up the road cheer a piece we gonna pass Spadefoot Pond," the deputy was drawling. "Off to the right cheer. More a lake than a pond."

"Oh, yeah," Waxy said from the back seat, where he was confined by handcuffs chained to a steel bar bolted to the floor. He didn't like the deputy's monotonous drawl at all, either, nor the cornball line of chatter that went with it.

"Save ole Spadefoot cheer, they's nary a body a water within a two-day drive or a two-week trot where a man can catch hisself a genuwine cutthroat trout. You have my oath on that."

"Yeah, yeah," Waxy said irritably.

The deputy shifted that sick cud of tobacco from one cheek to the other. "Big fellas, too, them cutthroat. They favor cold water, cold and runnin'. That's why they never seen this fur south save in ole Spadefoot. She fed by deep springs, I heah, and they so pure icy, a man mought freeze the knuckles off a hand if he troll it outen the boat more'n a few minutes at a time. Take my oath on that."

Waxy decided he'd like to take his yokel oath and shove it.

"But that's what make them cutthroat grow so big and frisky," the deputy drawled on. "Real cold water. Back a few weeks I hooked me a fair beauty. Weighed a smeddum over six pound gutted and scaled. Sweetest eatin' flesh a man ever set tooth to. You got my godly oath on that."

"I don't like fish," Waxy said.

"You missin' out," the deputy said. "There's ole Spadefoot now. Stretchin' out younder behind that thin stand a pines. She's all a five mile wide at her widest and ever cubic foot's as fresh and clean as the day the good Lord set her down cheer. Won't never see a prettier sight this side of paradise in a coon's age, Lustig. Which in your case means now or never. Yessuh, man, now or *never.*"

"Thank you very much," Waxy said with heavy sarcasm. "You must be working a shift for the county chamber of commerce."

The deputy's studied reply was to turn his stubbled face slowly, leftward and expectorate a globoid of tobacco juice through the open window upon the balmy morning air. This was one more thing about the shtup that Waxy didn't like—the damn chewing and spitting. Each time the crazy fool spat, which was about every four or five minutes, the breeze carried a fine spray through the open back window, flecking the left side of Waxy's face. Son of a bitch!

"Hell fire, Lustig," the deputy continued, "you ought to be downright grateful for a tour like this. Ain't ever jailbird gets a chance to enjoy Mother Nature, like this, between one cell and another. If I was in your britches, boy, I'd fill my lungs with this fine air and feast my blasted peepers on ever God-given thing in sight. I'd look at fence post, I would, and phone pole and outhouse. I'd raise my blighted eyes to the sky and count the clouds, I would. And I'd get me a lastin' sightful of the piney woods down to the last crimpin' tree and all the green grass down to the last little ole blade. Yessuh, in your britches, I'd sure hope to get me a bellyful of Mother Nature's bounty before the powers locked me up again behind cement and iron and thrun away the key."

"I'm sure as hell getting a bellyful of you, Homer," Waxy said.

"My name ain't Homer."

"Well, Clyde, then."

"Ain't Clyde, neither. Now if you was only half as smart as you think you are, Lustig, you mought have noticed when I was cuffin' you at the county jail that I wear my name pinned to the pocket of my shirt. And proud of it. Floyd T. Herrington's what it says, and that's what it's always been since I was knee-high to a weevil. Floyd T. Herrington."

"What's the T stand for—tochis?"

"Stands for Thomas is plumb what it stands for. I was christened in honor of my daddy's youngest brother who got hisself blown to smithereens over in France durin' World War Number One." The deputy meditatively masticated his cud of tobacco. "Uncle Thomas," he said after a moment. "Never so much as laid eyes on him. Never seen a picture of him, neither, and here I am bearin' his name. Funny thing how names come about."

"Funny as a crutch."

"Take ole Spadefoot. As a tyke, I figgered it was named after an Injun tribe. Injun names was on so many watery places cheerabouts—Tallahatchie, Tangipahoa, Natchez, Yazoo—a tyke was almost bounden to figger any wet spot that wasn't called Smith or Jones must of come down from the Injuns. Anyhoo, that was my way of thinkin' back then."

"Good thinking, Floyd."

"My Daddy was a great one for spinnin' Injun yarns. In his youth, he wandered some, and he run into all sorts of folk, includin' northern Injuns. I heard him tell of Flathead and Blackfoot before I knew shot from Shinola. The way I see, I must a reckoned the Spadefoot was Southern cousins of the Blackfoot. That's how fur from the truth a tyke's idee can take him. They wasn't· never no Spadefoot Injuns cheerabouts. I know that now. They never was no such tribe as Spadefoot. Matter fact, what this body a water is named after—" the deputy chewed and spat "—it's named after the little ole spadefoot frog. Yessuh, the little ole spadefoot frog."

"Did the county trust you with lunch money?" Waxy asked.

"Warty little cuss craves sand. Hunkers down under it. Happy with a foot a sand on his back. Won't come out for air save at night. Or to breed. But won't breed worth a damn lessen it's rainin' like the pure start of a flood. My daddy use to say you can tell when a spadefoot's right smart of its kind when it got brains enough to go *out* in the rain. My daddy had a comical turn to him."

"He should of been in pictures," Waxy said.

"My daddy's wit was dry," the deputy said.

"Speaking of dry, Floyd," Waxy said, "I haven't had so much as a drink of water since daybreak, and I'm hungry, too. Are we going to stop somewhere for lunch?"

"Appetite," the deputy said. "That's one damn thing you killers got in common. Eat like hogs, all of you."

"Who said I'm a killer?"

"I recollect the case of Stevie Harris. You recollect Stevie, don't you?"

"Never heard of him."

"Suppose not. Goes back a spell when they was still hangin' killers in this state. Well, young Stevie Harris caught his gal—name of Mary Jane Lukens—in a fiddlin' position with a Creole dishwasher behind the revival tent at a church picnic. Snatched up a cleaver that was somehow layin' to hand and clove that pretty gal damn near into two separate sections, and then he hacked off the better part of the Creole's left arm and was aimin' at vital parts just as some members of the congregation pitched in and got the lad under control. Creole died a while later. Loss a blood. Stevie mought have gone to jail for a year or two iffen he had been a proper sort, but he done more than his share of drinkin' and brawlin' and bustin' the wrong jaws cheerabouts, and so they tried him first degree for splittin' up pretty Mary Jane and found him guilty. Well, suh, from the day he was sentenced till the day his neck was stretched, ole Stevie Harris begun to pack away the vittles like eatin' was goin' out a style, which it sure as Satan was in his particular case. In the sixty day or so that come between judge and hangman, Stevie added ninety-two pound to his natural weight. You got my oath on that. Ninety-two pound. I was the one walked him to the scales the last night of his life. Hangman had to switch to a stouter rope than the one he plan to use in the first place."

"Don't you ever stop?" Waxy asked.

"Nervous habit, eatin' like Stevie Harris did," the deputy said. "Leastwise that's what Doc Volney said. Some folks eat like all get-out when they nervous. Some caint swalley so much as a glass a water."

Waxy moaned as if in pain.

For the next five minutes, the deputy drove in silence. He was a sedately slow driver, moving along this secondary highway a few miles per hour under the posted speed limit of fifty. Traffic was scant. Waxy studied the back of the deputy's leathern neck with an itchy feeling of repugnance. Three creases cut across it, pocked and bristly. Something about this scrawny neck set Waxy's stomach rumbling on its own emptiness.

"Well, are we going to have lunch or not?" he finally asked.

"Right soon now," the deputy said. "I'm gettin' a mite hungry myself."

"What's right soon mean?"

"It means noon. Leastwise I figger on noon. Noon's when I count on reachin' the state line. They's a fair to middlin' café there. Calhoun's Place. Straddles the border. Calhoun barbecues a real tasty rib. You partial to barbecue ribs, Lustig?"

"I won't say no to anything. How long before we reach this place?"

"Fifteen, twenty minutes. Why, man, you ought to know that. You ain't exactly a stranger to these parts."

"Meaning what?

"You been here before."

"It's possible."

"Hell fire, man, it's a pure fact."

"If you say so, Floyd," Waxy said wearily.

"You just after hearin' me say so."

"Well, you hayshakers may be able to tell one bush from another, but they all look alike to me."

"You mought sharpen up your look."

"I mought," Waxy said.

The road was taking a wide curve across an expanse of marshland. Rearing from the ooze, tall and feathery, were the omnipresent cypress trees. On higher ground beyond them to the right flourished a contrasting growth—white oak and black gum—but Waxy, whose recognition of local flora was limited almost solely to the cypress, didn't know what it was. Still, he began to find the immediate scene vaguely familiar and somehow depressing. Yes, he might have been here once before, just passing through. Since migrating south from Cleveland ten years earlier, he had passed through dozens of similarly dismal countrysides, and they were all easy to forget. Waxy stirred uneasily.

"You recollectin' some little thing?" the deputy asked.

Waxy deigned not to reply. He listened glumly to his growling stomach.

"Use to hunt in this here region a few year back,"

the deputy went on. "Back up in the high ground there midst the black gum and white oak. Coon and possum. And I bagged me a bobcat once. They's black bear up there, too. You never find a critter more quarrelsome than a full-grown black bear. But I had me a good ole hound in them days, best hound a man ever had, and he weren't afeard of black bear or grizzly. He treed that there bobcat I bagged. Yessuh. Raymond, I called him. After another ole hound I owned back in my beardless days. But this here Raymond I speakin' of now, he the sort of hound a man finds once in his whole damn life." The deputy's drawl was assuming a slightly rhapsodic lilt. "He weren't much to look at, mind. He was tan cheer, brown there, with sprinklins of black and white. Sad-eye ole boy, long-hangin' ears. He sure didn't have no fancy pedigree. He had a goodly mixture of stray dog bred into him, ole Raymond did—everythin' bred into him except quit. He was the most hang-on dog I ever did see. He pick up a scent, and nothin' on God's green earth shooken him off it. I take my oath. And when ole Raymond spoke up, you could hear that bayin' two mile away."

Waxy was on the verge of dozing off.

"Now here's a place you mought recollect right well," the deputy said.

Waxy opened his eyes.

The car was slowing down. To the left across the road a gap-toothed picket fence, buckling and sagging, ran half the length of a black-dirt yard, terminating at a gateless gatepost. Several bantam hens were pecking at the barren ground behind the fence. The one-story frame house, once white, was a watery gray with a wide streak of brown running through it at one corner from a rust-eaten rain gutter. Off to the rear of the house stood an unpainted clapboard shed, listing slightly, its open door hanging by a single hinge. Two huge hogs nosed side by side in a nearby wooden trough. Walking toward them was a boy in faded blue overalls, carrying a bucket and now looking at the car slowly passing by.

Waxy recognized the place immediately, although it had deteriorated a hell of a lot since the one and only time he'd seen it before; must've been about three years ago.

The deputy must have observed the expression on his face through the rearview mirror because he said, "Reckoned you mought find a bad memory or two cheer."

Waxy suddenly experienced an intimation of danger—he didn't know why. "These back-country shacks look all the same to me," he said.

"Nossuh, this little ole shack is some different."

"Yeah? How come?"

"Leastwise, to my way a thinkin' this ole shack is some different. This ole shack belong to a gemmun name Mister Ormond Woodruff until he die a few year back. He kept the place trim so long as they was a breath a life in him, Mister Ormond Woodruff did. Not like the trash what's livin' cheer now. Nossuh, Mister Ormond Woodruff was as fine an ole gemmun as ever walk God's green earth. I don't suppose a short-memory murderer like you'd recollect his name at all."

"That's the second time you've called me a killer," Waxy said. "Lay off, man. I never killed anybody in my life."

"You just a mite forgetful, Lustig. Why you think they want you in New Orleans if it ain't for murder?"

"I'm testifying in a trial. I'm a witness for the prosecution."

"Why, sure you are. And the reason you goin' to be such a good witness, Lustig, is you were part of the gang that robbed that there bank in New Orleans and killed the guard."

"I didn't pull the trigger," Waxy said.

"Maybe not that time," the deputy said. "But I warrant you pull the trigger many a time when nobody was lookin'. I take an oath on that."

"You and your oath can take a flying—"

Heedless of any voice but his own, the deputy plodded on. "Mister Ormond Woodruff, he sized up you and your pardner good and careful the night you busted into his abode and began your roughhouse. He tooken the measure of both you yella buggers inch by inch, and don't you never forget it."

"We hardly laid a hand on the old man," Waxy said, a plaintive note in his voice.

"Yessuh, and Doc Volney hardly had to take more'n ten stitches in the side of Mister Ormond Woodruff's head."

"He went for a shotgun, man."

"Why, sure he did. Any gemmun worth his salt'll go for a shotgun when a couple sons a bitches break into his abode and demand service. Yessuh, Lustig."

"All we wanted was something to drink, something to eat. We'd been on the run for three days."

"You should of applied for welfare, Lustig. Anyhoo, Mister Ormond Woodruff give us a detailed description of his assailants. He got your gold tooth into it. And that streak of white runnin' through your black hair like maybe they's a drop of albino blood somewhere. And he heard your pardner call you Waxy and you call him Cosmo. So I reckon one of the ones you go to New Orleans to testify against ain't nobody else save your ole pardner Cosmo Sienna. I swear you killers stick as close together as chaff in a high wind."

"You got killers on the brain, Floyd."

"I know what I know."

"Yeah, and not much else."

"One damn thing I know, Lustig, it was you shot the dog. Mister Ormond Woodruff saw you with the pistol in your hand."

"The dog?"

"Yessuh, the dog what begun barkin' soon as you

trash set foot on Mister Ormond Woodruff's property. You shot that dog down in cold blood."

Waxy blanched at the rekindled memory. He could see the dog coming around the house like an express train. Barking like mad. Then, when it stopped barking, he could see its long white fangs gleaming from the light in a front window. "Hell, man, I shot that crazy dog in self-defense. It was ready to tear us apart."

"You was trespassin', and they's nothin' Raymond hated more'n trespassers."

"Raymond?"

"Yessuh, Lustig, that was my ole hound Raymond you done killed. Mister Woodruff was kindly boardin' Raymond whilst I had a broken leg on the mend. And a yella weasel like you come down the pike and shoot ole Raymond in his prime. You couldn't done none worse iffen you shot my best friend."

"Sorry about that," Waxy said. "Maybe I should have just stood there and let the dog tear out my throat."

"You should a stood wherever in hell you come from," the deputy said, his drawl taking a cold edge.

This cat is a bloody weirdo, Waxy thought.

A few moments later, he saw up ahead a rambling red structure underneath an enormous sign that advertised CALHOUN'S: *Each Morsel A Memory.* He breathed a big sigh of relief.

The deputy piloted the cruiser into the gravel parking lot and headed it for a space beside a tan sedan with a heavy antenna rising from the trunk. In the front seat were two middle-aged men in flowered sport shirts and Panama hats. These hats, Waxy noted, were in somewhat better condition than that worn by the country clown.

The men got out of the sedan, their holstered revolvers proclaiming them fuzz in mufti, and shook hands with the deputy. Papers were exchanged with a little conversation.

Finally, the deputy opened the cruiser door nearest Waxy and unlocked him from the chain attached to the floor bar.

"We goin' tie on the feedbag now," the deputy said. "Then these New Orleans detectives takin' you on from cheer."

"That's the best news I've heard all day," Waxy said.

Grabbing him powerfully above the right elbow, the deputy assisted him, still handcuffed, from the back seat and walked him briskly toward the restaurant entrance. The detectives brought up the rear.

Inside, the deputy asked a gray-haired woman, whom he addressed as "Miz Ellen," for "a table kinda off by its lonesome," and she smiled understandingly and ushered them to a far corner of a room that had only a few customers.

While the detectives were seating themselves, the deputy said in a stage whisper to Waxy, "You got a call from Mother Nature, man, this the time to speak up."

At first, Waxy didn't understand what the bulbenik was driving at.

"The men's room," the deputy said.

"Oh, yeah, sure," Waxy said. "I could use it."

"Order me a bottle beer," the deputy told the detectives.

In the men's room, Waxy said, "I've got to use one of the stalls, Floyd. It would help without the handcuffs."

"Why, sure," the deputy said, producing a key, "but don't you try nothin' fancy."

From within the stall Waxy began to hear a series of sounds: the flushing of a urinal, water splashing in a sink, the releasing click of a paper towel from its dispenser.

Then he heard the deputy's tiresome drawl. "I goin' to wait on you outside the door, Lustig. Don't you tarry none, now."

As soon as he heard the door close, Waxy emerged

swiftly from the stall and looked for a way out. There was a single narrow window in the room, and it was barred. Waxy realized many restaurateurs barred rest-room windows to prevent deadbeats from leaving the premises that way after a hearty session with food and drink. He also realized that such bars over the years, by a process of metal corrosion and wood rot, often become laughably loose in their fittings; and these bars, to judge from the streaks of rust, just might be ready for manual removal.

There were two of them about 12 inches apart. With both hands, he seized one of them and shook it. It moved but just a perceptible fraction of an inch. He twisted it. It turned easily in its fittings, but that's all it was going to do.

He took hold of the other bar without much hope and gave it a mighty two-handed tug. It came away from its upper and lower moorings with a sharp squeal. He held his breath. Had that dumb deputy heard the sound? The door remained imperturbably shut. Good.

Waxy measured the available window space with his eyes. About 24 inches. Not too tight a squeeze sidewise for a man who prided himself on a 32-inch waist.

Prior to making his wriggling exit, he began to place the iron bar on the floor, and then he thought better of it. It might serve as a handy weapon. He shoved it across the windowsill and let it fall to the ground below. In less than a minute he was outside himself—outside and free.

Retrieving the bar, he surveyed the immediate prospect. He was at the rear of the place. Farther to the rear were thickets and marshland. That obviously was not the sensible way to go. The corner to his right, if his sense of direction was reliable, led to the parking lot. That's where mobility was. Once in the parking lot, he would be able to move out a car whether the ignition key was present or not. Then he remembered that the stupid deputy hadn't bothered to remove the keys to the cruiser ignition. Wonderful. Perfect.

Grinning wolfishly at his good luck, Waxy began to walk rapidly toward the restaurant's rear corner. As he rounded it, he came face to face with the deputy, who was also grinning.

"Hell fire," the deputy said, "if I ain't caught Waxy Lustig in a flat foot attempt to escape official custody."

Waxy came to a dead stop and looked fearfully at the revolver that was being leveled at him. Its barrel appeared to be as big as a cannon's.

"Yessuh," the deputy said, "it sure do warm the cockles of my heart to catch a murderin' son of a bitch like you dead to rights."

"I'm not trying to escape," Waxy said.

"Course not. You just takin' a long hike. And whilst you about it, you ready to attack a sworn deputy sheriff with an iron bar. That's what you doin', Lustig."

"Hey, man. I surrender. Here, take the damn bar. I don't want it."

"But I want you to have it," the deputy said. "Why I rid down cheer day before yesterday and personally hacksawed that there bar. So I want you to have it as kind a farewell present from me and ole Raymond."

The deputy's eyes were as chillingly gray as ice on a sunless winter day. Waxy didn't like those eyes at all—but he didn't have to look at them long.

THE MOONLIGHTER

by James Holding

It's funny how some little thing like a word or a movement can suddenly bring alive again in your mind an incident from your past that you haven't even thought of for years. That's what happened when I paid the bald, paunchy bartender for my Negroni.

With an hour to kill in a strange town, I dropped into a place near the railroad station called Gallagher's Tavern. It was empty. At two-thirty in the afternoon, there wasn't a soul in the joint aside from me and the bald bartender. I sat up on a bar stool and ordered a Negroni.

"A Negroni," he confirmed, giving it an upward inflection that could have been contempt. He began to mix it for me quite adeptly.

I suppose it isn't the commonest drink in the world, a Negroni, but it's my favorite—ever since I heard it referred to somewhere as "a velvet hammer." I like the phrase, even if I'm not crazy about the flavor. I'm an admirer of phrases. In fact, I much prefer alliteration to alcohol, expressive English to expensive Scotch. Most of my friends call me "Professor" Carmichael for that reason. I talk like a professor, they say. I don't really, but they think I do, which comes to the same thing. I'm not a bona-fide professor, of course; more like a student—of the fast and easy buck.

But the bartender didn't know anything about that. He just thought I was some kind of a nut for ordering a Negroni at two-thirty in the afternoon.

I took a sip and looked around the tavern. It was a crummy place, shabby and depressing, but I only wanted to kill an hour.

When I turned back to the bartender, he was looking at me. "That'll be sixty-five cents," he said.

I was surprised. "I just may have another," I said. "You want me to pay you drink by drink?"

"If you don't mind," he said. "It's a rule of the house. With a clientele like mine, I can't be too careful."

I happened to be in funds, so I handed him a twenty-dollar bill with a careless gesture.

He took it and turned toward his cash register on the back bar. Then he made one of those little unexpected movements I mentioned a moment ago. He held my twenty-dollar bill under the electric droplight behind the bar and took a good long look at it, front and back. His action brought vividly back to me, even after fifteen years, my first timid venture into, well, call it crime.

"What's the matter?" I said, amused. "Is that a rule of the house, too? I can assure you the twenty is perfectly good."

He nodded and rang the register. "It's legit," he agreed. Without apology, he placed my change before me on the bar.

Now my memories, stirred up by the fellow, were rushing through my mind with the warm nostalgia a middle-aged libertine must feel for his first teen-age romance. I said to the fat bartender, "What's your name?"

"Bothwell." For the first time, he allowed a touch of emotion to enter his voice. "Crazy name for a bartender, isn't it?"

"Not at all. It's a solid, rather imaginative name, it seems to me. Perhaps your folks had a liking for Mary Queen of Scots?"

This erudite reference went over his head. "I wouldn't know," he said. "I never knew them."

I clicked my tongue. He began to polish an old fashioned glass with a soiled rag. "You know, Bothwell," I said tentatively, "what you just did with my twenty puts me in mind of something that happened to a friend of mine some years ago."

He raised one eyebrow. "Oh?"

"Yes. Fellow named Hank. He's dead now." I felt an almost overpowering urge to talk about it. The fellow's name wasn't Hank. Nor was he dead. He was actually a man named Carmichael, currently killing an hour in a strange town. "Would you care to hear about it?"

Bothwell was not an eager audience. "Suit yourself."

"Well," I said, "to judge from your recent reaction to my twenty-dollar bill, you can distinguish a counterfeit bill from a good one." I decided to show off a little. "But do you know the approximate total of counterfeit U.S. bills produced in 1945, say, when World War II was ending?"

Bothwell shook his head.

"A mere $59,000. And do you know that this modest production of counterfeit money swelled to $2,200,000 in fiscal 1961?"

Bothwell grunted. I couldn't tell whether he was bored or impressed by my knowledge.

I went on, "And do you know, further, that counterfeit output has now reached the rather staggering total of over four million dollars a year? Over four million dollars!"

"What are you," Bothwell said, wiping off the bar with the same soiled rag he had used on the old fashioned glass, "a Fed?" He said it with the air of a man who doesn't care much either way.

I laughed. "No. I pick up a lot of odd information in my job, though."

I expected him to show a little interest in what my job was, but he didn't. So I trotted out another interest stimulator. "Back during the Civil War, do you realize that thirty-three percent of all the notes issued by our state banks were believed to be counterfeit?"

Bothwell grunted again. So I gave him the story starter. "And did you know, Bothwell, that the rapid advance of technology in the printing industry has made counterfeiting so simple that even a twenty-two-year-old kid, still wet behind the ears, can successfully engage in it, given the proper opportunity and the necessary initiative?"

"Now that," said Bothwell, "I didn't know."

"Neither did my friend Hank," I said, "until he saw it in the *Financial Journal* one day while reading over the shoulder of a man in the subway."

I thought this a rather provocative introduction to the story. Bothwell, however, seemed unmoved. He raised his other eyebrow at me, that was all.

I went on, anyhow. "My friend Hank was very young in those days, twenty-two. He was holding down his first job after graduating from Dartmouth, a very menial job; messenger boy, printer's devil, boy-of-all-work in a printing plant. It was a university press, the printing establishment of a famous college, as it happens. Hank started at the bottom, but he intended to work up as fast as possible to the top, so he read extensively in the field of printing and studied the various printing processes diligently. He asked his boss, the plant manager, a fellow named Colbaugh, as many technical questions about printing and plant operations as chance allowed, and he observed, with an unusually keen eye, how the craftsmen in the plant went about their various jobs. Thus, despite the fact that he served in a very minor capacity indeed, he soon won the attention and approval of the plant manager, Colbaugh."

"That figures," said Bothwell. I smiled. He was at least listening now, and I still had half an hour to kill.

"Yes," I said. "Hank was accorded a sign of this approval one evening. Colbaugh invited him to his home to show him his collection of coins, something Colbaugh had never done before for any six-month neophyte in the plant. Colbaugh was quite a collector. He specialized in nickels, for some reason not clear to Hank. Hank couldn't fail to notice, though, the almost avuncular attachment—there was no other phrase that described the old boy's attitude so aptly—to a batch of perfectly ordinary old nickels whose purchasing power was so low as to be well beneath the notice of an ambitious lad like Hank. Nevertheless, Hank pretended an interest in Colbaugh's hobby out of politeness, and Colbaugh went into considerable detail about one particular coin he desperately wanted in his collection: some nonsense about a buffalo nickel with only three legs. Hank paid very little attention until Colbaugh casually remarked that the coin would cost him in the neighborhood of three hundred and sixty dollars to acquire because of its rarity."

I paused, waiting for Bothwell to say something, to evince some surprise, perhaps, at the high price of old coins. He put down his rag, braced himself on both stiff arms against the bar, and looked at me. He was interested, obviously. But he said nothing.

"'Three hundred and sixty dollars!' Hank said to Colbaugh in amazement. 'You mean one little five-cent nickel is worth that much?' Colbaugh said sure, and that he had paid Goodblood & Co., his coin dealer, a lot more than that for some of the coins in his collection. Hank went home to his rented room on the West Side that evening quite impressed. And it was the very next morning, on his way to work on the subway, that Hank happened to read that article in the *Financial Journal* I told you about, Bothwell."

After asking my permission with his eyebrows, Bothwell lit a cigarette. He exhaled a long plume of smoke and said, "I was wondering when you'd get back to that."

He went up a notch in my estimation at once. He seemed to have at least a rudimentary appreciation of how a competent story teller constructs a yarn. I nodded and took another sip of my Negroni.

"As I told you, Bothwell, the *Financial Journal* article dealt with counterfeiting. From it, Hank learned for the first time that the old-time counterfeiters had to be true artists. They were forced to hand etch the design of a ten- or twenty-dollar bill on steel engraving plates—a delicate, painstaking, time-consuming process—and then print a few bills at a time on a flatbed press. It took months, sometimes years, to make a few thousand dollars worth of passable counterfeit bills. But, said the article, the development of offset lithography has changed all that. Modern high-speed printing equipment now permits the counterfeiter to turn out counterfeit bills at a furious pace and with a fairly high average of accuracy, too. All you have to do, the article went on, if you want to be a counterfeiter today, is to expose a few genuine bills to chemically presensitized plates—as simple as taking a snapshot, Bothwell—then mount the plates on a press, push a button, and presto! Instant money! Counterfeit, of course. But passable, spendable money."

Bothwell, for him, grew animated. "No kidding?" he said.

"No kidding. Well, when Hank read this over his fellow commuter's shoulder, he suddenly realized that here, presented to him upon a printing plate, so to speak, was the opportunity of a lifetime. And do you know why, Bothwell?"

Bothwell shrugged.

"You won't believe it," I said, remembering the exquisite thrill that had accompanied my own realization of the fact fifteen years ago, "but the university printing plant in which Hank had been laboring so faithfully for six months was an *offset* plant! Think of it, Bothwell. All the equipment for do-it-yourself counterfeiting handily available to him every day!"

"Pretty lucky."

"Hank thought so. Through incredible luck, he believed, he had been selected from the thousands of other young businessmen in the city as the specially favored darling of destiny. His mind filled at once with golden dreams of affluence. He would produce millions of counterfeit dollars and become one of the world's richest and most influential men. He was sure of it. So wasting no time, he made his first move in that direction that very day. On some pretext or other, he borrowed the plant manager's key to the back door and had a duplicate made of it during his lunch hour. And that night, he became one of the first practitioners of what I understand is today called 'Moonlighting,' Bothwell. You are familiar with the term?"

Bothwell nodded.

"Yes, well, beginning about midnight that night, with the help of his key to the plant's back door, Hank instituted a night shift in the plant—a one-man night shift. He was it. Alone in the plant, and calling on all his hardly accumulated knowledge of offset lithography, it took Hank only a few nights to prove that the *Financial Journal* article had told the unvarnished truth. On his fifth-night trick he turned out four hundred dollars worth of very creditable twenty-dollar bills in six minutes by the clock."

I paused briefly. Bothwell swished his dirty rag across the bar in front of me and glanced into my glass to see if I was ready for a refill. I wasn't. I drink Negronis rather slowly because I don't much care for their taste. Or did I mention that? Bothwell lifted one eyebrow at me again. I took it for an invitation to continue.

"So there was Hank," I said, "with four hundred dollars in hand and the prospect of millions more where they came from. As any twenty-two year old would be, he was wildly impatient to start spending this easy wealth. And what do you suppose he hit upon as an exciting way to pass his first counterfeit bills?"

With the long-suffering air of a man answering the silly questions of a child, Bothwell obligingly said, "What?"

"Did I tell you that Hank was a lad who dearly loved the little ironies of life? No? Well, he was. That's why he decided to spend his first homemade money for one of those three-legged buffalo nickels that his boss, Colbaugh, was so pathetically eager to acquire for his collection. It struck Hank as a truly beautiful bit of irony to pay three hundred and sixty dollars in phony twenty-dollar bills for five cents worth of genuine money in coin, you see? Especially as the five-cent coin, because of its rarity, could undoubtedly be exchanged at any coin dealer's or collector's for three hundred and sixty dollars in *genuine* twenty-dollar bills, which Hank could then spend with far more safety than counterfeit ones. Do you follow me, Bothwell?"

Bothwell pursed his mouth and made a deprecatory gesture with one hand.

Mollified, I continued. "In a way, this was a pleasing concept, don't you agree? And completely workable, too, as Hank discovered when he visited a coin dealer named Petrarch, whose name he had picked from the Yellow Pages because Petrarch's shop happened to be near Hank's rooming house on the West Side. There was something about Petrarch, a slender dark-haired man, that inspired immediate confidence in Hank, so he left an order with Petrarch for a three-legged buffalo nickel in good condition. Petrarch accepted a twenty-dollar deposit. *Not* one of Hank's homemade bills, of course. And promised Hank to have the coin in hand for delivery in a week's time. It seems he knew just where to put his hand on a three-legged buffalo nickel in the collection of a recently

deceased collector, which was being sold off piece-
meal to settle up the estate."

Bothwell took another peek into my Negroni glass. I
covered it with the palm of my hand and kept talking.

"Hank went back to his moonlighting and happily
manufactured a million dollars worth of bogus twenties while he was waiting for the week to pass. During
that week, too, he developed a sense of caution. He
decided that once he had cashed in his three-legged
buffalo nickel for genuine dollars, he would use the
money to transport himself and his counterfeit fortune
to another city where he would be completely unknown and thus better able to devise a safe and practical method for disposing of it." For the sake of sus-
pense, I stopped talking and drank the last of my
Negroni.

Bothwell said grudgingly, "Very smart."

Ostentatiously, I looked at my wrist watch. "Well,
sure enough, when Hank went back to Petrarch the
coin dealer at the end of the week, the precious three-
legged buffalo nickel was waiting for him in a neat
glassine envelope with the price stamped on the flap—
three hundred and sixty dollars. Hank handed Petrarch
seventeen counterfeit twenties, thanked him, and left
his shop. He felt very exhilarated. He had successfully
withstood his baptism of fire. A sense of euphoria filled
him."

"What's that?" Bothwell asked. He was hooked now,
I saw, listening with both ears.

"Well-being," I explained. "And no wonder, eh?"

Bothwell slowly wiped up a nonexistent stain on the
bar top.

"I suppose you can guess what Hank did next, can't
you, Bothwell?" I asked.

"Sure. Tried to sell the three-legged buffalo to
Goodblood & Co."

I rotated my empty glass on the bar and let the tension build. When I looked up, Bothwell was staring

straight at me. "That's right," I said, "but I'll bet you can't guess what happened next."

Bothwell's rag stopped in midswipe. "You want me to try?"

I nodded. It was a patronizing nod, I'm afraid.

"Okay," Bothwell said. "Hank offered his three-legged buffalo nickel to Goodblood & Co. for three hundred and sixty dollars. But they wouldn't buy it. Right?"

I goggled at him. Could he be brighter than he looked? "That's right," I admitted, slightly nettled. "But I'll lay you six, two, and even that you can't guess *why*. That's the whole point of the story."

"I'll take that bet," Bothwell said without a moment's hesitation. "The three-legged coin was a counterfeit. Petrarch had merely removed the fourth leg from the buffalo on an ordinary buffalo nickel and sold it at a fancy price to a sucker named Hank."

I gaped at Bothwell, as though he had two heads. "How," I managed to get out at last, "could you possibly know that?"

He grinned at me, showing a set of shiny dentures. "Speaking of life's little ironies," he said, "why did you think I took such a close look at your twenty when you paid for your drink? I've lost my hair, and I've gained fifty pounds, but my last name is still Petrarch. How about another Negroni, Hank? On the house?"

HONEYMOON CRUISE

by Richard Deming

When the employment office sent me down to the Miami Yacht Club to be interviewed by the owner of the Princess II, I had no idea she was tin heiress Peggy Matthews. I was told to ask for a Mrs. Arden Trader.

The Princess II was moored in the third slip. It was only about a thirty-five footer, but it was a sleek, sturdy-looking craft which appeared as though it could weather any kind of seas. No one was on deck or in the wheelhouse.

I climbed on deck, stuck my head down the single hatch behind the wheelhouse, and yelled, "Anyone aboard?"

A feminine voice from below called, "Be right up."

A moment later, a slim brunette of about twenty-five came up the ladder. She wore white Capris and a clinging white blouse that showed off a lithe, extremely feminine figure, thong sandals that exposed shapely feet with carmine toenails, and a white sailor hat. Her features were slightly irregular, her nose being a trifle aquiline and her chin line being a little short, but her face was so full of vitality and there was such an aura of femininity about her that she was beautiful, anyway. Lovely dark eyes, a suggestion of sensuality about her mouth, and a creamy suntan probably helped the general effect.

I recognized her at once from news photos I had seen. Only a few months before, on her birthday, she had come into full control of an estimated fortune of twenty million dollars, which had been left to her in trust until she was twenty-five by her widower father, tin magnate Abel Matthews. Matthews had been dead about ten years, but until Peggy's last birthday the terms of the trust fund had required her to struggle along on the piddling sum of about a hundred thousand a year. Now she was one of the richest women in the world.

"Aren't you Peggy Matthews?" I asked.

"I was," she said with a smile which exposed perfect white teeth. "I've been Mrs. Arden Trader for the last couple of days. Are you from the employment agency?"

"Yes, ma'am. My name's Dan Jackson."

She looked me up and down, and suddenly a peculiar expression formed on her face. Even now I can't quite describe it, but if you can imagine a mixture of surprise and gladness and apprehension, that comes close.

I think there must have been a similar expression on my face, except for the apprehension, because I was having an odd emotional reaction, too. Just like that, on first meeting, static electricity passed between us so strongly, it seemed to crackle like twin bolts of lightning.

I still don't believe there can be such a thing as love at first sight, but I learned at that instant that there can be an almost overpowering physical attraction between a man and a woman the first moment they look at each other. I had experienced it a few times in much milder form but never with this sort of thunderous impact.

We stood staring at each other in mutual dismay, hers probably from guilt, mine because she was already married. It was incredible that this should happen with a bride of only two days, but it was happening. There was no question in my mind that my impact on her was as strong as hers on me.

We gazed at each other for a long time without speaking. Finally, she said in a shaken voice, "Did the employment agency explain the job, Mr. Jackson?"

I took my eyes from her face so that I could untangle my tongue. "I understand you need someone with navigational and marine engine experience to pilot the Princess II on a Caribbean cruise and also double as a cook."

She turned and looked out over the water. "Yes," she said in a low voice. "It's to be a honeymoon cruise. My husband can pilot the boat all right, but he's not a navigator and knows nothing about engines. Neither of us is a very good cook, either. Incidentally, our marriage is to remain a secret until after the honeymoon because we don't want to be met by reporters at every port."

"All right," I agreed, still not looking at her.

I did risk a glance at her left hand, however. She was wearing both a diamond and a wedding band. I wondered how she expected to keep it a secret when people were bound to recognize her at every port of call. But that was none of my business.

She suddenly became brisk and businesslike. "May I have your qualifications and vital statistics, Mr. Jackson?"

"In that order?"

"As you please."

"I'll give you the vital statistics first," I said. "Age thirty, height six-one, weight one ninety; single. Two years at Miami U. in liberal arts with a B average, then I ran out of money. My hobbies are all connected with water: swimming, boating, fishing, and as a chaser for rye whiskey. No current romantic entanglements."

"I'm surprised at the last," she said. "You're a very handsome man."

I decided to ignore that. It didn't seem a good idea to involve myself as a third party on a honeymoon cruise if the situation were going to become explosive. I wanted to know right now if we were going to be able to suppress whatever it was that had sparked between us at the instant of meeting and keep our relationship on a strictly employer-employee basis.

"Now for qualifications," I said. "I did two years in the navy, the second one as chief engineer on a destroyer. I took an extension course in navigation and chart reading, intending to buck for a reserve commission, but changed my mind before my hitch was up. I finished the course, though, and am a pretty good navigator. I'm also an excellent marine mechanic. I had my own charter boat out of Miami Beach for two years. I lost it in moorage when Betsy hit, and there was only enough insurance to cover my debts, so I've been unable to finance another. Since then I've been odd-jobbing at any sea job I could get."

I looked directly into her face as I spoke, and she gazed back at me levelly. Whatever had caused the lightning to crackle between us was gone now, I was both disappointed and relieved to find. Her manner remained the brisk, almost brittle one of a businesswoman conducting a personnel interview. She still held an immense physical attraction for me, but now that she wasn't sending out rays of static electricity, I wasn't responding by sending them back.

She asked, "How about your cooking ability?"

"I'm no chef, but I've been cooking for myself for some years and have managed to remain healthy."

"That's not too important so long as you're adequate," she said. "We'll probably dine either with friends or in restaurants at our ports of call. You can furnish references, I presume?"

"They're on file at the employment office, which

has already checked them. All you have to do is phone."

"Very well," she said. "I think you'll do, Mr. Jackson. The salary is five hundred dollars plus your keep for a one-month voyage. Is that satisfactory?"

"Yes, ma'am."

"We'll leave tomorrow morning about ten. Our first port will be Southwest Point in the Bahamas, which should only take about four hours because the Princess II cruises at twenty-one knots. I'll outline the rest of the voyage after we're under way. Now, would you like to look over the boat?"

"Sure. Where's Mr. Trader?"

"Shopping for some last-minute supplies. We'll start below with the engine."

I judged the boat to be a couple of years old, but it was in excellent shape. I started the engine and listened to it for a time, and it seemed to be in top condition. There was a separate generator engine for the lights when we were in port, and the main engine was idle.

The galley was clean and shipshape, with an electric range and electric refrigerator, the latter well stocked with food. The food cabinet was well stocked with canned goods, also. There was a bunk room that slept four, and off it was a small head and a salt-water shower.

Just she and her husband would occupy the bunk room, Peggy Trader explained. There was a leather-covered bench in the pilothouse which folded out into a fifth bunk, and I would sleep there.

Her manner was entirely impersonal as she conducted the tour. Once, as we were moving from the bunk room into the galley, she accidentally crowded against me in the close quarters, but I sensed no reaction from her at the physical contact.

She merely said politely, "Excuse me," and continued through the hatch.

I knew the instantaneous physical attraction between us hadn't been just my imagination, but apparently she had decided, after her one brief lapse, to bring the matter to a screeching halt. I couldn't help feeling a bit rueful, but at the same time I was relieved. I needed the money badly enough so that I probably would have risked taking the job even if she had thrown herself into my arms, but I preferred not to break up a marriage before it was even fairly under way. If she could restrain herself, I knew I could.

I reported aboard at nine the next morning. Peggy's husband was present this time. Arden Trader was a lean, handsome man of thirty-five with dark, curly hair and a thin mustache. He had an Oxford accent and treated his bride with the fawning indulgence of a gigolo.

Later, I learned he had been the penniless younger son of an equally penniless English duke and had been existing as one of those curious parasites of the international set who move from villa to villa of the rich as perennial house guests.

I knew he was a fortune hunter the moment he flashed his white teeth and gave me a man-to-man handshake. I wondered why Peggy had allowed herself to be suckered into marrying him. I learned that afternoon.

The plan for the cruise was to sail east to Southwest Point the first day, a distance of about a hundred miles. After a two-day layover, we would head for Nassau, and after a similar layover there, we would cruise to Governor's Harbor. From there we would island hop to Puerto Rico, then hit the Dominican Republic, Haiti, Point Morant on the east tip of Jamaica, then head back northeast through Windward Passage to Port-de-Paix on the northern coast of Haiti.

The last would be our longest single jump, a distance of about two hundred and fifty miles. With a cruising speed of twenty-one knots, we could make it in about ten hours, however, so no night sailing would be required during the whole voyage.

After Port-de-Paix, we would touch at the island of Great Inagua, island hop from there back to Governor's Harbor, then cruise nonstop back to Miami. With all our scheduled stops, ranging from one-day layovers to two or three days, we would spend more time in port than at sea during the one-month voyage.

At noon the first day out, I called Arden Trader to take over the wheel while I went below to prepare lunch. When it was ready, as we were in no hurry, we cut the engine, threw out the sea anchor, and all lunched together.

After lunch, I pulled in the sea anchor and got under way again. The sea was rolling a little, but it wasn't rough, and the sun was shining brightly. We were clipping along at cruising speed when Peggy came into the wheelhouse wearing a red bikini swimsuit.

"Arden wants to try a little fishing," she said. "Will you cut to trolling speed for a while?"

Obediently, I throttled down until we were barely moving. Glancing aft, I saw Arden Trader seated at the stern rail with a sea rod in his hands. Peggy made no move to go back and join him after delivering the message.

"He probably won't troll more than fifteen minutes if he doesn't get a strike," she said. "He bores rather easily."

I didn't say anything.

She moved over next to me in order to look at the chart book lying open on the little ledge between the wheel and the pilothouse window. The nearness of her scantily clad body made my pulse start to hammer so hard I was afraid she could hear it.

"Where are we?" she asked.

I pointed silently to a spot a little more than halfway between Miami and Southwest Point.

She said, "We should be in by cocktail time, then, even if Arden decides to fish as long as an hour, shouldn't we?"

"Oh, yes."

There was no reason for her to remain where she was, now that she had seen the chart, but she continued to stand so close that our arms nearly touched. I didn't have on a shirt. In fact, I was wearing nothing but a pair of my old Navy dungarees and a visored yachting cap, not even shoes. She was so close I could feel the warmth of her body on my bare arm.

Although the sea was fairly calm, our decreased headway caused the boat to roll slightly. One swell a little larger than the rest caused a heavier roll to port. Instinctively, I leaned into it, and at the same moment she lost her balance.

She half turned as she fell against me. My right arm went around her waist to steady her as she grabbed for my shoulders. Her full bosom, covered only by the thin strip of the bikini halter, crushed against my bare chest. The bolts of lightning that crackled between us made that of yesterday morning seem like summer lightning. We remained rigid for several seconds, staring into each other's faces. Her lips parted, and her eyes reflected the same mixture of surprise and gladness and dismay I had caught when we first glimpsed each other. Then she straightened away from me and glanced out the aft pilothouse window. I looked over my shoulder, too. Her husband was fishing with his back to us.

"I shouldn't have hired you," she said quietly.

I faced forward and gripped the wheel with both hands.

"I knew I shouldn't have when I did it," she said. "Don't pretend you don't know what I'm talking about."

"We'll head back for Miami tomorrow," I said. "You can have the employment agency send you another man."

"No, I don't want to. It's too late."

With her gaze still on her husband, she reached out

and gently squeezed my bicep. I tingled clear to my toes.

"It's ridiculous," I said tightly. "You're a bride of three days. You must be in love with him."

Her hand continued to caress my bicep. "I'm not going to try to explain it, Dan. I was in love with him until you came aboard yesterday. I took one look at you, and everything turned topsy-turvy. It did for you, too. I could see it in your eyes. I can feel it in your muscles right now."

"Stop it," I said, keeping my gaze rigidly fixed ahead. "It's impossible. Why did you marry him?"

"Because I hadn't met you," she said simply.

"That's no answer. You must have been in love."

Her hand left my arm and dropped to her side. "I went into it with my eyes wide open," she said. "I've had a hundred offers of marriage—women with money always do—but I'd given up ever finding the man I dreamed of. The rich ones were all fearfully dull, the charmers all fortune hunters. I'm twenty-five and tired of being single. I hardly needed a rich husband, so I decided to settle for a charmer. Arden has been pursuing me for a year. Last week at a house party in Mexico City, I gave in. We were married there, then flew to Miami to pick up my boat for a honeymoon cruise. On my second day as a new bride, I had, finally, to meet the man I've been looking for all my life."

I continued to grip the wheel and stare straight ahead. The whole situation was incredible. A series of wild thoughts ran through my mind.

I'd always considered myself a confirmed bachelor, but suddenly the thought of having Peggy for a wife was so appealing, I've never wanted anything more. Her money had nothing to do with it, either. I would never marry for money because it had been my observation that men who do usually earn it. It had never occurred to me that I might fall in love with a rich woman.

I wasn't sure this was love, but no woman had ever held as strong a physical attraction for me, and I was sure I wanted to marry her. And it was hardly a disadvantage that she was one of the richest women in the world. Would it be sensible to turn her down merely because a few villas scattered around the world, a few yachts and foreign cars went with the deal?

Then the bubble popped. She already had a husband.

"Aren't you going to say anything?" she asked.

"Uh-huh. Do you plan an annulment?"

"From Arden? Impossible. He would hold me up for a half million dollars."

"Can't you afford it?"

From the periphery of my vision, I could see her frown. "Nobody can afford to throw half a million dollars down a hole. My father spent too many years building his fortune for any of it to be tossed away capriciously. It's not a matter of being able to afford it; it's a matter of principle."

"Then I guess you'll just have to stay married to him," I said.

There was a yell from the stern. "Strike!"

I cut the engine and looked over my shoulder. Trader was straining back in his seat, and a hundred yards behind the boat a sailfish broke water.

Peggy said, "We'll postpone discussion until later," and hurried aft to stand by with the gaff.

There was no opportunity to resume discussion that day, however. Trader lost his fish, and it discouraged him from further fishing. He devoted his attention to his bride for the rest of the day.

About five p.m. we berthed at Southwest Point. Trader and Peggy dressed and decided to go into the settlement for dinner. Trader invited me to go along, but I knew the invitation was only politeness, so I refused.

I had a lonely meal and afterward sat on the stern rail smoking a cigarette. The night was warm enough so that I didn't bother to put on any more than I had worn during the day. I had finished my cigarette but was still seated there bare chested and barefooted when they returned about nine.

Arden Trader had donned a white linen suit to go to dinner. Peggy had put on a dress but hadn't bothered with stockings. She wore thong sandals on her bare feet.

There were two inflated rubber mats with removable canvas back rests on the stern deck. Without the back rests you could lie full length on them for sunbathing. With the back rests in place, they made deck-level lounging chairs. Peggy sank onto the one right in front of me, leaned against the back rest, and kicked off her sandals.

"Let's enjoy the moonlight for a while," she said to her husband. "How about a cigarette?"

He knelt beside her with his back to me, placed a cigarette in her mouth, and lit it. After taking one draw, she took it from her mouth, put her arms about his neck, and drew him to her.

Ever since she had left the wheelhouse that afternoon, I had been stewing about what transpired there. I had finally decided that if she wasn't going to leave her husband, we were not going to have just an affair. I still wanted her as a wife more than I've ever wanted anything, and maybe if she had been married ten years, I might have settled for having her just as a mistress. But I wasn't quite rat enough to cuckold a groom on his honeymoon.

Apparently, my soul-searching had been for nothing. I could think of no reason for her deliberate show of affection in front of me other than that she had decided to let me know in definite terms that the scene in the wheelhouse had been a mistake. I looked away, not wanting to see her kissed by Trader.

I felt something touch my left foot and glanced down. My pulse started to pound when I saw her right foot rubbing against my instep. Her carmine-tipped toes wiggled in urgent demand for some response.

With her arms wrapped around her husband, the gesture seemed more likely to be an invitation for a clandestine affair than a signal that she wanted a more permanent relationship. Since I had already decided against settling for that, my conscience told me to withdraw my foot.

My desire for her was stronger than my conscience. I raised my foot and pressed its sole against hers. Her toes worked against mine and along the sole of my foot in a lascivious caress, all the time her arms tightening around her husband's neck until finally it was he who broke the kiss.

As he started to rise, her foot drew away from mine, and I dropped mine back flat on the deck. Trader sank onto the other mat and lit a cigarette.

"I'm beginning to like this married life," he said to me with a grin. "You ought to try it, Dan."

"I may if I ever meet the right girl," I said, getting to my feet. "Think I'll turn in. It's been a long day."

"Good night, Dan," Peggy said softly.

"Night," I said without looking at her, and headed for the wheelhouse.

The following morning when I climbed down on deck, Arden Trader was screwing some kind of bracket to the timber immediately right of the hatchway which led below.

"Morning," I said. "What's that?"

"Morning, Dan," he said affably. "I'm installing an outside shaving mirror I picked up in town last night. The head's too small and too poorly lighted to get a decent shave."

He lifted a round shaving mirror from a paper bag and slipped the two small vertical shafts at its back into holes in the top of the bracket. Then he moved the bottom of the mirror in and out to demonstrate that it could be adjusted to suit the height of anyone using it.

"Now all I need is a basin of hot water and my shaving equipment," he said as he started below. "You can use it when I'm finished if you want."

I did use it from then on.

I had no opportunity to be alone with Peggy during the two days we were in port because Trader was playing the attentive groom. By the second day, I couldn't stand his constant little attentions to her and, since I wasn't needed aboard because they were taking their meals in town, took the day off and spent it on the beach by myself.

On the third day, we pulled out for Nassau. As the trip would take six hours, we got under way at eight a.m. About ten, Peggy came into the pilothouse, again wearing a bikini.

"He's taking a nap," she said, and with no more preamble moved into my arms.

I spiked the wheel so as to have both arms free. Hers went about my neck, and her body pressed against mine as our lips met. We were both trembling when she finally struggled from my arms and stepped back. It was none too soon.

She backed clear to the pilothouse door. We were both so out of control, if her husband had walked in at that moment, neither of us could have concealed our naked emotion from him.

"What are we going to do?" she whispered.

My good resolutions lay in shreds. I didn't care what we did so long as it meant being together in some way. If she wanted to shed Trader and marry me, I would be happiest. But now I was willing to settle for just an affair if she wanted that. If she had suggested solving our problem by holding hands and jumping over the rail, I would have at least considered it.

I jerked out the spike and gripped the wheel with both hands in an effort to control my trembling. "What do you want to do?"

"Do you love me?"

"Do you have to ask?" I demanded.

"I want to hear you say it."

I took a deep breath. "I love you. I'm absolutely nuts about you."

She closed her eyes. "I love you, too," she said almost inaudibly. "I've never felt such overwhelming love. Do you want to marry me? Answer me truly, Dan."

"There's nothing I want more," I said in a husky voice.

Her eyes opened, and she seemed to get a little control of herself. In a more normal tone, she said, "I couldn't just have an affair, Dan. Despite my behavior, I'm really a quite moral person. I'm not a prude. If I were single, and we were alone out here and planned to get married when we reached port, I wouldn't insist we wait until the proper words were spoken. But there's some Puritan strain deep within me that makes it impossible for me to violate my marriage vows."

"We aren't going to have an affair," I told her. "I've already told you I want you for my wife."

"But I have a husband."

"You shouldn't have any trouble getting an annulment after this short a marriage. Why do you think it would cost you a half million?"

"Because I know Arden. I know him so well, I made him sign a premarital agreement waiving all claim to my estate except whatever I decided to leave him in my will. I didn't think it wise to put him in a position where he could become rich if I died."

I turned to stare at her. "If you thought him capable of murdering you, why in the devil did you marry him? What possessed you?"

"Oh, I really didn't think he might try to kill me. But he's a fortune hunter, and you don't place temptation in the hands of men such as Arden. Because he is a fortune hunter, I know he'll hold me up if I ask for an annulment. My guess that his price for cooperating will be a half million is based on sound experience. That's exactly what it cost each of two women friends of mine to shed fortune-hunting husbands."

"Wouldn't your premarital agreement cover that?"

"That only applies in case of my death," she said. "Actually, I could get out of paying him a red cent if I wanted a legal battle. No court would grant him any kind of settlement. But there's a pattern of blackmail men such as Arden use. If I refuse to pay him off, Arden will fight me in court with every dirty tactic he knows. He'll drag my reputation through the mud by filing countersuit for divorce and accusing me of infidelity with a dozen men. The tabloids will have a field day."

I said sourly, "You knew all this in advance of marrying him. How the hell did you bring yourself to do it?"

"I assumed it was going to last, Dan. How was I to know you would come along?"

I took my gaze from her and looked ahead again. "If you don't get rid of him, how are we going to marry?"

"Oh, I intend to get rid of him," she said softly.

"By paying him off?"

"There's a much simpler way, Dan. Who would suspect anything if a brand-new groom fell overboard and was lost at sea on his honeymoon? The wife might be suspected after a ten-year marriage or even after a year—but not after just a week, Dan."

A sudden chill doused the warmth I still felt from having her in my arms. "Murder?" I said shakily.

"There wouldn't be a chance of suspicion. Who could suspect a love triangle when I'm on my honeymoon and you and I have only known each other a few days? It's even incredible to me that we're in love. How could the thought ever enter the heads of the police?"

The logic of what she said was penetrating my mind even as I was rejecting the thought. Under the circumstances, who could possibly suspect? My throat was suddenly so dry I had to clear it.

"There would be some suspicion after we announced our marriage."

"Why? No one knows you're only a temporary employee. I'll simply keep you on in some permanent capacity—say as my social secretary. I'm the only woman in my set who has never had one, and it's about time I acquired one. You'll show sympathy for my bereavement, and I'll show appreciation for your sympathy. Gradually, your sympathy and my appreciation can ripen into love. It won't be the first time a sympathetic male friend has ended up marrying a grieving widow. I think it would be safe at the end of as little as two months."

Again her argument was so logical I had no answer, except that it takes more than mere certainty that you won't be caught to condition your mind to murder.

"It has to be that way or not at all," she said in a suddenly definite tone. "I'll leave you to think it over." She turned and left the pilothouse.

I was still thinking it over when it came time for the noon mess. By then, we were passing through Northwest Providence Channel. I had deliberately kept to the center of the channel, and land was barely visible on the horizon on both sides. The water was calm, with only a slight roll, and the sun was shining brightly. There wasn't another vessel in sight.

Arden Trader had emerged from below in swim trunks about eleven o'clock, and both he and Peggy were lying on the inflated mats at the stern, deepening their already rich tans. I yelled for Trader to come take the wheel while I prepared mess. He rolled off his mat, leaned over Peggy, and gave her a long kiss. Jealousy raged through me so hotly I had to turn my back to get control of myself. When he came into the wheelhouse, it was an effort to keep my voice calm while I gave him his bearing.

The sight of his kissing Peggy had brought me to a

decision. Peggy came into the galley only a moment
after I got there and stood looking at me expression-
lessly. "All right," I said.

Her nostrils flared. "When?"

"Right now if you want."

"How?"

"Why don't you go out and suggest a swim before
lunch? The water's calm enough. I'll do the rest."

Without a word, she turned and left the galley. I
waited a moment, then followed, pausing astern while
she climbed to the pilothouse. A moment after she entered, Trader cut the engine, then they both emerged.

"Okay, Dan," Peggy called. "You can throw out the
sea anchor."

I was already standing next to it. I tossed it overboard and let down the wooden-runged ladder strung
with rope so that swimmers could more easily get
back aboard ship. "Think I'll have a dip with you," I
said. "I'll put on my trunks."

When I came back out on deck, Trader and Peggy
were already in the water. Trader was floating on his
back about four feet from the boat, his arms outstretched and his eyes closed. Peggy was treading water near the rope ladder. I motioned her aboard. Quietly, she climbed up on deck. Trader opened his eyes
and looked up at her.

"Be right back, honey," she said, and ran below.

Trader closed his eyes again.

It had been my intention to swim up behind him
and give him a judo chop, but his outstretched position made him vulnerable to a safer form of attack.
Taking a running jump, I launched myself feet first at
his stomach, bringing my knees to my chest and snap-
ping them straight again with terrific force just as I
landed. The air whooshed out of him, and he was
driven deeply under water in a doubled-up position.

I must have caught him in the solar plexus with one
heel, temporarily paralyzing him, because when I reversed myself and dove after him to grab his shoul-

ders and push him even deeper, he barely struggled. I forced him down and down until my own lungs were nearly bursting, then reversed again, got my feet against him, and gave a final shove which drove him deeper and shot me toward the surface.

I made it only a microsecond before I would have had to breathe in water myself. Starting under with no air in him, I was sure Trader couldn't possibly survive. But when I recovered my breath and had climbed aboard, I crouched at the rail and studied the water for a good ten minutes just to make absolutely certain. Then I called Peggy from below.

When she came up, her face pale beneath its tan, I said tonelessly, "There's been an accident. I think he had a cramp. I was on deck with my back turned and didn't see him struggling until I happened to glance around. I tried to reach him, but he went under before I got there. I kept diving for nearly an hour in an attempt to spot him, but he must have sunk straight to the bottom. That's my story for the record. Yours is simply that you were below when it happened."

She stared at the gentle swell of water in fascination. "Will he come up?" she whispered.

"Eventually, if something doesn't eat him first, which is more likely. Not for days, probably."

She gave a little shudder. "Let's get away from here."

"We have to stick around for at least an hour," I said. "I spent an hour futilely diving for him, remember? If we head straight on, somebody just might check to see when we left Southwest Point and when we arrived at Nassau. It would look fishy if there weren't enough of a time gap to allow for our hour of waiting around."

"Why say we waited an hour?" she asked. "We'd know after ten minutes he wasn't coming up."

"You're a brand-new bride," I said. "You wouldn't give up hope after ten minutes. We'll do it my way."

"Do we have to kill the time right here?" she asked

nervously. "There's no mark on the water where he went down. Run a few miles and throw out the sea anchor again."

With a shrug, I hauled in the sea anchor, pulled up the rope-strung ladder, and went tops to start the engine. Peggy went along with me and stood right next to me, with our arms touching, as I drove the boat through the water at full throttle for about five miles. Then I reduced speed until we were barely making headway, scanned the horizon in all directions to make sure no other vessel was in sight, and finally cut the engine altogether. I went aft, tossed out the sea anchor, and lowered the ladder again, just in case another vessel came along during the next hour and I actually had to start diving.

Peggy had followed me from the pilothouse. She emitted a deep breath of relief and threw herself into my arms, clinging shakily.

We were only about two hours out of Nassau. We arrived about three-thirty p.m.

No one showed the slightest suspicion of our story. As Peggy had surmised, it didn't even occur to the police that it might be a love-triangle murder when they learned she had been a bride for less than a week and she had never seen me until two days after her marriage. Their only reaction was sympathy.

Since we said we had waited in the area for a full hour after Trader went down, they didn't even bother to send ships to look for the missing man. A couple of helicopters scanned the general area for a couple of days in the hope of spotting the floating body, but it was never spotted, and Arden Trader was finally listed as missing at sea, presumed dead.

Since Peggy's secret marriage wasn't revealed to the press until the drowning of the groom was simultaneously announced, both got wide news coverage. But again there wasn't the slightest intimation that it could have been anything but a tragic accident.

Peggy owned a half-dozen villas in various parts of

the world, and one of them was at San Juan. When the police at Nassau released us, we continued on to Puerto Rico, where the grieving widow went into seclusion. News reports said that the only people accompanying her to the villa were a female companion and her personal secretary, neither of whose names were reported.

The "female companion" was a middle-aged housekeeper who spoke nothing but Spanish. I, of course, was the personal secretary.

The villa had its own private beach, and we spent an idyllic two months on a sort of premarital honeymoon. Long before it was over, there was no question in my mind about being in love. The physical attraction was just as strong, but that wasn't Peggy's only attraction anymore. I was as ludicrously in love as the hero of some mid-Victorian love novel.

At the end of two months, Peggy thought it safe to emerge back into the world and for us to be quietly married. She had been in correspondence with one of her several lawyers meantime, and the day before the ceremony was to be performed, she presented me with a legal document to sign, a waiver of all rights to her estate except what she voluntarily left me in her will.

"You think I might murder you for your money?" I growled after examining it.

"It's my lawyer's idea," she said apologetically. "While I'm not legally bound to follow my father's request, it was his expressed wish in his will that if I had no heirs, I leave most of my estate to set up a research foundation. If we have children, naturally the bulk of the estate will go to them, and of course I'll see that you're well taken care of. But just suppose I died the day after we married? I have no other living relatives, so you would inherit everything. Would it be fair for my father's dream of a Matthews Foundation to go down the drain?"

"I'm not marrying you for your money," I told her.

"If you died the day after we married, I'd probably kill myself, too. But it's not worth arguing about." I signed the document.

The ceremony was performed before a civil judge in San Juan, with our housekeeper and the court clerk as witnesses. Peggy wanted only a plain gold band, and it cost me only twenty-five dollars. The diamond she wore, I discovered, had not been given her by Arden Trader but had been her mother's engagement ring. She said she preferred to continue to wear it instead of having me pick out another.

As in the case of her previous marriage, Peggy didn't want the news released to the press until we had completed a honeymoon cruise so we wouldn't be besieged by reporters at every port of call. I pointed out that she was too well known to escape all publicity, and, unless she wanted to pretend deep gloom at each stop, people were bound to guess we were on a honeymoon. She said she didn't plan to withhold the news from friends and acquaintances but was going to request them not to relay it to any reporters, so there was a good chance we could keep the secret from the general public until we completed the cruise.

"It won't be a tragedy if reporters find out," she said. "I just want a chance for us to be alone as long as possible."

For our cruise we decided to complete the circuit of the Caribbean we had already started. This time there would be only two of us aboard, however.

We got as far as the island of Great Inagua when we ran over a floating log in the harbor, broke a propeller shaft, and lost the prop. The spare parts weren't available anywhere on the island, but I knew I wouldn't have any trouble finding them back at our previous stop, Port-de-Paix.

A packet ship plied every other day from Great Inagua to Haiti, then on to the Dominican Republic and finally to Puerto Rico. I checked the schedule and discovered that if I caught the one on Friday, I could catch the return ship from Port-de-Paix to Great Inagua on Saturday.

Peggy knew some people named Jordan on the small island where we were laid up, and as they were having a house party on Friday night, she decided not to accompany me.

I got back with the new propeller shaft and propeller about four o'clock Saturday afternoon. The private boat slips were only about fifty yards from the main dock, and I could see the Princess II as we pulled in. A slim feminine figure in a red bikini was on the bow waving to the ship. I doubted that she could make me out at that distance from among the other passengers lining the rail, but I waved back, anyway.

When I lugged my packages aboard the Princess II, Peggy was no longer on the bow. She was leaning back into the canvas back rest on one of the air-inflated mats on the afterdeck. A tanned and muscular young man of about twenty-five, wearing white swim trunks, was seated on the stern rail.

As I set down my packages, Peggy said, "Honey, this is Bob Colvin, one of Max and Susie Jordan's house guests. My husband Dan, Bob."

The young man rose, and we shook hands. He inquired how I was, and I said I was glad to meet him.

"Bob was planning to take the Monday packet ship up to Governor's Harbor, then fly from there to Miami," Peggy said. "I told him if he wasn't in a hurry, he might as well leave with us tomorrow and sail all the way home. He can sleep in the pilothouse."

Counting our two months in seclusion at San Juan, our honeymoon had now lasted long enough so that the urgency to be completely alone had abated somewhat for both of us. I don't mean that my love for Peggy had abated. It was just that both of us were ready to emerge from our pink cloud back into the world of people. My only reaction was that it would be nice to have someone to spell me at the wheel from time to time.

"Sure," I said, and knelt beside my wife to give her a kiss.

She kissed me soundly, then forced me to a seated position next to her and pressed my head onto her shoulder. Smiling down into my face, she began to stroke my hair.

With my face in its upturned position, I could look right over her shoulder into the shaving mirror attached to the timber alongside the hatch leading below. By pure accident it was slanted slightly downward to reflect the deck area immediately in front of the inflated mat.

In the mirror I could see Bob Colvin's raised bare foot. Peggy's bare toes were working lasciviously against his and along the sole of his foot.

A COFFIN FOR
BERTHA STETTERSON

by Donald Honig

The murder happened in 1890, but you can still hear of it from certain of the old people to whom the story was bequeathed by parent and grandparent in solemn or breathless sentences.

Capstone at that time was a place of farms and woods and small round hills, all of which, except for a few patriarchal trees, is gone; the farms buried under facades of two-family houses, the hills paved and in some places leveled and not even called hills anymore. Lying across the East River from Manhattan and accessible only by ferry, Capstone was considered quite remote, and there were a lot of farmers who had been across the river only two or three times in their lives.

Beyond the dairy farms, in the back of town, was where Jacob Vandermeer lived. His had been an old family, descended from Dutch settlers who had come to Capstone in the 1700s.

When he was forty, Vandermeer, who was a tall, thickly built, long-bearded, taciturn man, finally took a wife. It all came as a sharp surprise, and not just because Vandermeer had always been such a solitary man, but more because of who the wife was. She was Bertha Stetterson, the judge's niece, and was reputed to be quite well off, having inherited some wealth

from her recently deceased parents. A small, shy
woman in her thirties, she had attended a young lady's school upstate and was considered refined, a fact
which doubtless intimidated most of Capstone's
earthy young men.

Why she married the big, brooding Vandermeer, no
one knew, except, as the talk went, that it was simply
because she was beyond thirty and had become desperate.

Soon after the marriage it became evident that Vandermeer was neglecting his farm. Weeds began to
grow over it. Cows and pigs and chickens from neigh-
boring places wandered over it, and the somber
farmer did not chase them. He simply sat on a chair in
front of his house and watched. He raised nothing,
sold nothing, had no income, but appeared undisturbed by it. It became obvious that he had decided
to become a gentleman, a squire, by virtue of Bertha's
money. What she thought of all this, no one knew. She
seldom appeared in town anymore.

Occasionally, Vandermeer drove his wagon into
town, which consisted then of the Dooley Boarding
House and the Capstone Hotel, a few stores and
blacksmith shops, and a feed and grain barn and a
tavern. He would sit on the porch of the boarding
house and smoke a pipe, never talking to any one of
the men, who had become accustomed to his sullen
quiet and who often winked at each other while he sat
there.

But finally one morning one of the men, unable to
contain his curiosity any longer, asked Vandermeer
the question which they had all been waiting to be
asked.

"You given up your farm, Vandermeer?"

Vandermeer sat there, smoking, the ashes flicking
down into his beard, staring straight ahead. For a
while it seemed as if he would never answer. (He did
that, too, sometimes.) But then, lifting the pipe stem
from between his teeth, he said.

"I've given up begging it for my living."

"Going to let it lay like that?"

"I believe so." The pipe stem slid back into his beard then, and the conversation was over.

The rest they reasoned for themselves after Vandermeer had departed. And it was confirmed for them later by Jonah Stetterson, the judge's younger (by fifteen years) brother.

"He won't work anymore. He just sits out there and smokes his pipe and takes occasional whiskey."

"How long can he keep that up?"

"Any man who can sit with lively company for three hours and not speak a single syllable," Jonah said, "can, I would say, sit the rest of his life in subsidized idleness quite easily."

"What's Bertha say about that?"

"She don't like it, of course," Jonah said. "But she's afraid to say anything. She's afraid of him."

"How do they live?"

Jonah looked troubled then. "That's what's bothering us," he said. "Seems that Bertha's got most of her money and all her jewelry there."

"Will she stay with him?"

"It took her thirty-one years to get a husband," Jonah said. "What do you think?"

A few weeks later, Vandermeer came into town again, on horseback this time.

"Wife's taken ill," he said, dismounting.

The men exchanged looks. Vandermeer bought some medicine and then rode away. The men on Dooley's porch sat in uneasy, incriminating silence.

Jonah Stetterson came by the next day.

"He won't let anyone in to see her," he said. "Not me or my wife, not even the judge. Said she's too weak. And he came to the door with a rifle."

"Didn't know he owned one," Dooley said.

"He owns one, all right," Jonah said. "He'll use it, too. He had that look in his eye. The judge says it's the look of a madman, and the judge has seen enough to know."

Jonah said to his brother that night, "We've got to get inside that house and see her. There's no telling what he'd do to her—if he hasn't already done it."

"But we can't just break in on him," the judge said. If the judge worshipped (and he was never seen in church, not Sunday nor any other time), then it was before the altar of the law, before the unbreakable scriptures of his legal beliefs.

"It's our niece that's fallen into his hands, Andrew," Jonah said.

"I know. I don't feel any less uneasy than you," the judge said.

"I'm going to try the house again tomorrow. If I can get in to see her, I'm going to persuade her to leave."

The judge sighed. "Ah," he said, "if I were but younger."

"Then let me handle it."

"You can be impetuous, Jonah."

"We need that now. The insolence of that man, not letting her family in to see her."

The judge sighed again. "Do what you can, Jonah, but let it be nothing that lies contrary to the law."

Early the next evening, Jonah crossed the farmlands toward the Vandermeer house. Entering the heavily wooded area that enclosed Vandermeer's neglected farm, he followed the path that made its way through the woods. It had begun to turn dark when he neared the farm. He paused at the edge of the wood. The evening was warm, windless, the woods perfectly still, the falling dark weaving together tree and leaf and sky into a single profound canopy. Then he began to hear the hammering. The hammer strokes were sharp, methodical, the thuds echoing flatly into the trees.

Jonah went quietly across the untilled furrows, listening to the hammering as if to some code, trying to decipher it, intrigued and disturbed. Vandermeer's chair, in front of the house, was empty. The hammering was coming from the back. Jonah could see the yellow flare of a lantern behind the house, casting a strange dark dancing over the trees. The front door was half ajar, looking quite mysterious, intriguing, irresistible. He went forward and entered the house. It was dark. He had been inside but once before, the night of the wedding. He went upstairs. There were two rooms there, one the bedroom, the other used by Vandermeer to store his tools.

He opened the bedroom door, pushing it slowly back. He moved into the room. And then he saw the bed.

"Bertha," he whispered.

But he spoke it to an empty bed. He did not believe what he saw. He went to the bed and touched it. It was cold, empty, the covers over it tightly. He looked about the room. Then he glanced out the window where the hammering was still constant, unbroken, the yellow light flaring toward the dark trees. He saw Vandermeer's back, with a Y of black suspenders, bent in work, the hammer swinging in slow, intent strokes.

Then Jonah left. Quietly and quickly he descended the stairs, went through the front door, past the empty chair, and across the weedy farm into the woods, followed by the inexorable beat of the hammer.

Later, he was facing his brother. The judge's countenance, never one of jubilation, was now quite severe in its gravity, its concern.

"She was not there, you say?"

"No," Jonah said, sitting forward, still breathless, flushed from his long run. "The bed was empty."

"Could she have been elsewhere in the house?"

"There were no lights. If she were there, she would have heard me."

"And he? Are you certain?"

"I saw it. He was hammering on it."

"You couldn't have been mistaken?"

"No," Jonah said. "I have seen enough coffins to know."

So the next day, at sunup, they—it was the judge and Jonah and another man, a farmer named Adamson—went there. They walked. The judge was dressed in his formal black, a derby upon his white hair. His face was set with judicial severity, and now with personal concern, too. They passed no words during the long walk across the farms and meadows and through the sun-shafted woods. Then across Vandermeer's farm. They saw him sitting on the chair, looking small and fierce with his black beard and growing larger and fiercer as they approached.

But before they had a chance to speak, Jonah laid his hand on the judge's arm. The judge looked at him, at his eyes, then looked around at the upright board at the side of the house. The board cast its path of shadow over a mound of fresh earth that had been rounded off. Ignoring Vandermeer, they went directly to the board. On it they read—it was printed large and neat in black crayon—the name of their niece and the date of her birth and the date of her death, the latter date being the day before. For a moment they stood in shocked silence; then they went to the sullen farmer. He was watching them, had been watching them with his eyes, without moving his head, his hands holding the rifle in his lap.

"Mr. Vandermeer," the judge said, his voice severe but controlled, "what does this mean?"

"I was going to come by this afternoon and tell you," Vandermeer said.

"Tell me what?"

"That my wife died."

"Died?" the judge said.

"She was never ill," Jonah said. "What have you done to her?"

"She was ill," Vandermeer corrected, his voice thick, patient. "And I've buried her."

"Murderer!" Adamson shouted, stepping forward. "We suspected . . ."

With a raised hand, the judge both silenced and restrained the farmer, his eyes never leaving Vandermeer's face. "Of what did she die?" the judge asked.

"Fever, it seemed," Vandermeer said, his small mouth moving in the deep black beard.

"Was there a doctor?" the judge asked. "Did you consult a doctor?"

"It did not seem to be that serious."

"Why didn't you call her family?"

"There wasn't the time."

"But you took time to build a coffin," Jonah said.

Vandermeer's eyes, which had been fixed impassively upon the judge, now shifted quickly, hostilely to Jonah, fixing him intently for a moment as if asking: How do you know that? How are you so sure? Then he said, "After she had gone, yes."

"And you interred her here," the judge said.

"Yes," Vandermeer said. "Where her remains won't fall prey to grave robbers." The allusion was to the recent desecration of the grave of the Capstone poet Benjamin McKinley, which had been opened in search of the poems which people believed had been buried with him. Also, the two men had recently been caught carrying a corpse in a wagon. They had stolen it while in the hire of a doctor in the Little Village section of Capstone. The doctor and the two men had been arrested, tried and convicted, and sentenced by Judge Stetterson.

"But you can't just bury people where you please," Jonah said.

"If you do it," Vandermeer said, "then you can do it."

"We've a right to bury her proper, Judge," Adamson said.

"No Christian man would think of that now," Vandermeer said. "Leave her be in peace now that she's passed on."

"You'd like that, wouldn't you?" Jonah said. "You think you can just—"

The judge silenced him. "You'd better come with us, Mr. Vandermeer."

"For what?"

"We're going to have the grave opened legally. You ought to be present when the papers are made out."

"You might ask why I'm sitting with a rifle," Vandermeer said. "I'm afraid of someone robbing the grave. Doctors do that, and madmen, to ply their deviltry on the dead."

"You're talking nonsense," Jonah said.

"Am I?" Vandermeer challenged. "I saw people in the woods just before you came. What were they there for? In fact, when I saw you coming out of the woods, I was about to fire on you. You took a chance, coming like that upon a man with poor eyesight."

"Nevertheless," the judge said, "I advise you to come along."

Vandermeer stood up, holding the rifle. "I'll come," he said. "I've nothing to fear. But the responsibility will be yours."

They walked back to town, the four of them. At the judge's house, the elegant white house on Grant Avenue, they obtained the papers.

"This is all unnecessary," Vandermeer said. "You're the judge. We could've dug right then."

"No," the judge said. "It's got to be done legally."

Then they went out and this time took the judge's buckboard and drove down to get Doctor Howell. Then the five of them drove the buckboard to the wood's edge and walked through upon the narrow path. As they emerged from the woods, Vandermeer stopped.

"Somebody's been here," he said.

"What do you mean?" the judge said.

"The grave's not as I left it."

"It looks the same to me," the judge said.

They walked across the farm.

"How many shovels have you got?" Jonah said.

"Two," Vandermeer said.

Vandermeer got the shovels out of his shed, and Jonah and Adamson began digging, plunging the long-handled shovels into the mound and digging and spilling with sharp, flashing thrusts. The judge and Doctor Howell stood by and watched. Vandermeer paced around them, fingering his unlighted pipe, watching the digging men, quite nervous. Several times the judge turned around and watched him.

At about four feet down, they struck wood. At the sound, Vandermeer ran over.

"I must protest," he said.

"But you may not," the judge said. He was standing over the pit now. "Open it," he said to Jonah.

"It's already been tampered with," Vandermeer exclaimed. "I can tell."

With the scoop of his shovel, Jonah pried open the coffin lid. It lifted easily. And as Jonah leaned it back against the earthen wall, it revealed an empty box.

"Vandermeer!" the judge cried. "Where is she? What have you done with her?"

Vandermeer peered down into the empty box, long and hard. Then he looked at the judge.

"I told you they were about," he said. "And you're no better than they are."

"I don't believe he ever buried her," Jonah said. He bit on his pipe. "The whole story is too fantastic. Grave robbers in broad daylight? How can a man tell such lies? I'll tell you what he's done: He's buried her out in the woods somewhere."

"But why the coffin, then?" the judge said. He gazed pensively into the fireplace. The logs were burned down, an intense redness glaring on them, occasional sparks bursting up, popping. "Why go to all that trouble?"

"Because he knew we would insist the grave be opened. Now he can say the body was stolen and can

even say that the blame is partially ours for making
him leave the place for an hour or two. He invents this
story of grave robbers lurking about, leaves for a little
while, then comes back and says they were there. He's
murdered her, taken her jewels and money, and
thrown her into the earth somewhere. If only I had
watched more closely that night, if only I had remained."

"He might have buried her days ago," the judge
said.

"But what are we going to do about it? We can't let
him get away with it. We *won't* let him get away with
it!" Jonah said, his voice sharp, angry.

"Using that tone of voice," the judge said, still
watching the dying fire, "you sound like a man who
wants to incite mob violence."

"I know your feeling about that sort of thing, but
are we going to let him do such a thing?"

"Would it make you feel better to see him hanging
from a tree?"

"Yes, considerably."

The judge sighed. "Ah, Jonah," he said. "But suppose that happens? Where, then, will we search for
our poor Bertha? Are we to forget her like that?"

"You're being taken advantage of, Andrew," Jonah
said. "He knows you only too well. He's taking advantage of your weakness."

"Upholding law and order is a weakness, then," the
judge said, making an ironic comment. "No, we'll first
find out what he's done with her. Then the law will
move against him, massively and decisively."

But the thinking in town was not as temperate. The
farmer, Adamson, had been sitting all day on Dooley's
porch talking about what had happened. Gradually, a
crowd of men had gathered around him.

"Killed her," Adamson said to each new man, and
the others, the ones who had heard it before, did not
seem to tire of listening. "Then dug a phony grave,

buried an empty coffin, and now claims grave robbers took her. But the grave was never touched. It
looked the same as when we had left it, no matter
what he says. Since when do grave robbers take that
much trouble to conceal what they've done?"

There were murmurs of concurrence.

"And now," Adamson said, "he's sitting out there
with her blood on his hands and her money in his
pocket."

"But where *is* the body?" someone would ask.

"Ask him," Adamson would say.

"You can't try a man unless you've got a corpse."

"Then let's have *his* corpse," Adamson finally
shouted when there were enough men there, when
they were ripe to hear it.

So they went. They mobbed together and left,
crossing the dark fields and meadows. On the way,
others joined. One who said they ought to call the
judge was shouted down. Adamson had the rope. He
drew the noose as he walked.

They crashed through the woods, each trying to be
in the front. But they made too much noise. As they
got clear of the woods, they saw the huge Vandermeer
running through the dark. With a whoop, they went
after him. He ran into the marsh. There was loud,
noisy splashing as they plunged in after him. It did
not last very long. Vandermeer went splashing
through the thick, shallow water, lost his footing in
the swirling mud, and crashed down, throwing up a
huge fan of water. When they hauled him to his feet,
the water was dripping from his beard. Adamson
thrust the rope into his face. There was a lot of deri-
sive shouting. Vandermeer snarled, broke loose for a
moment, and threw Adamson into the water. Immediately, Vandermeer was subdued again and dragged
back through the marsh to his farm.

"I told the truth," he said angrily as they stood him
under a tree, two men holding his arms.

"You'll have to do better than that," Adamson said.

But Vandermeer said nothing further. He stood straight and tall, his powerful chest swollen out, the beads of water clinging to his beard. His tiny red eyes watched them all as if trying to fix them in his memory.

But before they had a chance to throw the rope around his neck, the judge came. Someone had run and told him. The judge stormed toward them, seething.

"Untie that man," he commanded.

They all looked at the judge, then at Adamson.

"But, Judge . . ." Adamson said.

"Untie him," the judge said.

One of the men undid the rope around Vandermeer's wrists. They stood around in a sullen circle, not looking at the judge but waiting for him.

The judge moved into the center of the circle.

"Vandermeer," he said, "another minute and you would have been dead."

"And still innocent," Vandermeer answered.

"What have you done with her?"

Vandermeer did not speak.

"Let's search the house," someone said.

"Stick by stick," said another.

"Vandermeer," the judge said, "I want your permission to search the house."

"You cannot have it," Vandermeer said.

"The gall of him!" one of the men shouted.

"Don't ask him, Judge!" cried another.

Vandermeer rubbed his wrists where the ropes had cut.

"I want these men off my property," he said to the judge.

They went, finally. Slowly, sullenly, they went, angry and frustrated and embarrassed. All except the judge. He stood there and watched the last of them trail into the woods. Then he turned to Vandermeer.

"You've murdered her," the judge said. "And you've done something with her. Hidden her somewhere."

"Buried her," Vandermeer said.

"But where?"

"Where I told you."

"Do you expect me to believe you?"

Vandermeer turned and went toward the house. He stopped when the judge called his name. Patiently, wordlessly, he listened.

"We're going to find her, Vandermeer. You ought to know that. You've already committed some small un-witting mistake that will give us our clue. We only have to remember everything you've said and done, sort it all out, coldly and logically, and then we'll know what you've done with her. One more thing," the judge said. "You know why I stopped them? Not for you."

Now Vandermeer spoke. "I know." He was facing the house, still rubbing his wrists. "For justice."

The judge was back several days later with a war-rant to search the house. Vandermeer made no objec-tion; he did not even bother to look at the paper the judge showed him. They searched the house, and they dug in the cellar, and they dug in the yard and all around the house. Vandermeer sat and watched them—phlegmatic, unconcerned—and the judge stood and watched Vandermeer. Then they searched the woods, looking for signs of digging. They dragged the marsh. But they found nothing.

People said later that it had been uncanny, the con-fident knowledge that the judge and Vandermeer had of each other, as if each had had access to the other's thinking. In the judge's great strength, Vandermeer believed he had found a weakness. Without a corpse, without any evidence of any kind, the judge could do nothing, no matter how positive the judge might be. Vandermeer's contention that the body had been stolen was highly questionable but could not be disproven. It was obvious why Vandermeer had gone to the trouble of building and interring an empty coffin, and why he was willing to run the risk of its being dug up. But why had he been so certain the body would not be found elsewhere?

A few weeks later, returning from a short trip South, Jonah was met at the ferry by his brother. They rode the rattling old buckboard up the dusty, unpaved Grant Avenue.

"What's happened?" Jonah said eagerly.

"Nothing much," the judge said, holding the reins loosely in his hand. "We've got Vandemeer in jail."

"You have?" Jonah exclaimed. "Then they found her."

"Yes, they found her," the judge said mildly, watching the sun-hot, dusty road.

"How? Where?"

"I'll tell you," the judge said. "I'd got to doing some deep thinking about our friend Vandermeer. I combed back through everything. I thought about that first time when we went to him. You mentioned something about having had the time to build a coffin. He gave you an odd look at that, as if to ask you how you knew he had built anything. Then another thing. He said his eyesight was so poor that he almost shot us when we came out of the wood; but yet when we came back, he was able to see, at the same distance, that the grave had been tampered with."

"But he knew full well the body wasn't in it."

"That's right. Even though he couldn't see that far, he said the grave had been tampered with because he was anxious to get his story rolling. That confirmed, just in case we weren't sure (and we *always* have to be sure), that his story of a grave robbery was a fabrication. Then his attitude. He was pretty cocksure the whole time, wasn't he? When we were searching the house, digging in the yard, in the wood, looking in the marsh. How could he be so certain, so *sure* we weren't going to find her? But there was one time when he wasn't so composed. That was when we first dug up the grave. He paced around like a big cat, nervous and upset. But otherwise he was always imperturbable, even when they were about to throw a rope around his neck. And he had good reason to be so confident that we wouldn't find her—because we had already looked in the place where she was."

"I don't understand," Jonah said.

"He had given himself away not just by being nervous when we dug up the grave but by being so impassive at all other times. It didn't make sense to me, the more I thought on it. So I told them to dig it up again. Vandermeer was furious, but we did it, anyway. This time we hauled the box up. Then we broke it open. He'd built it with a false bottom. That's where we found her. That's where she was all the time."

"Well I'll be damned," Jonah said. "And you know how she died?"

"Of a skull fracture."

"How did he explain that?"

"He said it explained itself."

THE JERSEY DEVIL

by Edward D. Hoch

Many a fish has been hooked by a "cast beyond the moon."

It didn't start out as a murder case, and Captain Leopold wouldn't have been so deeply involved in it if he hadn't offered Fletcher a ride home that night. They'd been working late at headquarters on a barroom knifing, and when the case was finally wrapped up, Fletcher remembered that his car was at the garage for repairs.

"I'll drop you off," Leopold said. "It's not out of my way." He knew Fletcher's wife was always nervous when he worked late, and he did what he could to ease the situation. Since his promotion to lieutenant, Fletcher was working more nights, and Leopold sensed that all was not well at home.

"Thanks, Captain," Fletcher said, climbing into the car. "I appreciate it. But it sure as hell is out of your way!"

The rain that had pelted the city all through the chill March afternoon had settled now into a misty drizzle that hardly showed in the car's headlights. They had gone only a few blocks when a sudden harsh message came over the police radio.

"All cars! Attention all cars in vicinity of Park and Chestnut! Investigate house alarm at 332 Park!"

"We'd better have a look," Fletcher suggested. "It's only a block away."

Leopold grunted agreement, already wheeling the car down a side street. "How many homes in this area have burglar alarms, anyway?" he wondered aloud. Though close to downtown, it was an area of middle-class houses and well-kept yards, with a reasonably low crime rate.

"That's the house." Fletcher pointed, and Leopold slammed on the brakes. "Look! Around the side!"

Two figures had broken from the shadows and were running toward the back yard. Leopold was out of the car after them, shouting, "Stop! We're police officers!" They kept running, lost in the darkness between houses, and he started after them. He brought his gun out, but he wouldn't use it unless he had to. For all he knew, they were only a couple of punk kids.

"Careful, Captain," Fletcher cautioned, coming up behind him. The yard was muddy from the rain and slippery.

Leopold couldn't see the two who had run, but he sensed they were hiding nearby. "Got a flashlight, Fletcher?"

At his words, a girl's voice shouted, "Run, Jimmy!" A dark figure broke from cover not five feet ahead of Leopold and sprinted toward the voice.

Leopold made a long grab and ripped at the man's coat pocket, but he was off balance and falling. He tried to right himself, but his feet slipped in the mud, and he went down hard, throwing out his left arm in an effort to catch himself.

Fletcher had come up fast, shining his light. "You all right, Captain?" he asked, reaching out a hand.

"Never mind me. Get after them!"

Leopold knew he wasn't all right. His left wrist had taken the full weight of his fall, and although the pain was not great, he couldn't move it. He sat in the mud for a moment feeling sorry for himself, then got carefully to his feet.

After a few minutes, Fletcher returned. "A patrol car caught the man on the next street, but the girl got away. How are you?"

"I think I broke my wrist."

"Damn! I'll have to get you to a hospital."

"All right," Leopold agreed. He didn't feel much like arguing.

Fletcher snapped his fingers. "Wait a minute! There's a good bone man right in the next block. I took one of the kids there. Come on."

"It's a little late for doctor's hours," Leopold protested. He knew it must be nearly eleven.

"Never mind that." Fletcher got him into the car and drove to the next block, searching for the doctor's sign. Finally, he stopped before an older house with a remodeled front. "This is it."

"Not too plush for a doctor's place," Leopold commented.

"He's paying alimony to two ex-wives. Come on."

The sign by the door read: *Arnold Ranger, M.D., Orthopedic Surgeon*. Dr. Ranger proved to be a youngish man with a ready smile and quick wit. "Always glad to help the police," he said when they'd identified themselves. "We'll have to X-ray that arm, but judging by the angle of the wrist, I'd call it a fracture."

Leopold followed him into the X-ray room. "It's been a bad arm for me. Last year a bullet nicked it."

The doctor washed the dried mud away and carefully laid the injured wrist on the X-ray table. "Were you chasing a murderer?"

"Only a burglar. Down in the next block."

"That must have been at Bailey's. He's had other robberies." After a few moments, he returned with the X-rays. "It's a fracture, all right. Both bones—the distal end of the radius and the ulna. It's quite a common thing, really, but you'll need a cast for perhaps four to six weeks, and full recovery will take two or three months."

"That long?"

Dr. Ranger nodded and motioned Leopold onto a narrow padded table. "I'm going to give you a shot now. It won't completely knock you out, but it'll relax you while I set the bones. Perhaps your friend could come in and hold the wrist in place while I apply the cast."

Fletcher came in then and stood by as the doctor worked. Leopold was aware that the entire operation seemed to be happening with remarkable speed. Almost before he knew it, the doctor was helping him off the table and back to the X-ray room for a final look. "All right," he said finally. "I'll fix you up here with a sling, and you come back and see me in four weeks. Keep the arm elevated for a day or two in case there's any swelling."

The plaster cast was strange and heavy on Leopold's left arm. It reached from just below his elbow to his knuckles, with a slight crook at the wrist. Though it probably weighed only a few pounds, it felt much heavier. "Thanks, Doctor," he grumbled.

"Oh, one thing," Dr. Ranger said. "Could I have your health-insurance number for my secretary? She's always after me for treating people in the middle of the night and forgetting the paper work."

Dr. Ranger saw them to the door, and Fletcher tried to help Leopold down the steps. "Careful here, Captain."

"Damn it, Fletcher, I'm not a cripple."

"Well, cripple or not, I'm not leaving you alone in that apartment tonight. You come home and stay in our spare room."

Leopold started to protest, but Fletcher was firm. "Just tonight. Tomorrow you can go back to your place."

"All right," he agreed reluctantly. "And in the morning I want to see the guy they arrested. I want to know what he was stealing that cost me a broken arm."

* * *

The morning was something of an ordeal for Leopold. The combination of a strange bed and the cast on his arm had made sleeping impossible, and he arrived at headquarters tired and not a little grouchy. After explaining what had happened to the first dozen people he encountered, he retreated to his office and shut the door.

It was an hour later before Fletcher ventured inside with the morning coffee. "How's it feel?" he asked.

"The wrist's not bad, but this damned cast is getting me down already. A month of it and I'll really be ready for a rest home somewhere." He'd investigated the cast already, tapping its hard outer shell and fingering the thin layer of cotton that seemed to line it.

Fletcher sipped his coffee. "Want to hear about the guy you were chasing?"

"I suppose so. Who was he?"

"Fellow named Jimmy Duke. Three previous burglary convictions, all in New Jersey. Nothing too startling otherwise. He's thirty years old, and he's spent seven of them behind bars."

"What about the victim, Bailey? That Dr. Ranger last night said there'd been a number of robberies there."

Fletcher nodded. "Bailey is a stamp collector, of all things! He works out of his home and does quite a business in selling stamps to other collectors, which explains the burglar alarm."

"Did this Duke get much from him?"

"Quite a lot. All the most valuable items, unfortunately. But you saved some of them."

"I did? How?"

"When you grabbed the man and ripped his pocket. That's where he was carrying some of the loot. The boys were checking the yard with their flashlights, and they found stamps all over in the mud. Luckily, they're protected in individual little glassine envelopes, so none of them were damaged. We figure the girl must have gotten away with the missing stuff."

Leopold sighed and tried working the fingers of his bad arm. "I guess I should leave this chasing burglars to younger men and stick to murder cases."

Fletcher opened an evidence envelope and showed him a collection of multicolored stamps. "These are the ones you rescued. Quite a collection."

Leopold, who knew very little about stamp collecting, studied them with a mixture of interest and scorn. "You mean these things are worth money?"

"I guess collectors think they're a good hedge against inflation, just like art." He pointed to one reddish-brown stamp. "They tell me this U.S. five-cent one is worth fifty-five dollars. And here's an airmail stamp worth around five hundred."

"There's enough of a market for stolen stamps?"

"Apparently, among dealers and collectors. Unfortunately, one of the most valuable stamps in Bailey's collection is still missing." Fletcher consulted the notes attached to the evidence envelope. "It's a rare Hawaiian Islands stamp, two cents, issued in 1851."

"What's it worth? A thousand?"

"Bailey bought it thirty years ago for twenty thousand dollars. It could be worth twice that today."

Leopold whistled softly and gazed at the stamps with new respect. "No wonder he needed a burglar alarm. A bank vault would have been an even better idea."

"Collectors don't like bank vaults, Captain. They like to take out their collections at odd times and look them over."

"What's this stamp here?" Leopold asked, pointing to a large brown one that had been partially hidden by the others. It seemed poorly printed and showed a crude drawing of a winged demon flying over a row of houses. Across the top were the words: *Jersey Devil—Ten Cents.*

Fletcher bent over to study it and shrugged his shoulders. "I can't imagine. Never saw anything like it before. It certainly can't be very valuable unless it's something left over from Colonial times."

"No, those houses are modern. It's no Colonial stamp."

"Well, anyway, we got them back for Bailey. He's coming down this morning to look them over."

When Fletcher had gone, Leopold tried to busy himself with the morning reports and a batch of paper work left from the previous day, but he was not yet used to the heavy plaster cast, and its intrusive presence was both annoying and frustrating. Finally, he gave up the attempt and went out to the squad room to alleviate his uneasiness.

As soon as Fletcher saw him, he motioned him over to the desk where he stood with a tall, elderly gentleman. "Captain Leopold, this is Oscar Bailey. He's the man who broke his arm saving part of your collection, Mr. Bailey."

They shook hands, and the elderly collector said, "I thank you for your efforts, Captain. I only wish you'd rescued the two-cent Hawaiian."

"Any lead on the girl yet?" Leopold asked Fletcher.

"None, but Duke will probably break down soon and tell us who she is. We'll get your stamp back for you, Mr. Bailey."

"I certainly hope so. The insurance wouldn't begin to cover its current market value." He waved the evidence envelope full of his stamps. "And now I understand I won't be allowed to take these until after this man Duke has been tried."

"I'm afraid that's correct," Leopold said. "They're evidence that a theft was committed. We'll guard them carefully, however."

"I hope so!"

"While you're here, I wanted to ask you about this item in your collection, this *Jersey Devil.*" Leopold pointed to the poorly printed stamp. "What is it?"

"Nothing. A joke. It has no value." Oscar Bailey was suddenly ill at ease, his eyes shifting.

"Is it from New Jersey? This Jimmy Duke has a criminal record in New Jersey."

"No. Forget about it." He turned to one of the detectives and started reading the inventory of missing stamps. Leopold stood there for a moment, then shrugged and walked away. It wasn't his case, anyway; he'd just happened along in time to break his arm.

Yet the case did bother him because he had broken his arm. The following day, he called the public library and asked if they could give him the name of some leading stamp collector in the area. They had two names for him: Oscar Bailey and an assistant professor at the university, a fellow named Dexter Jones.

That afternoon, driving as well as he could manage with one arm in a sling, Leopold went out to the university campus. It had been some years since he'd been called there to investigate the killing of a student by his roommate, and the place had changed considerably. New buildings were under construction everywhere, and the old ivy walls were almost obscured by workmen and steel scaffolding.

His last visit had been on a glorious autumn day, but this one was quite different. The off-and-on drizzle of the past few days had started again, dampening sidewalks and spirits, and the sight of a muddy puddle at one construction site only served to remind him of his fall two nights earlier. He entered the fine arts building grimly and sought out the office of Dexter Jones.

Jones proved to be a graying, middle-aged man with glasses and what appeared to be a large mole on his nose. Eyeing Leopold over his glasses, he asked, "What happened to your arm?"

"Broke it chasing a burglar."

There was a grunt of sympathy. "I had an accident myself this morning. Tip of a match flew off and burned my nose here." He pointed to the molelike mark. "Looks terrible!"

"I understand you're an expert on postage stamps, Professor."

"It's only a hobby, but ever since the newspaper ran an article on me two years ago, the local library recommends me as some sort of expert. What can I do for you?"

"I want to ask you about a stamp called the Jersey Devil."

Dexter Jones lifted his fingers from a scratch pad he'd been toying with. "The Jersey Devil?"

"It was recovered after a robbery at Oscar Bailey's house."

"Did you ask Bailey about it?"

"He was quite vague. I was hoping you'd be more direct."

"Is it an official police matter?"

"The robber was from New Jersey. If the stamp was from there, too, it might be a connection."

"I see." He thought about it some more before replying. "Very well, I have nothing to hide. The Jersey Devil is the name of a semisecret, privately owned postal system operated in competition with the government."

Leopold wasn't certain he'd heard correctly. "A private postal system? Isn't that against the law?"

"Yes. Which is why it's secret."

"But who would use such a thing?"

"Various groups who need to conduct their business without fear of mail checks and interceptions by the government. Some quite respectable banks have even been known to use it."

"The whole thing is a bit hard to believe."

"Not at all. The government today exercises an amazing amount of control over the mails. Second- and third-class mail can be opened under certain circumstances, and first-class mail can be delayed and recorded. It's only logical that criminal elements, dealers in pornography, sellers of sweepstakes tickets, drug peddlers, and the like will use some other method of communication."

"But who's behind the Jersey Devil system?" Leopold insisted.

Dexter Jones paused to light his pipe. "A man named Corflu, who runs a trucking company in New Jersey. I've never met him, but I understand he's quite a colorful character."

Leopold stood up. There seemed nothing more to be learned about the Jersey Devil. "Thank you for your time, Professor. It's been most interesting."

Jones gave him a final grin. "Always glad to help the law."

On the way back to his car, walking through the puddles that remained from the March drizzle, Leopold wondered about one thing. He wondered about the name *Oscar Bailey*, which had been scrawled on the scratch pad with which Jones had toyed.

Nothing happened for two days, and Leopold pretty much forgot about the Jersey Devil and tried to busy himself with as much of the office routine as possible.

It was Friday morning when Fletcher walked into his office and dropped the bombshell. "How's the arm, Captain?"

"Heavy."

"Didn't you say you talked to a Professor Dexter Jones about that odd stamp the other day?"

"Sure. What about him?"

"Nothing, except he was murdered last night. Apparently, Jones was working late on campus. He left some test papers on his desk and started home around eleven. His car was in the faculty parking lot, and someone was waiting there for him. Shot him twice in the chest."

"Robbery?"

"Not unless the guy got scared off."

"Did Jones live long enough to say anything?"

"Not a word. Killed instantly."

"What about his personal life?"

"Divorced years ago. Wife and children out on the West Coast somewhere. Apparently, he was popular with the faculty and students. No sign of trouble there."

"Girls?"

"Nothing there. He wasn't one to fool around with his students if that's what you're thinking."

Leopold remembered his conversation with the cheerful, pipe-smoking man, and he felt somehow as if he were partly responsible for what had happened. Was there something he could have done? Had he asked the wrong questions or failed to ask the right ones?

"I'll be working with you on this one," he announced to Fletcher. "I feel I'm part of it already."

"I don't think you should, Captain, with your arm."

"Nonsense! I'm not going to sit here rotting away for the next month. Besides, I may have a lead that could help us." He told Fletcher about the name on the scratch pad. "I think it's time I had a talk with Oscar Bailey."

Leopold was becoming quite skilled at one-handed driving, though he wouldn't have liked going any distance that way. Returning to the scene of his misadventure gave him a brief moment of apprehension, and he was especially careful going up the front steps to Bailey's house.

The tall, elderly gentleman met him at the door and seemed surprised. "Leopold, isn't it? Captain Leopold? What brings you here, sir?"

"A few questions if you have the time. You may not have heard yet, but one of your fellow philatelists was murdered last night—Dexter Jones, out at the university."

"Jones! Murdered, you say?" He took a step backward and sank into a chair. Leopold stepped in and shut the door behind him.

"Were you a friend of his, Mr. Bailey?"

"Not especially, but at my age the death of anyone is something of a shock, a reminder of one's own mortality. Who killed him?"

"We don't know. I thought you might have some ideas."

Bailey waved a gnarled hand. "I hardly knew the man. We met a few times at stamp shows some years back, and he phoned me once or twice to discuss special stamp issues, but really we saw very little of each other. In a sense, we were rivals, and in this business it's usually best for rivals to keep away from one another."

"Then you wouldn't know if he had any enemies?"

"No."

"He didn't happen to phone you during the last few days?"

"I don't . . ." Oscar Bailey hesitated, through uncertainty or design. "Yes, now that you mention it. He called to inquire about the theft, to find out what was missing."

"Wasn't that unusual if you were not close friends?"

"Oh, he was just curious, that's all. Wanted to gloat, I suppose."

"Is there any possibility the thieves might have tried to sell him your stamps? I understand the girl got away with a valuable Hawaiian one."

"Anything's possible, but I doubt if they'd try to sell it this close to home. New York would be better."

Leopold nodded. It confirmed his own conclusion. "Then there's the matter of the Jersey Devil. I know all about it, so there's no need to be coy, Mr. Bailey."

"I know nothing about the Jersey Devil."

"That's odd, since Jones told me before he was killed that it was a private postal service used for extralegal purposes."

Oscar Bailey's face reddened a bit. "That may be so. My interest is in stamps and postmarks and covers only. The stamp you mention came my way, and I added it to my collection."

"Do you know a man named Corflu, a New Jersey trucker?"

"I may have heard the name. I don't remember."

Leopold could see he was getting nowhere. Bailey wasn't about to discuss the Jersey Devil with any detective. "All right," he said. "Thank you for your help."

"Are you going to get back my two-cent Hawaiian?"

Leopold merely looked at him. "First, I'm going to find out who killed Dexter Jones."

Jimmy Duke, the stamp burglar, was out on bail, and it wasn't until the following day that Leopold located him at his apartment in a run-down section of town. The day was sunny for a change, with the first hint of spring in the air, and Leopold felt good. Even the weight of the cast on his left arm was becoming bearable.

Duke, a stoop-shouldered young man with straight black hair and a pencil-thin mustache, didn't recognize him. "You another cop come to check on me? I ain't skipped town. You can see that, copper."

"I want to ask you some questions."

Then, seeing the cast on his arm, Duke's forehead twisted into a frown. "Are you the guy that broke his arm trying to grab me?"

"I'm the guy."

Duke thought about this, twisting his face into another unlikely shape. He reminded Leopold of nothing so much as a great rubber-faced rat. "Well, what do you want now?"

"The girl that was with you. Where can I find her?"

"Hell, man, they kept me up all night asking me about the girl! I don't know no girl!"

Leopold stepped closer to Duke. "Look, buster, I was there, remember? I heard a girl's voice call your name. She made off with some quite valuable stamps in case you don't read the papers."

Jimmy Duke lowered his head and sulked. "I don't

know her. I met her in a bar, and she came along with me."

"What's her name?"

"I didn't ask."

"Who put up your bail?"

"My brother in St. Louis."

Leopold sighed. "Look, Jimmy, I'm trying to get some information."

Duke's face twisted into something approaching a smile. "First names now, huh? The friendly copper! That's a real gas, that is!"

"I'm on a murder case, Duke. A stamp collector was murdered two nights ago, and it could tie in with your robbery. You were already out on bail then. How'd you like to face a murder charge?"

"You know I didn't kill anybody!" The words had gotten through. He was scared.

"If you didn't, maybe the girl did. Who is she, Duke?"

"I don't know."

"If she's such a good friend, why hasn't she split the rest of the loot with you?" It was a shot in the dark, but Leopold had a hunch it was true.

Jimmy Duke thought about that. He rummaged around for a cigarette and finally said, "All right, copper. Her name is Bonnie Irish. At least that's the name she uses. She's done some go-go dancing at clubs around town."

"Where does she live?"

"Rooms with a couple of other girls, but don't waste your time. She skipped town after the other night. Probably in New York trying to peddle that stamp for thirty or forty grand, like the papers said."

Leopold nodded. He had the feeling the rat-faced man was telling the truth. "Don't leave town. We may want you again."

"Don't worry, copper. I'll be here till the trial."

During the next three days police and detectives searched the area for the dancer named Bonnie Irish, but she truly seemed to have dropped from sight. The two-cent Hawaiian had not yet turned up in any of the normal New York channels, and Oscar Bailey was growing increasingly restive.

"He calls twice a day," Fletcher told Leopold the following Tuesday morning. "But I suppose we can't blame him."

"I do have an odd feeling of frustration on this case, Fletcher. Any leads on the Jones killing yet?"

"Nothing. I know you don't buy it, Captain, but I'm leaning toward the theory that the killer was a holdup man who panicked and ran. Nothing else fits. The guy had no enemies."

"Maybe you're right, Fletcher. Damned if I know."

On Wednesday, Leopold's arm began to itch beneath the cast. He was restless and irritable and anxious to do something. Finally, he called Fletcher in and announced, "I'm driving over to Jersey to talk to this Mr. Corflu about his private postal system." Something in a phone-company report had brought Corflu to mind.

"Like hell you are, if you'll excuse me, Captain. You've been driving around with one arm far too much already." Fletcher unrolled his shirt sleeves and buttoned the cuffs. "I've got no other leads to follow. I might as well drive you over myself. You're sure we won't upset the Jersey authorities?"

Leopold, giving reluctant agreement to Fletcher's accompanying him, answered, "We're not going to arrest anybody. If this Corflu is violating federal laws, it would be up to the post office department to get after him. I'm just interested in the murder of Dexter Jones, and that's what I want to talk about."

"You really think Corflu had Jones killed because he told you about the Jersey Devil?"

"It's farfetched, I'll admit. But Bailey certainly seems afraid to talk about it."

Traffic was light on this cloudy weekday morning, and they made good time. The offices of Corflu

Trucking Company were on the outskirts of Paterson, in a low, rambling warehouse that had been converted to house a fleet of modern diesel trucks. Leopold and Fletcher were impressed by it, but they were even more impressed by Benedict Corflu himself.

He greeted them wearing a grease-stained shirt and pants, poking his head up from beneath a pickup truck that was belching smoke as the motor coughed. "Be with you in a minute," he shouted over the motor's uncertain roar. If they had come expecting a crime king in a padded office, this was surely the wrong place.

When at last he emerged, passing a wrench to one of the other men, he proved to be a balding, middle-aged man with a tuft of sandy-red hair over either ear. The hair, sticking out like twin horns, gave Leopold the fleeting impression that here indeed, in the flesh, was the Jersey Devil.

"What can I do for you men?" he asked, wiping the grease from his hands with a soiled cloth. It was hard to pinpoint his age or much else about him, but Leopold guessed him still to be under fifty. When he walked, he threw his body to one side slightly, perhaps as a result of some old injury.

"Is there somewhere we could talk in private, Mr. Corflu?"

"My office. Up this way." He led them up a worn wooden staircase to a floor of offices above the garage. Here a dozen or so girls were engaged in general office routine, and they hardly looked up as Benedict Corflu passed through.

His office, overlooking the truck service area, was small and functional, with open shelves holding stacks of papers and printed bulletins. Against one wall, behind his desk, was a large map of the metropolitan New York area, showing everything from Newburgh south to Trenton and from the Pennsylvania state line east to New Haven.

"This is your operating area?" Leopold asked, motioning toward the map.

Benedict Corflu nodded. "Everything within fifty miles of Manhattan and a bit farther than that in spots." His face relaxed into a smile. "But you men don't want to talk about trucking."

"That's quite right," Leopold said. "How did you know?"

"The car you came in has Connecticut plates. It's also got a police radio in it."

"I'm Captain Leopold, and this is Lieutenant Fletcher. We're investigating a murder and a robbery that might be connected with it. There's a possibility you could help our investigation."

"Oh, I doubt that."

Leopold just smiled and reached out, placing the Jersey Devil stamp, in its little glassine envelope, on the desk before him. "We want to talk about this."

Benedict Corflu raised his eyes slowly, and the twin tufts of hair stood out more sharply than ever. "So?"

"We understand you operate a private postal service in illegal competition with the United States government."

Leopold had expected almost any reaction to his words, ranging from outright denial to flustered confusion. He did not expect the reaction he got. Corflu leaned back in his chair and said, "Of course! That fact is known to a good many people in the government. During the great mail strike, restrictions were even lifted briefly to allow me to operate legally. The post office department actually leased some of my trucks to haul mail out of New York City."

"That may be, but I can hardly believe they could condone the issuance of private postage stamps like this one."

Corflu waved a greasy hand in dismissal. "Rubbish! Stamps are only external symbols. I furnish a service, a needed service. Are you aware that mail—even first-class mail—can be seized and opened in this country of America? Are you aware that a sealed first-class letter can be held by authorities for more than a day while a search warrant is obtained to open it? The Supreme Court has even ruled the practice to be constitutional! What protection is there anymore for the average citizen? What protection is there for pure and simple privacy?"

"Who needs it? The criminal element? Isn't that whom you serve with your mail system?"

"I serve anyone who still believes in the right to privacy. The government allows me to operate in violation of the law for the same reason it winks at numbered Swiss bank accounts and illegal distilleries. Our operations are a tiny percentage of the total volume, and putting us out of business might be more difficult than it appears. The specific operations I conduct are carefully planned and executed in a manner designed to challenge existing laws rather than openly break them. My arrest would open up a maze of legal problems, which I am prepared to exploit to the fullest."

Leopold felt himself in a sort of wonderland, listening to a man who bragged of breaking the law and almost dared the law to arrest him. "I didn't come about your postal system," he replied. "I came about a murder."

"You said that. Who was murdered?"

"A stamp collector named Dexter Jones, last week in Connecticut. Another collector named Oscar Bailey had been robbed a few nights earlier. I think the crimes are somehow connected. One of the stamps stolen from Bailey was a Jersey Devil."

Corflu nodded. "I read about it. I remember, now that you mention it. The papers didn't mention the Jersey Devil, but they did say a valuable two-cent Hawaiian was still missing."

"That's correct."

"Worth how much?" he asked.

"Perhaps thirty or forty thousand dollars."

"I fear my poor Jersey Devils will never bring a price like that, Captain."

"We want the stamp back, and we want the murderer of Dexter Jones, Mr. Corflu."

"Why do you come to me?"

"Because the phone company records show that Jones placed a long-distance telephone call to you the day before he was murdered and the day after he told me about the Jersey Devil."

Benedict Corflu was silent for a time, perhaps considering the possibilities as he formed his reply. Finally, he said, "Yes, that's correct. I'd never met Dexter Jones, but we did talk occasionally on the phone. I was sorry to learn of his death."

"Why did he call you that day?"

"As a collector, he's been interested in the Jersey Devil stamp issue. He'd called me a couple of times before. This time he had two things on his mind. First, he wanted to warn me that a detective had been asking questions about the Devil stamps. I assume that was you."

Leopold nodded. "What else did he say?"

"That he'd been approached by someone regarding the missing two-cent Hawaiian. There was no picture of it in the papers, and this person wanted to know exactly what it looked like."

"Do you know if the person was a girl?"

"He didn't say. He only told me that he felt himself in the middle of things. Apparently, he'd told this person he'd have to see the stamp to be certain, and he was undecided whether he should tip off Bailey. They were bitter rivals, you know, and I think he was almost pleased at the robbery. Still, he didn't want to get in too deep."

"He asked you your advice?"

"In a sense, yes." Corflu smiled slightly at the memory. "Jones was an honest man, but even honest men can be tempted at times. I really believe he was sounding me out on the availability of a market for the stolen stamp. I suppose it follows logically—a man who prints illegal stamps would be interested in buying stolen ones."

"He put it to you like that?"

"No, no. But the implication was clear. He could get his hands on the stolen stamp if there was a buyer for it."

"And you told him what?"

Benedict Corflu smiled once more. "I advised him to call Bailey or the police. I advised him not to get involved."

"Spoken like a law-abiding citizen."

"Which I am."

"You heard nothing more from Jones?"

"Nothing. But you know that. You have a list of his calls."

Leopold got to his feet. The arm beneath his cast was itching again, annoying him with the persistence of its presence. "We may have more questions, Mr. Corflu."

"My door is always open."

On the way back, along the Garden State Parkway, one of Corflu's trucks seemed to follow them for some distance. It made Fletcher nervous, and he rode with his .38 service revolver in his lap until the truck turned off at the state line. It was that sort of a day.

Nothing happened for a week.

Leopold had never had a case like it, and the feeling of absolute frustration grew with every passing day. There was no sign of the girl, no sign of the missing stamp, no further news of the Jersey Devil. Oscar Bailey continued to phone every day, and Jimmy Duke continued living alone in his apartment, awaiting trial.

It seemed obvious to Leopold that Dexter Jones had been killed—by either Bonnie Irish or Jimmy Duke—when he took Corflu's advice and told them he was going to call the police; but the obvious was not always the case, and at least one other possibility had inserted itself into Leopold's reasoning. They had only Corflu's word for the contents of that telephone conversation. Perhaps Jones had, indeed, obtained the two-cent Hawaiian from Bonnie Irish and in turn delivered it to Corflu. A man like Corflu might well have killed him rather than pay him the stamp's value.

So Leopold continued to puzzle over the facts, or lack of them, and wait for the sort of break that always came sooner or later.

The break, when it did come, was from a most unexpected source: Benedict Corflu himself, on the phone from his Paterson office. "Leopold, this is Corflu. Remember me?"

"I remember."

"Some news has reached me which might be of interest to you."

"Oh?"

"Regarding a young lady named Bonnie Irish. Are you still looking for her?"

Leopold signaled Fletcher to pick up the extension phone. "We certainly are! Where is she?"

"A friend of mine in New York has been contacted by her. She has some stamps for sale."

"I'll bet! The two-cent Hawaiian, for instance?"

"That one was not specifically mentioned, but others from the Bailey robbery were. There's no doubt this is the girl you want."

"Where is she now?"

Corflu sighed into the telephone. "That I cannot tell you. But the day after tomorrow she is to be in New York City, meeting with my friend."

"He's willing to cooperate with the police?"

"When I told him there was murder involved, he thought it would be best. He wants me to be there, too, when he meets the girl."

"Tell us where and when," Leopold said. For the first time in weeks he actually forgot his broken arm.

The mid-Manhattan offices of Royal Stamp Sales were located on a dim side street off Sixth Avenue,

behind shop windows cluttered with faded and probably worthless stamps from all parts of the world. It
was not a place any passerby would be likely even to
notice, but on this particular morning there was a
great deal of activity. Corflu's friend, pleading a bad
heart, had allowed himself to be replaced behind the
counter by Corflu himself, free of grease and dressed
surprisingly in a conservative shirt and tie. Two New
York City detectives were also on the scene, working
as clerks behind the counter with Corflu. They would
make the actual arrest if one were to be made.

Leopold had been relegated to the sidelines, given
an observation post in a hotel lobby across the street,
but Fletcher was to play a key role in the stake-out.
Dressed as a mailman, with peaked cap and leather
mailbag, he would enter the stamp shop immediately
after the girl, blocking her escape route.

"I feel foolish in this outfit," Fletcher complained,
standing with Leopold in the lobby of the shabby hotel.

"But you can follow her in without alarming her.
Remember what Chesterton wrote in one of his Father Brown detective stories? 'Nobody ever notices
postmen somehow.' It's just as true now, except when
they're out on strike." He reached out with his good
hand to grip Fletcher's arm. "Could that be her?"

A girl in her early twenties, who certainly had a
dancer's body, was walking down the opposite side of
the street, studying the numbers on the shop doors.
Fletcher adjusted his cap and moved out of the lobby
door. When she reached the entrance of Royal Stamp
Sales, the girl paused a moment, seemed to brace her
shoulders, and then entered. Fletcher was only a few
steps behind her.

Leopold waited impatiently, running his right hand
over the hard plaster of his cast. It must have been
less than a minute, but to him it seemed like five. He
cursed softly to himself, then moved out. Traffic was
heavy on the side street, and it took him a moment to

get across. He couldn't see through the dusty windows
of the stamp store, but just as he reached the front of
it, the door was flung open, and the girl came running
out, holding a small pistol in one hand.

She saw Leopold and started to raise the gun, but
he swung his cast and knocked it out of her hand,
feeling the arrows of pain shoot up his arm at the
force of the impact. Her face twisted in alarm, and
she turned to run, but now Fletcher was out of the
door behind her, mailbag and all, grabbing her in a
bear hug that knocked the remaining fight from her.

"She got the drop on us, Captain," Fletcher explained. "I didn't figure her having a gun that handy."

Leopold grunted as he stooped to recover the gun.
"Miss Bonnie Irish, I presume?"

She twisted in Fletcher's grip and spat, "Go to hell!"

Inside, Benedict Corflu and the two New York detectives were sorting through the little pile of glassine
envelopes she'd left on the counter. "Is that everything?" Leopold asked.

"Everything but the two-cent Hawaiian," Corflu replied. "It's not here."

Leopold swore and looked down at the gun in his
hand. "Well, we've got Bonnie Irish, but that's about
all. This gun is a .22 caliber, and Dexter Jones was
killed with a .32."

The case went into another of its periodic slumbers,
only this time it seemed that nothing would awaken it.
Bonnie Irish denied any knowledge of the Jones killing, and they could hold her only for her part in the
Bailey robbery. The two-cent Hawaiian was still missing, and Oscar Bailey was still demanding its recovery. Benedict Corflu went back to his trucking business and apparently to the Jersey Devil postal system
as well.

Finally, one sunny day in April, Fletcher asked,
"You think we're going to have to give up on that
Jones killing, Captain?"

"It hasn't been even a month yet, Fletcher. Something will turn up. If only the girl would break down and tell us what she did with that damned stamp . . ."

"Maybe it was never stolen. Maybe Bailey just added it to the loot for insurance purposes."

"You think I haven't considered that?" Leopold grumbled.

"Or maybe the girl gave it back to Jimmy Duke, and he's got it."

"No, we've been watching him. She didn't go near him before her arrest, and she hasn't been able to raise bail yet to get out of jail."

"So where does that leave us, Captain?" Fletcher said wearily.

"Nowhere. Back with our stickup-man theory, I guess."

Leopold shuffled papers and looked unhappy. After a time, Fletcher asked, "How's the arm coming? Isn't it about time for the cast to come off?"

"Tomorrow, I hope. I go back to Doctor Ranger tomorrow."

Leopold arrived at the doctor's office fifteen minutes early the following morning. He was anxious to know about the arm, anxious to get the heavy cast off and to feel himself a whole man again.

"How've you been?" Dr. Ranger asked, coming in smiling. He wore a white jacket this time and seemed much more the doctor than he had on Leopold's first, nighttime visit.

"I'll be better when this thing comes off."

"We'll see." Ranger picked up a small electric saw and went quickly to work on the cast. He made a line of small cuts, tracing the route of the saw, and then cut in deeper. Leopold felt the tickle of the saw against his skin as it broke through the cast. "Had any interesting murders lately?"

"One that's had me stumped. It grew out of the night I broke this thing."

"Oh?" Dr. Ranger made his cut on the other side of the cast and started to pry it apart. "Not that university professor I read about? Jones?"

"That's the one."

"Any leads on who killed him?" The cast came off, and Leopold stared down at his thick, scaly wrist. "Don't move it," Ranger cautioned. "This is only an inspection. We have to X-ray it."

"No leads," Leopold said, flexing his fingers.

Ranger carried the two parts of the discarded cast to the next room. "I'll just take you in for X-rays now." He positioned Leopold under the machine, cautioning him again not to move his wrist. "You know, I knew Jones slightly. Hadn't seen him for years, though."

"Oh?"

"Gray-haired fellow with glasses and a wart on his nose?"

"That's the fellow," Leopold agreed.

"I thought so. Met him once at a convention. That's why I was interested in your progress on the case." The machine hummed as the X-rays were taken.

"Couldn't you just look at it through a fluoroscope?"

"The pictures are a good record, and besides, you're exposed to less radiation this way." Ranger came out in a moment with the X-rays. "You think it was a bandit that killed Jones?"

"Probably. How does the arm look? Is the break healing OK?"

The doctor clipped the film sheets to a lighted cabinet. "The fracture is still very much in evidence, but all this is new bone growth. I think we can put you in a plaster splint for a few weeks. It'll be a lot easier on you than the cast."

Leopold followed him back to the examining room. "You mean it's still not healed?"

"Not yet, but I don't think you can lose position. A splint to keep the wrist in place should be enough." He produced a flat piece of fabric-covered plaster material and soaked it in hot water until it was malleable. "We'll shape this against the bottom of the wrist for support. It'll harden as it cools." He began to wrap it with an elastic bandage.

When he'd finished, Leopold got to his feet and stepped into the next room before Dr. Ranger could speak. "I'll be wanting this cast you took off," he said, reaching for the two pieces. "Just for a souvenir."

Dr. Ranger kept smiling. "Oh, I'm afraid that will be impossible," he said, and stepped around Leopold and quickly yanked open a drawer of the supply cabinet.

Leopold caught the glint of the pistol from the corner of his eye, and he swung the heavy cast as he turned, bringing it down hard on Ranger's hand. The doctor gasped in pain and dropped the gun.

"Hope I didn't break it, Doctor," he said, putting down the cast and drawing his own pistol. "Now, let's talk about the murder of Dexter Jones."

Lieutenant Fletcher brought coffee and placed it carefully on Leopold's desk. "Do you want to explain it to me, Captain? Just how in hell did you know Doctor Ranger killed Jones?"

"I suppose I didn't know for sure until he tried to pull that gun. Murderers don't seem to throw weapons in the river like they once did, Fletcher. But then I suppose he felt he was safe enough."

"But *why* did he kill Jones?"

"You told me yourself that Ranger was paying alimony to two wives. The prospect of thirty or forty thousand looked awfully good to him, and when Jones threatened to blow the whistle about the stamp, Ranger had to kill him."

"The stamp? You mean the two-cent Hawaiian?" Leopold nodded. "But where was it?"

Leopold held up half of his heavy plaster cast and pulled back the cotton lining a bit. "Right here, Fletcher. I've been carrying it around with me for four weeks without even knowing it."

"Inside the cast!" He stared at the old, crudely printed stamp.

"Remember how muddy my wrist was the night I fell and broke it? And remember how they found the loose stamps from Duke's torn pocket on the ground? When I fell, this stamp in its little protective envelope just stuck to the mud on the underside of my broken wrist. I couldn't feel it there through the pain and tightness, and I couldn't turn my wrist to see it there. In the darkness, you never noticed it, either. Doctor Ranger found it when he was wiping the mud away before setting the bones. As luck would have it, that one stamp was the most valuable of them all, but of course Ranger couldn't know that then. I remember at the time he was sure the robbery was at Bailey's, though I only said it was in the next block. He was so sure because he saw the postage stamp clinging to my arm."

"But why did he put it inside your cast?"

"It was a spur-of-the-moment thing, of course. He saw that the stamp was a two-cent Hawaiian and saw its design and color, but he couldn't know it was so valuable. It might have been worth no more than five dollars. He didn't want to keep it himself, to commit himself to the act of stealing it, until he knew more. But in case it was valuable, he certainly didn't want just to give it to me. So he tucked it under the cotton lining for protection and poured the plaster cast over it. He knew I'd have to come back to him to get the cast removed, and by that time he'd know more. He could either keep the stamp then or destroy it or even pretend to 'find' it when he removed the cast."

"What about Jones?"

"He called Jones to learn the stamp's value either because he remembered meeting him once or because the library referred him there. He could hardly call Bailey, after all. But Jones saw in the newspaper about the missing stamp, and he guessed the good doctor wasn't asking a hypothetical question. At first, he planned to help Ranger sell the stamp, but two things changed his mind. I came calling about the Jersey Devil stamp, which worried him, and then Corflu advised him to tell the police everything. When he told Ranger he was going to do that, the doctor saw his forty grand going out the window. Once we knew Ranger was involved, we'd suspect that I somehow brought the stamp to him with my broken wrist. So he went out to the university and killed Dexter Jones."

"Just like that."

"Just like that. I didn't really start suspecting him, though, until this morning in his office. He said he'd known Jones years ago, and he described him. He said Jones had a wart on his nose. It probably looked that way in the darkness of the parking lot, but it was really a burn he'd gotten the day I visited him. So I knew Ranger had seen him just before his death and that he was lying about it for some reason. Then I remembered how he'd guessed the robbery was at Bailey's that first night, and how he'd been quick to get the cast out of my sight after he removed it. I took a chance and asked to keep it. That's when he really lost his cool and went for the gun."

"All that for a postage stamp," Fletcher mused. "Well, at least the case is wrapped up, and you've got the cast off your arm, Captain."

Leopold reached out to touch it on the desk. "You know, I think I'll miss it. There were times when it came in handy."

THE GARAGE APARTMENT

by Joyce Harrington

Although not recommended heartily, this may be one way to fix a troublesome problem.

I don't know why I should feel this way," Sylvia Hawkins mooned into a cup of cold black coffee. "I drink too much coffee these days. And now I'm talking to myself." She sighed.

Sylvia rose wearily from the kitchen table and sloshed the bitter brew into the sink. She rinsed the cup and opened the dishwasher. The door sprang out of her wet fingers and slammed the cup to the floor.

"Not another one," she groaned. It was the third out of the set of coffee mugs to go in a month. One broke in the move from San Francisco. Last week, one mysteriously fell off its handle while full of hot coffee. Now this. The cups must be jinxed. Imagine Judy giving her a jinxed moving-day present. Sylvia sighed again and got out the broom and dustpan.

The thought of Judy, immersed in the trials and errors of first-time motherhood, brought a pang of regret. Sylvia would have enjoyed being nearby—not to meddle, just to be there, to watch her first grandchild grow and to help Judy over the rough spots. Instead, she was three thousand miles away, getting settled in a new home, getting oriented in a new community, while John was grasping the challenge of an even more exalted position with the company.

Ah well, that had been the pattern of their lives for more than twenty years. Seven different cities—never more than a few years in any one place. No wonder Judy had dug in, married a native Californian, and had no desire ever to go anywhere again.

Jody, on the other hand, was a born wanderer. The world was his back yard. No pair of twins was ever more unalike. Now Jody, a dropout from Stanford, was somewhere in South America teaching an emerging Indian tribe to grow bigger and better plantains and to wear shoes.

Sylvia realized with a start that she was leaning on the broom, the dustpan filled with shards of broken cup about to slip from her forgetful fingers. "Dreaming again. Miles away." Miles away but with her eyes fixed out the back window, focused on the red brick garage across the lawn. Or rather, on the windows above the garage—the blank white windows with the shades pulled down.

"I wonder if Mrs. Pickens is busy cooking up some new complaints."

Sylvia grimaced with distaste and dumped the broken cup into the trash can. Put the broom and dustpan away, she mused. Funny how she had to keep telling herself what to do next.

Roaming the first floor of the house, Sylvia caught her reflection in the tall mirror over the fireplace in the living room. She stopped, staring. Did she really look that bad? The glass was old and slightly distorted, but still . . . The old brown slacks that she wore for doing odd jobs were wrinkled and bunchy, and her blouse was faded and missing a button. Bad enough, but were her shoulders really that slumped? Did her face really look that old? Not old exactly, but sour. She moved closer to the mirror and tried a hesitant smile.

"Oh, no! That's even worse. No makeup, that's what's wrong. I'll put on some makeup."

Upstairs, Sylvia took off the ill-fitting slacks and

the old blouse. She left them in a heap on the bedroom floor. From her closet she selected a bright pink shirtwaist dress. The dress seemed a bit tight at the waist.

"Am I dreaming, or am I becoming hippy in my old age?"

The full-length mirror on the closet door didn't lie. There was even the beginning of a stomach. Sylvia forced her shoulders back and stood tall.

"That's better. Not perfect but better."

At her dressing table near the window, the cruel morning light showed frown lines around her eyes and tiny pouches under her chin. The pink dress reflected color up her throat, but her face gleamed back at her, yellowish and frightened. Frightened?

"What am I afraid of? Of getting old? That's absurd. I'm Sylvia Hawkins, forty-six years old and in good shape. Just a little tired, that's all."

With quick fingers she dug into a jar of face cream and slathered her face with fragrant goo. She massaged and slapped and pinched until her face tingled under the mask of white cream. She finger-painted circles on her cheeks and made grotesque faces at herself, laughing aloud at her near-hysteria.

The doorbell erupted shrilly into the silent house.

"Oh, damn! Just a minute." She quickly tissued off the cream and ran to the door, feeling shiny-faced and greasy.

"I'm sorry to bother you," the lumpish creature announced. The chewed-over bun of a face showed no regret at all, and the dry raisin eyes peered intently over Sylvia's left shoulder. She wore a sleazy wool coat of dusty magenta with three gaudy buttons and a stiff black Dynel wig.

"Oh, Mrs. Pickens. Good morning. Won't you come in?"

"No, I don't have time. I have to get to work. I can't afford to be late. I can't spend my mornings giving myself beauty treatments. What a pretty dress. So youthful."

"No. Yes. Thank you." Sylvia felt herself shrinking under the envious barrage. Ordinarily, Sylvia could hold her own in a gently murmured cat fight, but this woman's hatred and jealousy were so transparent, her own weapons so meager. Sylvia remained polite and tried to feel sympathy for the stunted creature.

"What can I do for you, Mrs. Pickens?"

"Oh, I don't expect *you* to do anything about it. But maybe you'll be good enough to have *someone* fix it. When Mr. Pickens was alive, he never let things get into a bad state. Fixed things right away, he did. It's the bathroom window. It's been stuck all winter, and now that spring is here, I'd like to be able to get it open."

"Yes, of course. Well, I could come over and have a look at it right now. Or if you'd like to leave me your key, I could have a repairman come over while you're at work."

The shapeless figure ballooned with indignation. "I don't believe in handing out house keys right and left. And I don't want *anybody* tramping through my apartment when I'm not there. Don't you read the papers? Don't you know about the crime rate? Think I want to get murdered in my bed? No, thank you!"

"Well, I'm sorry . . . I didn't think . . . I'll try to get it fixed later this afternoon. What time will you be home from work?"

"I always get home at four o'clock. I don't suppose you noticed that. I usually take a nap as soon as I get home. My job is very tiring, very exhausting. But if you're going to get the window fixed, I guess I'll just have to skip my nap. Four o'clock, that's when I get home."

"I'll see you at four, Mrs. Pickens. Have a nice day."

"I'll have a hard day as usual. And if I don't hurry, I'll be late. Maybe you have time to stand here gabbing, but I don't."

She turned abruptly and minced down the porch steps as if her shoes pinched. At the ornate iron gate, she turned. "If you can't take care of that window, maybe that handsome husband of yours can do something about it."

Mrs. Pickens smiled. The smile became a leer, and the black eyes challenged Sylvia. Sylvia blinked and looked again, but the dumpy figure was waddling self-importantly up the street, the black curls bobbing and gleaming artificially in the brilliant sunshine.

Sylvia closed the door and drooped against its massive frame. "So that's it. She wants John to fix her window. She thinks I'm lazy and frivolous and incompetent. She practically accused me of both spying on her and ignoring her in the same breath. She wants to get John up in her apartment." It ought to be funny, but it wasn't, somehow. Poor old thing. Sylvia wondered how old Mrs. Pickens was. Fifty? Sixty? It was hard to tell with that absurd wig she always wore.

Sylvia felt a sudden damp chill and realized that her dress was clinging wetly to her back, that stains of darker pink had spread under her arms, that cold drops trickled between her breasts and down her sides.

"Oh, damn! What now?" It was as if all the things she could have said, should have said, to the vile Mrs. Pickens were pouring out of her skin, drenching her in cold disagreeable sweat. She felt dizzy and slightly nauseated.

She pulled herself up the stairs, clinging to the banister, and collapsed onto her unmade bed.

"What's wrong with me? Maybe I should see a doctor." She thought back to her last visit to the smiling young Dr. Weng in his cheerful modern office near Golden Gate Park. She remembered the Chinese doctor doll that reclined, coyly naked, on his polished walnut desk. He'd told her that in the old days, well-bred Chinese ladies never disrobed for their doctors. Instead, they delicately pointed out their aches and

pains on the pale ivory body of the doll forever smiling placidly upon her teakwood couch. From there it
was all guesswork, and the delicate ladies often died
smiling placidly.

The dizziness passed, and Sylvia sat up cautiously.
"No placid smiles for this delicate lady. I'll have to
find a doctor and make an apointment."

Yet the thought of the effort involved in locating a
doctor dismayed her; phoning comparative strangers
for their recommendations, explaining vague symptoms to a possibly unsympathetic ear. After all, what
symptoms did she have? A slight dizziness and an upset stomach. A touch of a cold sweat. All gone already.
Probably something she'd eaten. Nothing to bother a
busy doctor about. Never mind the thin aura of foreboding that hovered constantly at the edge of her
consciousness. The unshakable feeling, however
slight, that something awful was going to happen. The
nightmares . . . She hadn't told John about her
nightmares. John had enough to worry about, getting
a new department organized, establishing himself
firmly as a senior vice-president and next in line to
head one of the company's far-flung enterprises.

Sylvia stood up, testing her equilibrium. The pink
dress, so gay and encouraging an hour ago, sagged in
tired wrinkles and still felt slightly damp. Her skin felt
itchy, as if somehow it didn't fit quite right.

"I'll take a shower and start all over again."

With the hot water cascading over her, washing
away the morning's megrims, Sylvia shampooed her
short hair lavishly and thought about all the things
she knew she should do to soften their newness in the
town. Some of the company wives had a bridge club,
and she had been invited to join. She would call and
attend the next meeting. She would find out about a
tennis court. Even this dingy little Eastern industrial
town would have a tennis court. She would plan a
dinner party. She would find some volunteer work to

do. Surely there would be some way she could be useful and get to know people in the process. She would make an appointment to get her hair done. Even though it was crisp and curly, it was beginning to straggle, and the gray was making noticeable inroads.

If the children had been younger and living at home, Sylvia would by now have met other children and their parents, would have attended PTA meetings, would have become involved. It had always happened automatically, without her thinking about it, when the children had been living at home. Well, she *would* get involved—that was the key to feeling at home in a new place—and she would do it today. Just as soon as she got the drapes hung.

Dressed for the third time that morning and carefully made up, Sylvia headed out to the garage for the ladder. She crossed the lawn, noting with pleasure a wide area at the back of the garden where daffodils nodded in the gentle spring breeze. "I'll cut some later," she decided. "They'll look lovely in the dining room. Maybe I'll take some to Mrs. Pickens at four o'clock. Make up for her lost siesta."

Trailing back across the lawn with the aluminum ladder balanced on her shoulder, Sylvia paused to gaze at the solid brick structure that was her new home. It was an old house, pretentious in its ponderous Victorian elegance. From the rear, the view was of peaks and gables and a funny series of three small arched windows at the back of the attic. They looked down on her critically under their rococo eyebrows.

"That attic could certainly stand some exploring. I'll have to set aside a day for that. I wonder if it's haunted."

She glanced back at the garage, a red brick rectangle lacking ornamentation of any kind. No ghosts there. Only the dreadful Mrs. Pickens. The windows of the garage apartment still showed blank and white. Didn't she ever raise her window shades?

Sylvia spent the rest of the morning perched on the

ladder in the living room, carefully positioning the rods for the new drapes. The luxurious fabric gave pleasure to her hands as she inserted hook after pronged hook into the pockets at the top of each panel. The result when she finished was more successful than she had hoped. The deep bay window with its cushioned seats, once angular and forbidding, had become a cozy nook for reading or daydreaming. The pale gold drapes brought the room into focus and diminished the heavy dark woodwork that crept halfway up the walls. Sylvia was heartened by her success, and the earlier unpleasantness of the morning retreated into a shadowy corner of her mind.

Over a diet lunch of yogurt and unsweetened tea, she thumbed through the Yellow Pages of the phone book, making notes of tradesmen and shops that might be useful. There was no listing for Window Repair, although several window cleaners advertised their services. Perhaps one of them could do the job. At any rate, she would have to look at Mrs. Pickens' stuck window before she would know what to tell a repairman. Perhaps she could fix it herself. Maybe all it needed was a little elbow grease. Mrs. Pickens might be disagreeable and ugly, but she didn't look particularly strong.

Now that the drapes were hung, the afternoon loomed empty and endless. For all her good resolutions, Sylvia could not bring herself to call the bridge club, did not make a hair appointment, did not go any further with planning a dinner party. Nor did she make any inquiries about finding a doctor. The dizziness had passed. Time enough if it returned.

When the phone rang at three o'clock, Sylvia didn't know where the hours had gone. The empty yogurt container with a crusted spoon inside it sat on the kitchen counter. Dregs of cold tea stained the bowl of her cup. The phone rang five times before she could tear her eyes away from the back window.

"Sylvia, are you all right?" John's voice carried more than a hint of anxiety.

"Yes, of course. What could be wrong? Are *you* all right?"

"Oh, well, I thought . . . the phone rang so many times . . . Yes, I'm fine." Now his voice was too hearty. Sylvia decided he had something bad to tell her. The cloud of foreboding had slipped back somewhere between the yogurt and the phone call. She realized that her teeth were tightly clenched, as if to hold back thoughts too dreadful to speak.

"I was busy, John. I hung the new drapes in the living room." Sylvia heard her own voice, brittle, like a cracking bone.

"That's good. How do they look?"

"Fine. Perfect." Sylvia paused and consciously relaxed her tense jaw. "John, Mrs. Pickens was here this morning. She said her bathroom window was stuck."

There was a silence at the other end of the wire.

"Did you hear me, John?"

"Yes. What are you going to do?" Now his voice was guarded, apprehensive.

"Well, I thought I'd go take a look at it. Can't do any harm. Can it?"

"I guess not. Look, Sylvia, I called to tell you that I'll be a little late getting home tonight. Carter has called a late-afternoon meeting that might go on until after six. I have to be there."

"Yes. Well, that's all right. I haven't any plans for this evening. It's funny," she continued. "You sounded so worried, I thought you were going to tell me some bad news."

"Oh, Sylvia, you shouldn't let yourself look for trouble everywhere." John sounded weary, but he suddenly shifted gears and forced brightness into his tone. "By the way, Carter said his wife was looking forward to having you join the bridge club. Why don't you give her a call?"

"I will. I promise I will. This afternoon. After I take care of Mrs. Pickens' window."

"Are you sure you can handle it?" A heavy layer of doubt underlined the question, and Sylvia flamed with resentment at the implication that she was unable to cope with Mrs. Pickens or her window or anything else.

"Of course I can handle it. Nothing very difficult. It's probably like all the rest of her complaints—sheer fabrication with a slight basis in fact. A moron could handle it." Sylvia felt her voice shrilling out of control. "On the other hand, I'm sure she'd much rather have you fix it. Would you like that better? We can let it go until the weekend, and then you can go up there and fix the window *and* the drippy faucet *and* adjust the thermostat *and* look for the imaginary leak in the roof. And then you can sit down and hold her fat little hand and listen to how much better things were when Mr. Pickens was alive and how difficult it is to be a woman alone."

"Sylvia, Sylvia. Hold on. I'll come right home. I'll be there in twenty minutes. Maybe I can make it back in time for the meeting."

Sylvia said nothing. What was she doing? Why was she acting like this? She can't expect him to come rushing home every time Mrs. Pickens had a brainstorm.

"Sylvia! Are you still there?"

"Yes. I'm still here," she whispered. "It's all right, John. I don't want you to come home." She searched her mind frantically for some way to reassure him. "I think I'll start cleaning out the attic. There's an awful lot of old junk up there. Who knows, I might find a hidden treasure. Or a ghost." She laughed, trying to put more mirth into the sound than she felt.

"Well, if you're sure you're all right."

"I'm sure. Good-bye, John."

"Bye. Don't forget to call Mrs. Carter."

Sylvia put down the phone and, for lack of a better

idea, trudged up the back stairs to the attic. From the inside, the three small supercilious windows seemed quaint and comforting. Afternoon sunlight poured through them, imprinting three golden arches on the dusty attic floor.

Along one wall, sagging shelves held stacks of old magazines. Trade journals mingled with ladies' fashions of bygone days. Sylvia was drawn to the picture magazines, years of them piled helter-skelter. She leaned against the wall and thumbed through the pages of her life. Here were college days reflected in Ike's grin; their honeymoon trip to Nassau against the background of GIs wintering in Korea; Judy and Jody toddling while Hillary and Tenzing struggled to the top of the world. No vague forebodings then. Everything was certain. Day followed night; peace and prosperity were just around the corner. Nightmares and cold sweats lay in an inconceivable future. Mrs. Pickens did not torment her with nagging complaints and beady-eyed envy.

"Mrs. Pickens! Oh, no!" Sylvia dropped the magazines on the floor. Her wristwatch remorselessly read four-thirty.

She flew down the stairs and through the kitchen, snatching up a pair of shears and the hammer as she went. The kitchen door slammed behind her as she ran to the daffodil patch and feverishly hacked six or eight yellow flowers from their stems. With the flowers and the hammer in one hand forming a strange bouquet, the shears clutched in the other, Sylvia ran to the side door of the garage. Into the small vestibule and up the narrow stairs she panted, arriving at the tiny landing and the apartment door in an agony of apology for her forgetfulness.

She knocked. There was no answer. She knocked again, louder this time, her hands encumbered by the tools and flowers she carried. The door shuddered open on angry squeaking hinges.

"That's another thing that's got to be fixed. That

door squeals like a sick cat." Mrs. Pickens stood there, squat and malevolent, in a tacky no-color chenille bathrobe. "I thought you weren't coming, so I went ahead and started my nap. I thought, 'Well, she's forgotten. She's not coming. She's so busy with tea parties and such, who can blame her if she forgets a little thing like a window that won't open.' You woke me up, so you might as well come in."

Mrs. Pickens stood back and grudgingly held the door open just wide enough for Sylvia to slide sideways into the room, which was poorly lit and smelled of ancient cooking and sour laundry. It was filled with odds and ends of heavy old furniture. Sylvia didn't want to look too closely lest she be thought prying and critical. She leveled her eyes somewhere between the ceiling and the back of a lumpy seat-sprung couch. The furniture seemed to be coming at her in waves. She felt that she would drown in a sea of old plush and clinging antimacassars.

"I brought you some daffodils. I hope you'll feel free to cut some any time you like. There are so many. More than I can use." Sylvia disentangled the flowers from the hammer and extended them to Mrs. Pickens.

Mrs. Pickens shrank from the flowers. "That's very kind of you, I'm sure. Of course, you couldn't know about my allergies. You'll have to take them away with you. I can't even touch them long enough to throw them in the garbage, or I'll be sneezing for a week. The window's this way."

Sylvia followed Mrs. Pickens into a long cramped bathroom. The window was at the narrow end, covered with a cracked pink-plastic curtain. Pink plastic shrouded a white claw-footed bathtub. Sylvia squeezed past Mrs. Pickens and the bathtub and laid her tools and the flowers down in the sink. She drew aside the pink curtain and looked at the window. She noticed that the catch between the upper and lower sashes was firmly closed.

"Mrs. Pickens, this window is locked." Sylvia exulted in her victory over the horrid woman. A small victory, to be sure, but nonetheless, one up for Sylvia. "No wonder it won't open."

"Of course it's locked," the petulant voice snapped back. "All my windows are locked. Think I want some cat burglar creeping in on me at night? But even when it's not locked, it won't open."

The dreadful illogic of this statement circled in Sylvia's mind like a snake biting its own tail. *It won't open even when it's not locked, but it's locked so no one can open it.* Sylvia picked the hammer out of the welter of crushed daffodils in the sink. With one hand she slid open the catch and tried to raise the window. The window refused to budge.

"I told you it was stuck. Didn't you believe me?"

Sylvia glanced over her shoulder. Mrs. Pickens stood preening in front of the bathroom mirror, twining black Dynel around fat white fingers. Her fingers looked like slugs crawling through the wig. The awful bathrobe gaped, and Sylvia glimpsed sagging white skin where green veins popped and exploded into frightful networks. Her ears rang, and she felt a wave of dizziness approaching from some distant well of fear. She turned back to the window and began tapping gently with the hammer across the top and all around the sash.

"I don't know what good you think that's going to do. Do you think I haven't tried that? I've pounded that window until I thought my arm would break. You're just going to leave hammer marks all around it, and the window still won't open. Well, it's your property, so you can do as you like."

The voice blared on and on while Sylvia tapped and strained at the window, praying for it to open and shut Mrs. Pickens up for good, praying for a breath of clean spring air to rush in and dispel the dizziness that was racing in upon her, trapped as she was in the narrow corner of white tile. The window remained obstinately closed.

". . . I said, why don't you just give up? You're not doing any good!" Mrs. Pickens shouted in her ear.

Sylvia hadn't noticed that the woman had crept so close. She leaped, and the hammer twisted in her hand. It struck the pane, and glass flew tinkling in all directions.

Mrs. Pickens loomed, gloating. "Oh, now you've done it! Isn't that just beautiful? Thought you knew what you were doing and just made things worse. I suppose you think you can put a new windowpane in, too."

Sylvia, crouched by the window, could think of nothing but how to stop the terrible voice.

"Be quiet," she murmured. "Please be quiet."

Still the voice went on. "Won't your husband be happy about this? Won't he think you're just the smartest thing in the world? Nobody can say the window's not open now. It's open all right. Permanently open."

Sylvia watched her own right arm raise over her head. Curiously, she watched it go up and up, the hammer in her hand. She watched it come down. Her body moved along with her arm, strong and slim and powerful. She saw Mrs. Pickens floundering in the bathtub, her wig knocked askew, a thin trickle of red dripping off its shiny black fringe. The voice was no longer saying hateful, hurtful things, but the spongy mouth worked and uttered sounds, ugly, gulping, flaccid sounds. It had to stop. Sylvia covered her ears, but she could still see the mouth moving.

"Stop," she whispered. "Please stop."

She scrabbled in the sink basin. Daffodils fell, broken-necked, to the floor. Her hand came up gripping the shears.

John Hawkins drove his car into the garage and crossed the lawn, savoring the mildness of the spring evening. The meeting had run late but had been successful as meetings go. The real work of getting the new line into production would fall on his shoulders,

and he looked forward to the next months of problems
and pitfalls to overcome.

The sky was darkening to gray with a few streaks of
pink as he approached the house. There were no
lights on. Could Sylvia have gone out? Good for her if
she had—but no, her car was in the garage. Maybe she
was sleeping. John shook his head and opened the
back door. She was sleeping altogether too much
these days. Dr. Weng had said she would be all right,
but still John worried.

He walked through the kitchen and the dining
room, flicking on lights as he went. There were no
dinner preparations under way. All right, he would
wake her up and take her out to dinner. He hurried
down the hall and into the foyer. The elaborate chan-
delier, when lit, showed no trace of her. He called up
the stairs.

"Sylvia? You up there?"

On the stairway, he let his feet sound heavy so that
she could waken and not be startled by his sudden
presence. He peered into the dark bedroom but could
see nothing and heard no sound of breathing. He
switched on the light. The unmade bed and the heap
of clothes on the floor set off a slight ping of alarm.
Sylvia wasn't sleeping. At least, not here. He toured
all the rooms on the second floor. Lights sprang up as
he searched the house. He remembered she'd said
something on the phone about cleaning the attic. He
raced up the back stairs, sure that he would find her
up there. An accident, maybe. Or a return of that dizziness that had plagued her after Judy and Jody had
both left home. And the business with Mrs. Pickens . . .
But Dr. Weng had said she would be all right.

The dim hanging bulb in the attic shone down on a
scattering of old magazines on the floor, but there
was no sign of Sylvia.

Downstairs again, he went through the arch into the
dark living room. When he found the light switch, he
suffered a momentary disorientation. The long awk-

ward room was changed; no longer did the ceiling seem impossibly high, nor did the walls tilt down an uncomfortable perspective. He remembered that Sylvia had said something about new drapes. They made the difference. It had become a reasonable room for reasonable people to live in—except for one thing. He whispered her name.

"Sylvia."

She huddled in the deep window seat, staring into the light as she had probably been staring into the darkness. She was hugging herself with rigid elbow-pointing arms, rocking and rocking. He sat beside her, adding his arms to her protective cocoon.

"Sylvia, what happened?"

She moaned, deep and guttural, without opening her mouth. He rocked with her and spoke softly, trying to ease her out of the trance.

"Sylvia, I'm here now. Everything's all right. I'm here, and you're safe. But you've got to tell me what happened."

At last, he felt her body lean against him. Her arms relaxed and fell limply into her lap. She opened her mouth wide, and he heard her jaw crack with the release of tension. Then she spoke.

"John? She's dead, John. Mrs. Pickens. I killed her."

"You killed her?"

"Yes. I killed her, and she's dead. She won't come back anymore."

"Well. That's good news. A little drastic, perhaps, but good. Don't you think so?" John held her closer and smiled into her pale upturned face. "Maybe we should hold a little celebration. Or a wake."

"What? Oh, yes. I see." She shivered slightly in spite of the comfort of his presence. "But John, it was so awful. I couldn't help myself. I just couldn't listen to her anymore."

"All right. Let's have it all. How did you do it?"

"With a hammer. And the kitchen shears. Up in the garage. Oh, John. The blood. It splashed all over the bathroom. All over everything. The daffodils." She looked down at her spotless dress.

John laughed. "Oh, Sylvia. When you do something, you really go all out. Couldn't you have arranged a neat little accident? Or a nice clean, incurable disease?"

Sylvia smiled faintly. "It's really finished now, isn't it? She can't possibly come back now, can she?"

"I wouldn't think so. But I'm no expert on these things. Why don't you call Dr. Weng and tell him what's happened? See what he thinks."

"Maybe I will. Tomorrow." Sylvia rose and stretched. "Right now I feel so free. A little shaky but free." She tried to laugh, but her laughter came out in dry, breathless sobs. "I think you're right, John. We ought to celebrate. There's a bottle of champagne in the refrigerator. Good old California champagne. I'll get the glasses, and we'll go up to the garage apartment and drink to the timely death of horrible Mrs. Pickens."

Sylvia's excitement was contagious. John had the bottle of champagne in his hand before his natural caution reasserted itself. He caught Sylvia's arm as she was opening the back door.

"Do you think it's a good idea to go up there, Sylvia? To . . . ah . . . return to the scene of the crime? Maybe we ought to just lock the place up for a while, forget that there is an apartment over the garage."

"John, dear, I could never forget. I need to see it again, to get it straight in my mind. I don't want to live the rest of my life with that last vision of her in a bloody heap in the bathtub. I need to get everything clear right now."

"If that's what you want, dear, it's all right with me." He opened the door for her. "Let's go and remove all traces of Mrs. Pickens from our lives."

Sylvia chattered gaily as they crossed the wide, dusk-shrouded lawn.

"I remember the first time I saw her. She was a short, stout, middle-aged lady, eager to talk to somebody about her problems. She used to corner me in an empty aisle at the supermarket and rattle on about her loneliness. I felt sorry for her. You would have, too, John, if you'd seen her. This was about a month after Judy's wedding. Jody had just left for South America, and I was beginning to have those dizzy spells. Just about a year ago.

"Then she started coming to the house. The first time it was something about needing help with some medical forms. She always had a reason for being there; I couldn't turn her away. Each time she came, she was uglier, more demanding, more critical, but still so lonely and unloved. When I realized that she never came when there was anyone else in the house, that I was the only one who'd ever seen her, well, that's when I really started to get frightened. I hated her, but I couldn't stop her from coming. And the dizzy spells were getting worse. That's when I . . . when . . ."

Sylvia's rapid chatter trailed off. She raised both arms and peered through the failing light at the thin white lines that scarred the insides of both wrists.

"Well," she continued, "when I got out of the hospital and started seeing Dr. Weng, she never came back. I didn't see her again until we came here. I thought everything would be different here. A new town, new people to meet, a whole new environment. No more Dr. Weng, but I thought I could manage on my own. And there *she* was, living in the garage apartment as if she'd been there for months, just waiting for me to arrive. Oh, John, I tried not to let it upset me. I tried not to let you know she was back. But she frightened me so. And made me angry at the same time."

John opened the door to the small vestibule at the side of the garage and held it for Sylvia to pass through. "Maybe we can clean this place up now and find a new tenant for it. A friendly tenant."

"That would be nice. Yes, I think that would be a good thing." Sylvia took a deep breath and started up the narrow stairs. At the top, she pushed at the apartment door. It squeaked loudly and swung halfway open. "It won't open any farther. I think it's warped." She turned to John. "Hold my hand," she whispered. "I'm not really frightened. I know exactly what we're going to find. But hold my hand, anyway."

Hand in hand, they entered the musty darkness above the garage. The cold champagne bottle in John's free hand sent shivers up his arm. Sylvia clutched the two glasses upside down by their stems. Together they tiptoed like trespassing children into the room, colliding with tables and chairs as they tried to find their bearings.

"Where's the light?" John asked.

"There's a pull cord here somewhere."

John groped in the air and tugged. A cold, dim overhead light sprang on and crept over the crouching bulk of the heavy old furniture that filled the apartment.

"We'll have to get rid of all this stuff. I wish we could pass it off as antique, but I'm afraid it's just old."

"The bathroom's over here. Come on, John." She pulled him eagerly to the door of the dark, narrow cavern. "I want you to see. I want to see."

The fluorescent light in the bathroom flickered and then flared harsh and blue as Sylvia depressed its switch. A faint breeze gusted through the broken window, bearing with it the smell of approaching rain. The pink-plastic shower curtain waved its tattered ruffles around the bathtub. Crushed daffodils lay on the white tile floor amid a sprinkling of splintered glass. Sylvia bent and retrieved the hammer from under the sink.

"You see!" she cried. "It's all just as I left it. Just the way it happened. Now look in the bathtub. You look in first, John."

John parted the shower curtain and gazed down into the tub. "I'd hate to have you coming after *me* with a pair of scissors in your hand!" he exclaimed. "We'll have to put a new bathtub in here."

"Open the champagne now, John. We'll drink to the end of Mrs. Pickens and pour a libation on the poor old bathtub."

The exploding cork ricocheted off the white tile wall, and foaming wine sprayed the starry wound in the bottom of the tub. Sylvia's kitchen shears lay bent and useless on the cracked white porcelain. There was nothing else in the tub. No blood. No body. John filled the champagne glasses.

Sylvia raised her glass and saluted the empty tub. "Good-bye, Mrs. Pickens, whatever you were. Alter ego, hallucination, dark sister. I'm not afraid anymore. I can grow old without being useless and lonely. I've killed my fears. I will not become you."

"Amen," said John. They each drank deeply. "Now let's go get some dinner. I'm starving."

"So am I. And tomorrow . . . Well, tomorrow's not too far away, is it? We'll see what happens tomorrow."

ATTRITION

By Clayton Matthews

Ward Roberts, forty-five, a bachelor, a tax consultant, and investment counselor, had his own small firm, quite successful, with five employees. He was content with his life. He liked the neatness, the dependability, the symmetry, of figures.

If Carla Strong, recently widowed, in coming to his firm for help in making out her income-tax return had chosen a time some weeks earlier, it was likely Ward would never have met her. But Carla came the week of April fifteenth, and the firm was snowed under. Ward happened to have a few minutes to spare between appointments, so—kismet, or so Ward liked to believe in the weeks that followed.

Carla was a natural blonde with a bubbling, freshly scrubbed beauty but a real scatterbrain about money matters. Her bookkeeping was atrocious. To Carla, a receipt was something you used as a cooking guide-line; guideline because it wasn't in her to follow any instruction, printed or otherwise, exactly. Her person was immaculate, but her housekeeping was not, and she was always late for appointments. Fifteen years younger than Ward, she looked even younger. Her first husband, dying of an early coronary, had left her a small fortune that Ward felt certain she would have frittered away if she hadn't been fortunate enough to come into his office.

She was, in short, all the things Ward was not, but he found her wholly delightful, and he tumbled into love with all the tumult that accompanies a first love. It was his intention to propose in the proper surroundings, with candlelight and wine, a bird under glass, perhaps even violin music in the background. It didn't quite work out that way.

He made reservations in the right restaurant and telephoned instructions to the maître d' as to exactly what he wanted. But Carla was late; not a few minutes late, which might have been all right, but an hour and a half late, and the restaurant Ward had selected took a very dim view of late arrivals. They never held a table over thirty minutes.

Carla was properly apologetic about her tardiness, and she had used the time to good advantage. She glowed, she sparkled, she was gorgeous, and Ward's annoyance slunk away without a whimper.

The restaurant they finally dined in was clean, the food more than adequate, and the words fell from Ward's lips without benefit of candlelight: "Carla, will you marry me?"

"Of course, Ward."

He gulped, he felt himself turning pale, he stammered. "You will?"

"Darling, did you think I wouldn't?" Her hand floated across the table and came to rest in his. "I thought you'd never ask me."

More was said, endearments exchanged, eternal fidelity sworn, plans made, but such was Ward's ecstatic state, he had little clear recollection.

When the waiter came with the check, Ward double-checked the figures, consulting the menu he had requested to be left at the table for just that purpose.

"Why do you always do that, darling?"

Ward didn't look up. "Do what?"

"I've noticed you always total up a check. Don't you trust the waiter?"

Ward glanced up with just a twinge of irritation. He forced a smile. "It isn't a matter of trust, dear. Everyone's capable of error."

"I've wondered, is all. I know you're not stingy."

Perhaps it was her last remark which prompted Ward to tip twenty percent instead of his usual fifteen.

Carla suggested a wedding date one month hence. Ward was agreeable.

They had their last evening out together three nights before the wedding. This time Carla was on time, and they dined at the restaurant Ward had originally picked as the site for his proposal. They dined well and wined well and were bubbly with wine and honeymoon anticipation as they rode the elevator up to Carla's floor.

Carla had forgotten her key. She dumped the contents of her purse on the floor and rummaged. From all fours she glanced up at him and giggled. "It ain't here, darling. It just ain't."

"Don't you always check for your key when going out?" he asked, a slight edge to his words.

She smiled serenely. "Who checks?"

Ward always did, but he thought it perhaps undiplomatic to bring that up just then. Instead, he went about unearthing a building super, who was grumpy at being routed out of bed at one in the morning.

The honeymoon went swimmingly. The days were glorious, the nights even more so. Ward acquired a mahogany tan and didn't think it possible to love anyone as much as he did his lovely Carla.

A couple of flies buzzed into the ointment in the form of telephone calls from the office. He'd left a number where he could be reached in the event the necessity arose. Carla thought he should have shut himself away from all such mundane considerations, but a man couldn't expect a woman to understand things like that, especially a woman like Carla.

Ward still totaled checks and made sure they weren't locked out of their suite. Carla voiced a few comments but always in a good humor.

They had decided to consolidate their two apartments into one large apartment, in a modern glass-and-steel building out on Wilshire. Arrangements had been made before they left for furniture for the new apartment, their personal belongings moved in, even their mail forwarded.

The first item requiring Ward's attention on their return was a stack of mail, some addressed to him, some to Carla, some to Mr. and Mrs. Roberts.

Carla groaned. "You open them, darling. Mine will be mostly bills, anyway. I'll leave all that in your very capable hands."

Ward attacked the mail with good spirits, good spirits which rapidly turned into dismay. He had assumed Carla's bills would be for clothes, et cetera, purchased for the wedding and the honeymoon. Ward had a horror of unpaid bills. His horror was doubled when he discovered some of Carla's bills dated back before he even knew her. Most creditors threatened dire consequences unless payment was prompt. A number of the threats were directed to the immediate attention of Mr. Ward Roberts. With what he considered admirable restraint, Ward called this to Carla's attention.

She pouted prettily. "You know how I am about money, darling. Just don't fuss so."

The new apartment had His and Hers bathrooms. Ward liked his toilet articles arranged just so in the medicine cabinet, so he could, if the necessity ever arose, find his razor in the dark, said razor always in the far right corner of the second shelf.

Two weeks after their return, he went into the bathroom one morning, reached for the razor, and his fingers closed on nothing. He finally found it on the bottom shelf behind a bottle of mouthwash. It was without a blade, and he was positive there had been one in it when he had put the razor away. He was careful about things like that. He asked quite casually, "Carla, have you been using my razor?" He hoped she hadn't.

"Yes, darling," she said blithely. "Mine is rusted shut. I used yours to shave my legs."

He concealed a shudder. "I like my things, razor included, kept in the same place."

"Darling, there's no need to raise your voice." She arched her eyebrows at him. "A fuss over a silly old razor?"

After a dangerous moment, he said, "Perhaps you're right. I've lived alone too long."

"That's it, darling. We'll both have to adjust a little."

It seemed to Ward *he* was doing all the adjusting.

Carla was a clutterer. She hit a room like a tornado. Sometimes, when they'd been out to dinner and came home late, she'd start undressing the moment she entered the front door and leave a trail of discarded clothes behind her all the way to the bathroom.

Ward began cleaning up after her, even emptying ashtrays. He got to the point where he would empty an ashtray holding only one cigarette. Carla chided him. He started doing it furtively behind her back. The fact that he didn't smoke caused him to feel even more guilty.

Now, instead of locking herself out, Carla developed the annoying habit of leaving the apartment door unlocked when she went out. Ward began double-checking the door, turning the knob twice to make sure it was locked.

Often Carla would leave dinner dishes overnight in the sink, especially if she'd had a few drinks. One morning, Ward got up earlier than Carla. When she came into the kitchen, she found him elbow-deep in dishwater.

"Ward, what on earth are you doing?"

"Washing last night's dinner dishes."

"Darling, I always do that after you've left for the office."

He said stiffly, "I don't like to get up in the morning and find the sink full of dirty dishes."

"Ward . . ." She sighed. "We simply have to talk."

She plugged in the coffee, helped him with the rest of the dishes, then led him to the table. She poured coffee for them and sat down across from him. "Ward, we have to reach an understanding. You're driving me out of my mind, emptying ashtrays behind my back . . ."

He was driving her out of *her* mind?

". . . checking door locks. Like the other night when we went out, you started worrying if you'd locked the door. You turned around and drove all the way back. Now I know I'm sloppy about some things, and I know you developed certain habits living alone, but sometimes you're a fussy old maid!"

Ward sat up indignantly.

She reached across to pat his hand. "Now don't get all fussed. We have to look at this sensibly. We're intelligent people. We have to adjust, or we'll be at each other's throats in no time at all. If I make a real effort to be less sloppy, can you try and be less picky, less demanding?"

Ward slowly relaxed. He found himself nodding agreement. They were adults, they were intelligent, and Ward was honest enough with himself to admit that perhaps he was too set in his ways. There was no reason he could see why he couldn't change. It wasn't even teaching an old dog new tricks; it was more a matter of forgetting old habits.

Both made a conscious effort. On Ward's part it was more than that. He set up a bookkeeping system, a double column, a list of Carla's bad habits and a list of his old-maidish efforts to counteract them. He prided himself on the fact that he soon had crossed out more items in his column than in Carla's.

Yet it seemed to work. There were no more dirty

dishes left overnight, ashtrays rarely overflowed, and his razor wasn't disturbed once. Ward paid Carla's overdue bills without comment and forcibly restrained himself from double-checking the door. There were a few lapses, naturally. Carla forgot occasionally and left a discarded garment on the living-room floor, and Ward sometimes absentmindedly emptied an ashtray.

One evening, nine months after Acapulco, Ward took Carla out to dinner and a show. They came home late and found the apartment door standing wide. Carla's mink coat and jewelry were gone, the silverware missing, as well as several of Ward's good suits, and a hundred dollars in cash.

After the first questioning and subsequent apartment check by the police, a young officer huddled with Ward and Carla in a quiet corner, notebook across his knee.

"Now, Mr. Roberts, we have a list of everything missing. But there's a puzzling thing— You stated you and your wife came home and found the door wide open. Yet there are no signs of the door being forced, the lock being jimmied—"

Ward, head down, hands locked together in his lap, whispered, "I'm afraid I left the door unlocked, Officer, when we went out."

Carla gasped. "Ward, you mean you actually went away and left the apartment unlocked?"

It was then that Ward decided he had to kill her.

Carla said, with a little laugh, "Of course, Officer, it's partly my fault, looking at it one way."

"How's that, Mrs. Roberts?"

"Well, you see, I have this bad habit of leaving doors unlocked when I go out. My husband is just the opposite. He double-checks. He fusses so it got on my nerves. We made a pact. I'd try not to leave doors unlocked, and he'd stop checking so carefully." She laughed again. "So tonight the shoe's on the other foot."

The officer smiled broadly, as though he could easily forgive her any such small transgression.

But it was too late for Ward. He could never find it in himself to forgive her. He could, of course, divorce her.

Automatically, his mind set up a double-entry column. A divorce wouldn't be easy to get. He had no solid grounds. On the surface, theirs seemed an ideal marriage. He supposed he even loved her still. Divorce would be expensive. He was confident he could safely predict Carla's reaction. His asking her for a divorce would hurt her; she wouldn't be able to understand it. But once her initial hurt was past, she would demand, and likely get, a huge settlement as a price for his freedom.

On the other side of the column: Carla's demise. Everything solved with one slash of the pen. And it would cost nothing. On the contrary, he would gain considerably financially. Carla had no relatives. Her first husband's fortune would fall to Ward, and judicious investment could double it within a few years. Not that Carla's money was any inducement for killing her; it was simply a dividend accruing from the larger purpose of ridding himself of Carla before he began skittering up the walls like a frightened bug.

Killing her presented no great problem that he could see, requiring no elaborate, intricate plan. He knew very little of murder, but it seemed to him the more involved the plan, the more likely eventual detection.

The same things that weighed against him getting an easy divorce were in his favor. What possible motive could he have for killing her? They were happily married. He didn't have a girl friend, and Carla didn't have a lover. And although not wealthy, he had no immediate need of Carla's money, which was his, anyway, for all practical pruposes, so long as they remained married. Carla had early turned it all over to him to invest. He had control of it and could do with it as he pleased.

Somewhere he had read that the police look for three things in a murder suspect: motive, opportunity, means, in that ascending order.

Motive? Insofar as the police were concerned, none. The opposite, in fact.

Opportunity? He had to have the opportunity, of course; he couldn't kill her long distance unless he devised some exotic method, which he had no intention of doing. He knew the police viewed a perfect alibi with suspicion. The thing he had to do was make the opportunity, at the same time make it appear he hadn't availed himself of it. Tax deadlines were approaching, and this gave him a reasonable excuse to work evenings at the office. He had before his marriage; no reason why he shouldn't now. And he had, in those days, sent his staff home and worked alone until midnight. This was what he started doing now, working later and later and always alone, after everyone had gone. Carla understood and was very sweet about it.

He waited a little over a month, working late four or five nights a week. Almost every night when he came home, Carla was already asleep. Twice during those weeks Ward found the apartment door unlocked when he got home.

Finally, he selected the evening. His dinner was brought in from a restaurant up the street. He ate heartily, disposed of the dishes, and left the office by the back door. He left the office lights burning. The likelihood of anyone coming to see him or telephoning at that hour was remote. It was a small risk he was prepared to take. He could always maintain he had been too busy to admit visitors or answer the phone. His staff could testify that this wasn't at all unusual.

The parking lot behind the building was dark, and there was an alley, walled by business firms also dark at this hour. The alley emptied out onto a busy street a long block away.

It was early, shortly after nine, when he parked two blocks away from the apartment building, but he couldn't risk a later hour. By the time he'd accomplished his purpose and returned to the office, it would be ten or later. He used his key to let himself in the rear door of the building and walked up the three floors instead of using the elevators. The short time he'd lived there he'd met only a few people casually. If he encountered anyone on the stairs, he would say the elevators had been busy and then postpone his plan until another night. Another time, same plan.

He met no one. There were four apartments on his floor. The corridor was empty. The apartment door was locked; he entered very quietly. There was a small light in the foyer, enough to guide him toward the bedroom. He drew on a pair of gloves as he crossed the living room. Not that it mattered about his fingerprints, but a prowler would certainly wear gloves, smearing doorknobs. The bedroom door stood open, light spilling out. Ward hid his gloved hands behind his back, arranged his features in a smile. There was no need. Carla slept, her hair loose about her face.

Ward approached the bed on tip toe. As he stood above her, Carla stirred, sighing as though his shadow disturbed her, and he froze. The faintest hint of her breath, martini scented, reached him, and he knew there was little fear of her awakening.

He took the other pillow, his pillow, one end in each hand, and folded it across her face. At the same time, he slammed a knee into her stomach, bearing down with all his weight.

Carla convulsed, thrashing wildly, a muffled sound coming from her. She struggled furiously for a minute or so, but her strength ebbed fast. Ward held the pillow over her face long after her struggles ceased, held it there until his arms grew numb. Finally, he straightened up, leaving the pillow over her face.

He glanced around the room. On the nightstand beside the bed was an ashtray full to overflowing, as well as another full one on her dressing table. With a feeling of satisfaction, he dumped the contents of both ashtrays into the wastebasket, scouring them reasonably clean with tissue. Thank Heaven, he wouldn't be confronted with *that* problem ever again!

Then he tipped the nightstand and lamp over onto the floor, disarranged the bedclothes a little more. He dumped all of Carla's jewelry into a brown paper bag he'd brought along for that purpose. Her purse was on the dressing table. He upended it, taking all the money he could find.

He started out, then hesitated beside the bed, his gaze on her diamond engagement and wedding ring. For the first time, he felt a stir of repugnance. He decided against it. The rings wouldn't come off easily, if at all. Carla had gained weight since her wedding day.

He went out quickly then, turning out all the lights and smearing doorknobs with his gloved hands. He left the apartment door standing wide and hastily departed.

His luck held. He met no one on the stairs going down or in the alley outside. Trash barrels lined the alley; trucks would be by in the morning for the weekly pickup; that was the reason Ward had selected tonight. At the end of the alley, he paused by one barrel, raised the lid and rammed the bag, crumpled into a wad, deep in the trash. The odds against the trash men opening every paper sack in a barrel were prohibitive.

Frugally, he kept the money. There was no way it could be identified.

Ward was back in his office at a quarter past ten. He even managed to get some work done before the phone rang. He let it ring six times before he picked it up and said in an annoyed voice, "Yes?"

A crisp voice asked if he were Ward Roberts of such-and-such an address on Wilshire. When Ward admitted that he was, the crisp voice said, "I'm Lieutenant Carter of the LAPD. Perhaps you'd better come home at once, Mr. Roberts. Something has happened to your wife."

Ward had been halfway expecting the announcement to come from an officer rapping at his office door, with a police car purring at the curb. The fact that he had been notified by telephone he accepted gratefully as a good sign.

The apartment thronged with police, both in and out of uniform. Lieutenant Carter was thin, slight, middle-aged, very polite, but with a disconcertingly direct gaze. After Ward, demurring that he'd rather do it now, had made the formal identification of Carla, Lieutenant Carter placed him in a quiet corner of the living room, fired questions at him in between the times he was called away into the bedroom. Twice he was gone for a long time. Ward early volunteered the story of apartment burglary and Carla's habit of leaving the door unlocked. Lieutenant Carter said he would contact the investigating officer.

After more than two hours, all activity suddenly ceased. Carla had been taken away, and all the police were gone except Lieutenant Carter and two of his men. The lieutenant dropped down on the couch beside Ward. He took out a pack of cigarettes, offered one to Ward.

"I don't smoke, Lieutenant."

"That's right, you don't. I noticed that. In your shoes, I'd've consumed a pack or more with all this waiting." The lieutenant fired his cigarette and leaned back with a sigh. "I've talked to the officer who investigated the burglary, Mr. Roberts. He confirmed the fact that your wife admitted her habit of leaving doors unlocked. The front door was open tonight, by the way. That's how your wife was discovered. A woman who lives on this floor saw the door open, ventured in, found your wife, and called us."

Ward said carefully, "That's what happened, then? A prowler found the door open and—"

"That could be the answer, yes. Your wife's purse had been rifled, her jewelry box empty. I suppose she replaced most of the missing items after the insurance was paid?"

"I believe so. I'm not sure I can list all the things missing."

"No need right this minute, Mr. Roberts." The lieutenant was studying his half-smoked cigarette. "You know, it's an odd thing, your not smoking."

"What's odd about that?"

"There were two ashtrays in the bedroom. Both were empty, wiped clean. That seemed a little odd. If you'll pardon my saying so, your wife didn't strike me as an immaculate housekeeper, yet both ashtrays were clean. Now even a finicky housekeeper who smokes will have a last cigarette before going to bed, perhaps even *in* bed. Being curious by nature, I searched and found several cigarette butts in the wastebasket. Two different brands. And several were without lipstick smears. Undoubtedly smoked by a man . . ."

"But that's impossible! I don't smoke. I told you!"

Lieutenant Carter glanced up. He said softly, "So you did, Mr. Roberts. With that fact in mind, I did some thinking, some more snooping. You see, the woman who found your door open was coming home, not leaving."

"I fail to see—"

"She had gone out an hour earlier on an errand. At that time, she saw a man leaving your apartment. What's more, she had seen this man on two other occasions recently."

Ward was drowning in a tide of outrage. "Carla and another man! I don't believe it. It's simply not true!"

"I'm afraid it is, Mr. Roberts. Checking through

your wife's purse, I found a telephone number tucked away. I've been talking to the man whose number it is. When he learned he might be under suspicion of murder, he talked freely. He met your wife a month ago and has been in your apartment several times. They hadn't quarreled, and he claims it was no intense love affair. He swears he didn't kill her, and I'm inclined to believe him. You know what I do believe, Mr. Roberts?"

Ward wasn't really listening. Carla had a lover? It was inconceivable!

"At the start, I could uncover no motive for your killing your wife—but now there is one. You discovered she had a lover. Tonight, you waited until he left, killed her, then tried to make it appear a thief had done it. You candidly admit to having no alibi, no verification whatsoever that you were in your office all evening. It's only a hunch, but I believe you may have gotten rid of the jewelry close by. Some of the boys are out searching now."

What was this man saying? That he had killed Carla because of a lover? Ward couldn't let him think that. No matter what happened, he couldn't let him think that.

He leaned forward. "It wasn't like that at all, Lieutenant. Let me tell you how it was . . ."

ANOTHER WAY OUT

by Robert Colby

Allen Cutler had returned so unobtrusively from his
annual two-week vacation that I was unaware of his
presence until the midmorning coffee break. We were
cohorts at Whatley Associates, a large commercial employment agency, Allen handling the placement of
technical or professional people, while I found jobs
for general office personnel.

There was a lounge at the back of the employment
mill, furnished with a coffee urn and a daily supply of
doughnuts. En route to this lounge, I saw Cutler in his
office and paused at the entrance. He was studying
cards in his job file and talking on the phone. A tall,
spare man nearing forty, he had an abundant crop of
pure white hair which was set off strikingly by a deep
tan acquired during his vacation.

Allen put down the phone and glanced up. He
flashed a quick smile at me, removed thick-lensed
glasses, pinched his prominent nose. At that instant,
some insidious aspect of his appearance stirred an un-
pleasant memory. It was a puzzling reaction, completely unfounded. Allen was a likable guy with
whom I had always been friendly, if not close. Possibly, without the black, heavily framed glasses which

he seldom removed, he reminded me of some forgotten enemy in the distant past.

"Don't just stand there, Don," he said. "Applaud, do a little dance. Cutler has returned, bringing order to chaos, hope to despair."

We shook hands across the desk, he restored the glasses, and gone was my vague impression that he recalled a sinister character from another time and context.

"Welcome back to unemployment," I said. "See you're flaunting a tan. Acapulco, I suppose. Or the Riviera?"

He snorted his contempt. "Nope, I rented a room right here at the beach and saved a bundle. What's the difference? You go to Acapulco, the Riviera, what do you find? Sand. Water. Sun. Girls in bikinis."

"So? Is that bad?" I asked him.

"That's good," he answered with a grin. "But the sun at the Riviera is the same one we got here. And anywhere you go, sand is sand, water is water."

"You forgot the girls in their bikinis," I told him.

"Wanna bet!" He chuckled. "It's you married slaves who forgot the girls in their bikinis long ago. Not me, buddy, not me."

Allen was a bachelor, embittered, it was rumored, by a disastrous marriage which had ended when his wife divorced him, grabbing the lion's share of his savings and property. He rarely spoke of his personal life, and his private existence outside the office was something of a mystery.

"Time for coffee and," I announced. "You coming?"

"I got two customers writing applications," he replied. "Be a sport, will ya? Bring me a dark coffee, light on the sugar. Okay?"

The rest of the day was a hectic scramble. The outsized Sunday ads had stacked job-hungry clients wall to wall in the reception room, while the phone rang incessantly. The oddity of Allen Cutler hovered at the edge of my mind but didn't take hold until near dusk when I sat with a highball in the silence of my own living room. Beverly, my wife, was an R.N. She was on the night trick and, having left me a little note, had departed for the hospital before my arrival.

I might have dismissed that sudden, startling image of Allen Cutler as merely an absurd distortion of reality, somewhat like an old friend seen abruptly in the crazy mirror of an amusement park, but my concentrated probing produced a conviction that Allen resembled some fugitive character in the news who had stuck in the back of my mind quite recently, during his absence.

I found the answer at last in a page of a newspaper ten days old. I had saved the page because a face illustrating a story seemed dimly familiar. I hadn't given it much more than a passing thought since the face was connected to a crime, but it did occur to me that perhaps the man had come to my desk in search of a job, so I had torn out the page and kept it.

Now I sat with it under a strong light and examined the face with a mental overlay of Cutler, sans eyeglasses, for the wanted criminal did not wear glasses. Further, his hair was invisible under a yachting cap.

It was not a photo but a composite drawing—and that was the real problem of identity. There are isolated examples of composites which so closely resemble a hunted criminal that it is a small miracle of collaboration between artist and witness. But usually a composite is not much more than a loose sketch of facial characteristics, the general aspects of facial structure and expression.

I understood these things. I had once earned almost enough bread to exist painting portraits, doing charcoal sketches and caricatures. I knew that if you erased the eyeglasses worn habitually and of necessity by Allen Cutler and covered his white hair with a visored cap, the newspaper composite was a pretty fair, if mechanical, likeness. I could see it now, I could see it absolutely, though I was quite certain that the untrained eye, even of a friend, would not be able to match Cutler to the sketch.

Of course, it might have been a purely accidental similarity, for there was no reason to suspect that the other side of Allen's coin was a secret life of crime. So again I read the newspaper report, searching line by line for a clue.

Two gunmen behind .45 automatics had held up the Merchants Security Bank minutes after an armored truck had delivered close to ninety thousand in currency. They had worn yachting caps and ornamental scarves about their necks. The scarves had been pulled up over their faces at the moment of entry, and only their eyes were revealed.

All might have gone well for the bandits, but a customer outside of the bank had approached the main door. Catching the picture at a glance, he had waved down a patrol car which had just then rounded the corner.

One gunman was killed in an exchange of shots as he left the bank. The other had taken a hostage, Miss Lynn Radford, a teller, and had escaped with the loot by a side door. The robber hustled her to a car in the next block and sped off.

As Lynn Radford explained it after she was released unharmed, her captor could not ride through the streets with a scarf over his face, so he had yanked it off. Thus, she got a look at him, though mostly he kept his head turned away from her, and the cap covered his hair. Miss Radford wrote down the tag number of the car, a beige Ford sedan, but as it turned out, the license plates had been stolen.

There was a rather fascinating sidelight to the case. The slain robber, Harley Beaumont, 38, was a computer programmer in the data processing section of Merchants Security. Recently divorced, he had not the least criminal record.

Cutler appeared to be a bird of the same feather, and that was a piece of the puzzle. Also, as described by Miss Radford, the robber was tall and slim and in his late thirties, as was Cutler. She thought he had pale-blue eyes, and so did Cutler, as I remembered, though his eyes were somewhat obscured by his strong lenses. He couldn't function without glasses, but he could have worn contacts during the robbery.

Finally, the robbery had taken place on the third day of his vacation. Harley Beaumont had also been on vacation.

It was exciting to speculate upon all these possibilities, but my elation soon died and was replaced by an insinuating depression. What if Cutler really *was* the stickup man in the composite? If I could prove it, did I have the heart to turn him in?

With a sense of relief, I decided that it was so far only a kind of game I was playing. I could take one more step before I was committed.

Next morning, determined to keep the secret even from Bev, who, anyway, was fast asleep when I left for the grind, I phoned Miss Lynn Radford at Merchants Security. After introducing myself with the information that I worked for Blaine Whatley Associates, I told her I had reason to believe that an acquaintance of mine might be the surviving partner in the bank robbery, the man who made her his hostage and escaped with some ninety thousand dollars.

It took a bit of doing, but I persuaded her to meet me at a restaurant where my "suspect" habitually had lunch so that she could take a look at him. I made the stipulation that since it was an extremely delicate matter to accuse a man who might be considered a friend of sorts, I did not want her to go out on a limb with the police until we had put our heads together secretly. She gave me her pledge of silence.

I asked her if she could arrange with the bank to leave half an hour before noon so that we could talk quietly before the luncheon crowd arrived. She said she would call me back and did so in a few minutes to say that she was leaving at 11:30 by cab. Having discovered that I really was with Whatley Associates, she sounded much less reluctant the second time around.

Lynn Radford arrived just behind me, wearing a modest yellow cotton dress and an expression of worried expectancy. She was a rather short young woman who could no doubt see her thirtieth year of earthly joys and sorrows approaching from no great distance. She was carrying too much weight for her size, and her small features were exceedingly plain. Her dark hair was so unstylishly busy with swoops and curls, it was almost a distraction.

Despite the harsh photo of her in the newspaper, I recognized her at once. I had taken the nearest booth to the door, and Miss Radford, with a hesitant smile, sank to the opposite cushion and peered at me in wary silence.

"Sorry about all this intrigue," I said, "but it seems necessary, and I do appreciate your help."

She shrugged but said nothing, and I asked if she'd like a drink.

She brightened. "I'd love a stinger," she said quickly. "I've been more relaxed having a tooth pulled." She smiled in a way that gave her uncomplicated face the first accent of personality.

I ordered two of the same, and she went on to say, "I just can't help being a bit nervous, Mr. Stansbury. Since the robbery, nearly every stranger looms as a kind of threat to me."

"Naturally."

"But you do seem a nice person, not at all scary."

"Little old ladies adore me."

"Go on," she said with a giggle. A waiter brought the stingers, and she gulped half her glass in one swallow. I explained that I had once been an artist and that because I studied facial characteristics with a professional eye, I had recognized the basic similarity between my suspect and the composite, while most people would fail to note the resemblance.

"What sort of man is he?" she wanted to know.

"He's pleasant, well educated, has a responsible job. Far as I know, he's never been in any trouble. But don't let that fool you."

"What about his appearance?"

"I was coming to that. He's tall and slender, he's thirty-nine and—"

"That fits him exactly," she said.

"And he wears thick-lensed glasses with a heavy black frame."

"Then you've got the wrong man," she declared firmly.

"Suppose he wore contact lenses for the robbery? It would be a kind of reverse disguise." I signaled the waiter to bring us another round.

Miss Radford leaned toward me conspiratorially. "You mean," she said, "that since he's normally associated with strong eyeglasses, he went to the trouble of buying contacts just for the holdup?"

"Yes, because if he's the right man, he can't see without magnification. It was a small detail, perhaps, since he never expected to show the rest of his face. But small details have solved a lot of crimes."

"How clever," she said, nodding rapidly. The waiter brought more drinks, and she went to work on her second.

"So be prepared for glasses," I warned her, "and try to erase them mentally. And don't forget, your man wore a cap on his head, and you didn't see his hair. It's pure white, and there's plenty of it."

"White hair!" she gasped, and shook her head. "No, no, the robber had dark hair, I saw his eyebrows, they were dark."

"So he used charcoal pencil to darken them."

"Thick glasses and white hair," she mused, hoisting her stinger. "You're asking a lot, but I'll try."

"Concentrate on the look of his nose, mouth, and jaw, the shape of his face."

"Yes, but how will I observe all that, just sneaking a look at him from a distance?"

"You'll see him close up. He can't miss us here by the door, and I'll introduce you as an old friend. His reaction should tell us almost as much as his appearance."

"Face to face?" she said anxiously. "Well, I thought–I mean, I never expected that you would ask me to— Listen, I think I'll need another drink."

I ordered lunch with her third stinger. She only nibbled at the lunch. She was flying pretty high, and we were on a first-name basis by the time Allen Cutler stepped into the restaurant and stood near the entrance, hunting a table. I had purposely sat facing the door, and I now casually waved him over.

He gave Lynn Radford no more than a quick, speculative glance and a polite smile. If he recognized her in that first instance, his composure must have been lined with solid steel. I introduced them casually.

"Lynn is an old friend of Beverly's," I fabricated. "Spied her coming out of a store and invited her to lunch. Why don't you join us? You're not going to find a decent table, and we'll be on our way in a few minutes."

"In that case . . ." he said.

I moved over and gave him room beside me. I beckoned the waiter, and while Allen ordered, I watched Lynn watching him. Mellowed by the drinks, she seemed in control.

"Do you live in town, or are you just shopping?" Allen asked her, as if only making conversation.

"I was shopping on my lunch hour until I met Don," she answered. She gazed at Allen steadily. "I'm a teller at Merchants Security."

"Merchants Security," Allen repeated, snowy eyebrows lifting above the ebony enclosure of his glasses. "I know it well, had an account there a while back, nearly a year ago."

"I was about to say that you do look vaguely familiar," Lynn declared boldly, "but now I'm at a loss to know why since I've only been with Merchants a little over three months. Say, do you always wear glasses?"

"Yes, I'm afraid so," Allen replied blandly, his face and voice undisturbed by the smallest ripple of tension. He plucked his Tom Collins from the table and sipped it lovingly.

"I should wear glasses myself," said Lynn. "My work is demanding on the eyes, and the strain is beginning to wear me down. I suppose it's just female vanity, but I'm thinking of contact lenses. Ever try them?"

"Yes," said Allen without a pause. "And they're a damn nuisance. I couldn't adapt to them. One night, I came in stoned, peeled them off, and dropped a lens. Tiny thing. I never could find it, so I gave up and bought these." He chuckled merrily.

"They look so powerful!" said Lynn, smiling. "May I try them on, just for laughs?"

"Sure," said Allen. Without hesitation, he reached up for them. The swift movement extended his elbow sharply. The elbow collided with his glass, the drink spilled over the table and trickled into Lynn Radford's lap. She stood to wipe up with her napkin.

A desperate gimmick, I figured. But I had been watching him carefully, and it appeared such a natural mistake. . . .

"Sorry, Lynn, how clumsy of me," said Allen smoothly.

"No harm," she answered coolly, and peered at her watch. "We'd better run," she said, and I called for the check.

I went with her to the bank in a cab. On the way, we compared notes.

"D'you suppose he did it on purpose?" she said. "The bit with the spilled drink."

"Probably," I answered. "What do you think? Is he the man?"

"I *think* he's the man, but I don't *know* that he is. The glasses, the hair . . . The hair is incredible. It throws me off completely. And there's something else—the tan."

"What about it?"

"The robber was wearing this dark blue paisley scarf. When he took it off, his face was pale in contrast. No tan."

"Allen claims he was on vacation at the beach, and since the robbery took place on the third day of his vacation, there was plenty of time for a tan."

"It's terribly confusing, you must admit," she said.

"What about his voice?"

"It doesn't help. This guy showed me a huge pistol, a .45, they tell me. And he said two words: 'No tricks!' He drove me into the suburbs, pulled to the curb, and barked two more words: 'Get out!' He said nothing else."

"How about the car he was driving? You must have had a look at it."

"Yes and no. I mean, I was awfully frightened, and my concentration wasn't exactly the best. The only thing I *really* looked at was the license tag. But it turned out to be a stolen plate."

"And the car itself? The paper said it was a beige Ford sedan."

"I told the police it *appeared* to be beige, but the paint was pretty well covered with dirt, and it was just a fuzzy impression. I'm not sure. I do remember that it was a Ford sedan, perhaps three or four years old but very ordinary inside and out in all respects. There must be dozens like it on the streets, and if I drove right up beside it, I doubt if I'd recognize it."

"Skip the car for now; let's get back to the man. He spoke just four words, but what were his mannerisms, his actions? What did he *do* that might help us? He didn't just sit there, did he?"

"Yes, he did. Once we got going, he just sat there driving, looking straight ahead, watching in the rearview."

"Once you got going? Did something happen before that?"

She nodded rapidly. "When he put me in the car, he raced around to the driver's side, and while he was getting in, I tried to climb out. He grabbed my arm and, after a little struggle, yanked me back again. That was when he showed me the pistol and said, 'No tricks.'"

"Anything else?"

She frowned. "Can't think of anything. Nothing important, that is. I did lose an earring that day, but it could have been lost anywhere, and I didn't mention it. Later, I got to wondering if it dropped off in the car or on the street when we were struggling. Should I have told the police about it, do you think?"

"Right now it seems a minor point," I said.

"Maybe to them but not to me," she whined. "That earring was very special because it belonged to a set given to me by a very special person long ago and far away."

She fumbled in her purse, brought up a lone earring, and dangled it in front of my face. "Isn't that *darling*, with the little heart and everything? It's real jade—at least I guess it is," she said hopefully.

To display polite interest, I took the earring from her and held it in my hand. It was a green heart of dubious jade, fastened to a gold chain, the heart bisected diagonally with a gold arrow. Beyond its sentiment, it seemed of no value.

"Very attractive," I said, and gave it back to her.

"I suppose it's silly to keep it now," she mused, "especially since he's probably married and forgotten me years ago." She dropped the earring into her purse with a shrug.

We were nearing the bank, and I said, "Well, what's the verdict? Apparently we haven't anything to go on but your memory. Is Allen the man, or shall we write him off?"

"Oh, no, not at all!" she cried. "I'm just being cautious. If you forget the eyeglasses and the hair, this Allen Cutler's face is very close. Oh, very! Put a cap on him, take off the glasses, and I'd likely say, 'That's the man!' "

"In that case—"

"But," she added hastily, "it doesn't mean I'm ready to accuse him openly to the police and the whole world. No, it would be foolish to go off halfcocked. Very dangerous. Think how embarrassed I'd be if I were wrong. And think of the harm it would do him. Why, he might even sue me. No, let's wait a bit. Close as you are, maybe you could dig up some piece of concrete evidence, any little thing that would convince me I'm right in going to the police. Because once I tell them he is definitely the man, they'll believe me, and they'll turn him upside down."

"Listen," I said, "I'm in no hurry to crucify a man who might be innocent. So I'll nose around, see what I can find. Meanwhile, if he's guilty, he'll know I suspect him, and he'll be apt to give himself away."

"Call me," she said, "the minute you have news. I hope it's soon because I'm cracking under the strain. I'm going on vacation next week unless you find some real reason for me to postpone it."

I told her we were bound to get some kind of break in the next day or so, but as it turned out, I was wrong. Allen did not betray the slightest sign of guilt. He was friendly, but no more so than usual. He kept the same hours and performed in his job with the same deliberation, his manner unruffled. He did not avoid mention of the meeting with Lynn Radford but spoke of it only in passing, as one might expect.

I tried his desk for a clue while he was out to lunch. It was locked. I made plans to open it somehow on Monday, the day I often stayed overtime to catch up.

I phoned Lynn Radford Friday morning and told her to go ahead with her vacation, that Allen Cutler was either the slickest operator on record or a paragon of innocence.

On Monday, I informed Blaine Whatley that I was staying over to do some paperwork. Naturally, I said nothing to Allen. People began to drift out of the office at five, and by six there was the silence of desertion. I checked to be sure I was alone, then went to Allen's office, a gadget with which I hoped to unlock his desk in my pocket.

Allen's door was closed. I opened it and went in. I had seen him leave, but there he was, sitting behind his desk, and munching a sandwich and going through a stack of papers. It must have been obvious from my look of gaping surprise that I expected him to be absent and was preparing to snoop in his office.

"Well, well," he said heartily, "I guess you heard the news, and you've come to say farewell to your old buddy. What marvelous clairvoyance that you should know I would come back to clean out my desk.".

"What news?" I said dumbly.

"Sit down, sit down," he said.

I sat, though something in his expression told me I should run. "What news?" I repeated.

"I'm leaving," he answered cheerfully. "Didn't Whatley give you the scoop? Well, I suppose not since I quit this afternoon at closing, and Whatley is too choked up to speak."

"You resigned?"

"Yup. I'll be gone for good in an hour. I offered to hang on a couple of weeks while Blaine found a new boy, but he was furious, didn't think he could bear the sight of me for another day."

"Sorry, but I just don't get it."

He took a bite of his sandwich. "For years," he said, "I've been living in a one-room apartment, squeezing a buck and saving my coin for the knock of opportunity. Today over lunch, I closed a deal with Len Kaplan. I'm buying him out."

"Kaplan? Peerless Employment Agency?"

"Right. It's not the biggest in town, but it'll be the best and maybe the biggest, too, when I reorganize

and build it to its full potential. I'm taking a couple of
Whatley's people along with me—Sandra Thompson
and Joe Briggs, as a matter of fact—and that's why
Blaine is sore at me. I had to offer them more dough
than that tightwad pays them, of course. But I want
people I can trust, people who are loyal. How about
you, Don? Certainly I could trust *you*. Certainly I
could count on your absolute loyalty. Would you care
to join up as my right arm?"

"Well, I don't know, Allen," I said with the straight-
est face I could muster. "I'm pretty well entrenched
here. There's at least a feeling of security, and I'm not
much of a gambler on new ventures."

"My, my," he crooned, "I do believe you're trying to
tell me you're in Whatley's camp, Don. Perhaps he
sent you to spy on the enemy, huh? Well, if there's
anything I can't bear, it's being betrayed by a friend."

"That's ridiculous!" I answered. "You must be kidding."

Methodically, he began to open drawers, piling
items on the desk, among these a great yawning .45
automatic which, however casually placed, appeared
to be aimed precisely in my direction.

"Strange," he muttered, "the sort of peculiar junk a
man accumulates in his desk which has no place in an
office." He picked up the weapon and held it care-
lessly canted toward my chest. "I don't know why,
Don," he said, "but of late I've had the feeling that
you've become hostile toward me."

"Not at all," I said hastily, forcing my eyes away
from the gun as if ignoring it would render it harm-
less. "I can't imagine how you got that impression, Allen."

"I always thought that we were rather good
friends," he continued, leaning back in his chair and
raising the barrel of the .45 slightly. "But now—"

"Nonsense!" I interrupted. "We *are* good friends, Allen. You mustn't assume, you mustn't jump to false
conclusions just because—"

"I have no conclusions, only intuitions," he snapped. He leaned forward suddenly and decisively, leveling the gun at my head. "And these intuitions tell me that you're an enemy, a dangerous threat to my future."

He thumbed back the hammer, cocking the gun with a snick of sound that caused a centipede of fear to scramble up my back.

"Put down that gun, Allen, and let's talk calmly!" I said in a voice that was anything but calm. "Now, listen, Allen, I was only curious, playing a little game. I never intended to turn you in, you know."

"Turn me in?" he mocked. "What does that mean, turn me in? For what? And who were you going to turn me in to? Whatley?" He laughed bitterly, lips sneeringly twisted as his finger took up slack in the trigger.

"It doesn't matter, I wouldn't believe you, anyway," he said as I groped for an answer.

He extended his arm, and the malevolent maw of the gun seemed about to swallow me. One eye closed wickedly behind the glasses, the other sighted.

Then he pulled the trigger.

The hammer fell, there was a spurt of flame. It came not from the barrel but from the bullet chamber, which had sprung open with a muted snap. Whereupon, using his other hand, Allen Cutler delivered a cigarette to his mouth and gave it fire from the narrow butane jet of his .45 caliber cigarette lighter.

Again he pulled the trigger, and the flame vanished. He placed the fake gun on the desk and leaned back, crossing his arms. His spreading grin became a snicker, a chuckle, a laugh. The laugh rose and fell, sputtered, began again, diminished convulsively, died with a gurgle.

Allen removed his glasses and peered at me through tears of mirth. Perhaps it was only the wash of my relief, but at that moment I could not see his resemblance to the composite bank robber. He was just an adult kid with a perverse sense of humor.

He knuckled the tears from his eyes and readjusted the glasses. He patted the .45 lighter affectionately. "Exact copy. Spied it the other day in one of those novelty shops where they got everything from itching powder to rubber snakes. Great little gag, what?"

"Yeah, great," I said limply. "Very funny."

"Makes you laugh so hard you think you'll die," he said. The smile left his face abruptly. "Look, Don, I wasn't pulling your leg about the job offer. Good people are hard to find, and I need you. Everyone has his price. What's yours?"

"Well, right now, Allen, I'm not ready to—"

"How about five thousand out front as a bonus? Say the word and I'll write you a check this minute."

"Five thousand?"

"Five grand, Don."

I saw the strings, smelled the bribe. Money paid for silence. "It's mighty tempting," I said. "But I'm the cautious type. Let's wait until you get rolling, then we'll see."

"Think about it, kiddo," he said. "And when you're ready, let me know."

He had a big fat smile on his face when I left, but his eyes were malevolent. I knew that when I had failed to accept his five-grand offer, he had become a dangerous enemy.

I went back to my office and waited nervously for him to go home. Fortunately, the clean-up crew arrived, and as if on cue, Cutler departed, a briefcase under his arm.

The big scare with the fake gun had not exactly endeared him to me, and now, twice determined, I reentered his office. His desk was empty, of course, but his wastebasket was loaded with discarded junk. I carried the basket to my office and sifted the contents minutely. There were stubs of pencils, a dried-up ballpoint, bent paper clips, torn business letters, cards and receipts for this and that, plus the leavings of his sandwich in waxed paper.

I uncovered no curious items until I pieced together with clear tape the torn fragments of a receipt for a valve job on his Mercury convertible, this accomplished by Hickman Motors, Inc., Lincoln-Mercury-Ford dealers, sales and service.

Nothing strange about that, no clue offered—until I noticed the *date* of this valve job. The motor overhaul had been done on the very same day of the robbery. Now, on that day, what if anything in the way of a car did Cutler drive while his Mercury was in for repair?

A big outfit like Hickman, I reasoned, would probably furnish a loaner. Nothing splendid, of course. Just a nice little transportation car, maybe from their used-car lot—like a beige Ford sedan.

I expected that Hickman's new-car sales and service departments would be closed, while no doubt the used-car lot would be open until nine. I used the phone, and in answer to my question about loaners, a salesman told me I would have no problem. When I turned my car in for repairs, the service rep would provide me with some sort of transportation.

Satisfied, I asked no further questions. In the morning, when the service department opened at eight, I would be on tap with a story which would surely uncover the beige Ford for my inspection. If so, when Lynn Radford returned, and I took her down for a close look at the car, she just might notice one or two items for identification which had escaped her memory in the excitement.

Now the whole caper was clear enough. In all seeming innocence, we arrange to have the old bus overhauled, drive off in a loaner, switch to stolen plates, rob bank, restore genuine tags, return loaner. Simple!

Just a little proud of myself, I stuck the Hickman repair ticket in my pocket, delivered the wastebasket to Cutler's vacated office, and went down to my car.

Next morning, when Hickman's service department opened, I was there. I went to the service desk and told one of the white-clad reps that I had lost my wallet, and it could be in one of the loaners—a beige Ford sedan. He scowled and said there was no beige Ford sedan in use as a loaner. Did I mean the *gray* Ford sedan?

I said I hadn't paid much attention to the color; that was probably it. He said no wallet had been turned in, or it would be in the desk drawer in the office where they kept lost articles. And as of a few minutes ago when he deposited a forgotten pen in the drawer, it did not contain a wallet.

I followed him out behind the garage to a parking enclosure where he pointed to a dusty, gray Ford sedan, which I judged to be a '66 or '67. I crossed to it, opened the door, and leaned inside. He was watching me, so I made a big search, hunting around on the floor in front while noting the color and appearance of the interior. Then I bent to peer under the seat where there were all kinds of paper and scraps, butts and other debris—plus something of shiny green and gold which positively startled me! I almost shouted.

I groped for it, sneaked it into my pocket, backed out, shut the door, and returned to him. "No luck," I grumbled. "Maybe it went to the cleaners with one of my suits."

Down the block I parked and took a good look. Sure enough, it was the mate to Lynn's earring, complete with gold chain attached to green jade heart with slanting gold arrow. If that didn't convince her we had the right man, what would?

There was then a long period of anxious waiting to reveal my find, but at last it was the Monday morning of Lynn Radford's return, and I phoned her at the bank. The vacation seemed to have given her a new lease—she didn't sound so fearfully tense. I told her only that I had a fascinating little memento for her to see and identify. I wanted to watch her spontaneous reaction when I lifted that earring from my pocket and waved it before her astonished eyes.

She asked me to drop by her apartment that evening and gave me the address. Around seven, I arrived in front of a modern high-rise and, as instructed, went up to 12D. She came to the door at once, wearing a pale-pink, flower-cluttered dress which did nothing to conceal the abundance of her flesh, jammed into that skimpy envelope of cloth. As usual, her terribly plain features were overwhelmed by a hairdo of frantic complexities.

"How nice," she said, and ushered me in with ceremonial bow and sweeping gesture. The living room was too large for its furnishings, which were an incongruous mixture of dreary old stuff and splashy-modern pieces.

We sat facing each other, Lynn primly upright, hands folded in her lap. "Well," she began before I could open my mouth, "I've been meaning to call you. Because in the oddest way you can imagine, I've become convinced that Allen is innocent."

"Is that so?" I contained my surprise with an effort. "How very interesting in view of—"

"Just wait till you hear!" she inserted. "Are you willing to listen to a crazy story?"

"I'll listen, but—"

"Now just hold everything," she said, "until I tell you some new developments I didn't mention before because they concern you and I was—well, *embarrassed.*"

"Mmm," I answered.

"First, Allen called me at the bank just as I was preparing to go on my vacation. He saw right through that dreadful attempt to identify him at lunch, of course, and he was simply wretched. He said it all started as a joke. Someone in the office noticed his resemblance to the composite and began to tease him. It went around harmlessly until *you* picked it up. You were angry and jealous because a while back Mr. Whatley had made Allen general manager, a job you had expected would be yours all along.

"So you schemed to convince me that I should go to the police," she went on as if scolding a child about to be forgiven magnanimously. "The point, Allen said, was to cast enough doubt, stir up enough ugly publicity in the news to have Whatley toss him out, innocent or not."

"Fantastic!" I sneered. "General manager! The man is a genius at twisting—"

"Wait!" she cried. "Hear the rest, and you'll see. Now, I didn't really believe him until he suggested that perhaps the best way to clear up the whole matter was to have me meet him at the police station for a conference with Sergeant McLean. He's the officer in charge of the case, you understand." She grabbed a breath. "Allen did feel, however, that there was a chance it would leak to the newspapers. And by the time the police declared him innocent, his reputation, his career, would be ruined. But he was willing to risk it if I thought that was the only solution."

"A masterpiece!" I said. "Prize-winning fiction."

"Well, I couldn't help admiring his openhanded courage," she gushed on, ignoring me. "I told him I didn't want to see him hurt and degraded if he were innocent, and there had to be another way out. Allen offered to meet me in any public place of my choosing to discuss it, and I asked him to come to this little bar near my apartment where I know the bartender, a guy who is kind of protective of me. Not that I was afraid. I mean, the top executive of a big employment agency like Whatley Associates could hardly be a criminal type."

Oh, no? She was so taken in, I was almost sorry to burst her balloon, full of Cutler's gas. I was about to show her the green jade earring when she rattled on again.

"Allen was already on tap when I arrived at the bar. He was beautifully dressed in this handsome blue suit and looked like anything but some cheap hood. I mean, you gotta admit, even if you have your personal reasons for not liking him, Allen is a gentleman! Anyway, we had a few drinks, and he talked in that ear-

nest, direct way of his, asking my advice on the pros
and cons of approaching the police or finding another
way out.

"Suddenly, he reached up and yanked off his
glasses and stared me right in the eye. And he said,
'Now there! Am I a hood, a gunman? Am I that cold-
blooded robber who took you hostage? If you think
so, got to the phone,' call the police. I'll be waiting
right here when they come."

"The two of us sitting there, eyeing each other so
grimly. It was just plain funny. We both caught the
humor of it, Allen began to smile, I smiled back, and
soon we were laughing ourselves sick. And before the
night was over, I knew that I had never seen him before, that Allen Cutler was no more a bank robber
than my own father."

She sank back with a sigh. Then in desperation, I
groped for the earring. I was going to dangle it in her
face, give her the entire scoop about the car.

"Remarkable tale," I said. "One of the wildest I've
ever heard. But now . . ."

She didn't hear me. "It certainly wasn't love at first
sight," she was saying, "but that's what it became. I
spent nearly my whole vacation with Allen. Does that
sound naughty? Well, just take a look at this, if you
please!"

Her chubby little hand shot toward me, displaying
an engagement ring which sparkled with considerable
candlepower—and a silver wedding band. "We pooled
our furniture and moved in here," she announced.
"The old junk is mine, of course. I just couldn't part
with it."

Everyone has his price, Allen had declared, and he
had paid the big one. How long would it be, I wondered, before he felt it safe to divorce her? Probably
not until the day after the statute of limitations ran
out for the robbery. A long time, Allen old buddy.

"Where's the happy groom?" I asked her.

"He's down at Peerless. They're renovating, nights

and weekends. I didn't dare tell him you were coming, but I do hope you'll be friends again."

Even then, just for a moment, I did ask myself if I would be doing her a favor or an injury by showing her the little green earring with the corny heart and arrow.

"Just consider it a bad joke that got out of hand," she was advising me. "Forgive and forget. Listen, it doesn't matter anymore. Allen could be guilty as sin, and I'd forgive him, I'd stand by him. I'd even lie for him. I mean, in this lonely world, isn't marriage the most!"

Against both of them, there was no chance. I recognized that, and I thought of the risk I had undertaken to bring in a robber, and then I remembered the offers that robber had made.

Lynn's dreamy, lovesick eyes slid toward me. "By the way," she said absently, "didn't you have something you wanted to show me?"

"It was nothing, Lynn. Look, it was probably just as he said. We almost made a terrible mistake. Tell you what, Lynn, I'll call him tomorrow. I'll call Allen first thing tomorrow. I really think I've outgrown Whatley Associates . . ."

THE SCIENTIST AND THE
STOLEN REMBRANDT

by Arthur Porges

Perceptiveness, innate in some, may yet yield lit-
tle without the virtue of insight.

Nobody loves an informer," Lieutenant Trask said.
"He's bound to be, by nature, the worst sort of selfish
opportunist, living with or near criminals and selling
them for cash. I always feel dirty dealing with one,
but no police department—at least, in a big-city, high-
crime area—could do very well without them. There
are administrative problems, too. He has to be paid
for useful tips, and budgets don't allow for that
openly. That means understood lies and outright book
juggling, with the commissioner turning a blind eye."

Cyriack Skinner Grey, erect in his wheelchair, may
have thought Trask too one-sided; it troubled his or-
derly mind, which stressed balance in everything.
Darwin, he thought wryly, made a point of writing
down every objection to natural selection the moment
it came to his attention, realizing, well before Freud,
that it was just such evidence one tended to forget
immediately.

"Yet he must have a kind of courage to mingle with
the very men, often desperate and brutal, he be-
trays," Grey observed.

"That I'll have to give him" was Trask's grudging
reply. "But often he has no other way to make a living, although, to be fair, it's also possible the very risk

involved—walking the tightrope—gives some excitement and direction to a shriveled little life, the sort most of these guys have."

Grey reached toward a button on the arm of his chair, then hesitated. "I was going to offer you coffee," he said, "but it's a warm day, so maybe you'd like something cool."

"What's on tap?"

"Limeade, made from fresh limes."

"Great. I'll take about a gallon."

The scientist turned a tiny faucet on his miniaturized refrigerator and drew a glass of the icy drink, handing it to Trask, who nodded his thanks.

"Delicious," he said, sipping the green liquid thirstily.

"Now," Grey said, "what about Max Rudolph?"

"He's a top fence, one of the best. Pays a fair price and has never squealed on a client. That's rare, believe me. He's the one, according to the informer, who bought the Rembrandt drawing from the thief, and he's the guy who'll peddle it for heaven knows how much. I understand Rembrandt was a superb draftsman, that his drawings bring as much as most top painters' finished oils or whatever. Here's this newly discovered preliminary sketch of *The Night Watch*, a famous work, for sale to the highest crooked bidder. It could net Rudolph a million, for all I know. The museum says it's beyond price. You don't just find new Rembrandts anymore."

"Why does a man buy something he can't sell, exhibit, or even admit owning?" Grey wondered aloud. Then, answering his own query: "Only a dedicated collector—a true fanatic. Somebody who'll gloat over it in private."

"That's about it," the detective said. "But there's one funny angle most people don't understand. Rich collectors are dynasty-minded, often from old families. They look ahead a hundred years. By then, all the museum people will be dead and gone—they're peasants with no pedigrees to go on that long. Ditto us cops and insurance adjusters. But their great-great grand-children will 'discover' a lost Rembrandt and can sell it, if necessary, for X millions by then. Weird, isn't it?"

"To me, yes, but not, obviously, to your illegal buyers."

"Okay," Trask said, giving Grey his empty glass and accepting a refill. "We got the tip. Rudolph is taking the Rembrandt on his boat out to sea a few miles, there to rendezvous with the top bidder." He paused, gave the scientist a wistful glance, and added: "Believe it or not, I didn't know Rembrandt from da Vinci a few days ago; I've learned a lot fast."

Grey's mouth twitched. "You've certainly done plenty of homework," he assured the lieutenant. "But don't forget you got me that Fragonard from the insurance people and picked up some background on that job."

"Nothing like this!" Trask said fervently. "However, as soon as we got the tip, I contacted the coast guard, and they sailed at once to intercept. Rudolph, who's damned wealthy himself—never convicted once, by the way; smart and lucky—has a great boat with an engine that could drive a liner, so he gave the coast guard quite a run for their money. He dodged in and out of fog banks, changing course, and used enough tricks to make Hornblower green with envy; but they have radar, so he didn't get away. They finally made him heave to, boarded his boat, and brought Max back to port, where I was waiting." He gulped the last of the limeade, put the glass on a table, and said, "Now comes the bad part. Up to then we were doing great, the U.S. and I working together like precision machinery. There's absolutely no doubt he had the drawing with him; aside from the tip, why else this trip to sea? It wasn't a good day for fun, I assure you; cold, wet, foggy, choppy waves, lots of bitter wind. Okay, I search the ship, and I'm a pro; I didn't miss anything. But no Rembrandt."

"Dumped at sea for later recovery," Grey suggested.

"Possible—barely—but not probable. For one thing, I'm pretty sure we surprised him. He had no idea he'd be intercepted. Then, too, according to the coast guard captain, it would take expert and lucky navigation to drop a small parcel, without a radio marker, in fog at that, and count on recovering it days later; currents, waves, wind, bad bottom—stuff all Greek to me but clear to sailors. I have to take his word on it. No, I can't help feeling the Rembrandt is still on Rudolph's boat—only I can't find it, which is why I'm here guzzling your limeade."

The scientist seemed a little taken aback, which was atypical. "This doesn't seem to be quite for me," he said. "Obviously, to search a boat from a wheelchair is even more impracticable than trying it on a house. I could send Edgar, but—" He shrugged.

"I didn't make myself clear," Trask said. "Of course, a physical examination of the ship is out of the question; besides, I've done that. No, what occurs to me is more of a 'purloined letter' approach. I'm certainly overlooking some obvious hiding place. Rudolph is a very ingenious and experienced fellow. My guess is that when the coast guard got after him, he led them a long chase in order to hide the Rembrandt—and did a mighty fine job of it apparently."

"So Edgar was wrong," Grey said, his deep-set eyes twinkling. "Some detectives do read detective stories after all; 'purloined letter,' eh?"

The detective grinned. "Edgar, the Miraculous Midget, was right; I don't read 'em. But in my police science course at the university, the professor was more literary and made us tackle a few of what he called classics. That was first on the list, and I've never forgotten it. Very clever story."

"You do have a point—about Rudolph and the boat. He may have come up with a far-out solution, one that an ordinary search, even by a pro—" here Trask had the grace to redden, "—might miss. Well, what do you want me to do?"

"This," the lieutenant said crisply, taking up his briefcase. "I've got detailed plans of the boat and photos—lots of nice, big, glossy ones, inside and out, from all angles. You know my cameraman; he's good. Now, if you were to study these and use that great imagination of yours . . ."

"I'm willing to try," Grey said, "but don't look for any miracles. What fooled you on the ground, the locale, so to speak, is probably too much for me, miles away with plans and pictures."

"Maybe so," Trask admitted. "But considering your track record, it just may happen that Mr. Max Rudolph will meet his match. By the way—odd coincidence—he's a Poe collector himself. Does that openly, but I wouldn't be surprised if he has a few stolen items of his own to gloat over. If there's ever a lost *Tamerlane*, which I'm told is the rarest of all Poe works and the rarest, almost, of anything in print, I'll know who might have it in a locked room!"

"Go away," the scientist said, smiling. "You're full of esoteric information today. I can't listen to all that and concentrate."

"I'm leaving. But work fast, if possible. We can't hold Max or the boat much longer; as it is, my neck is way out. I had to trump up, with help from Captain Haskill—the coast guard man—some idiotic charge about not having proper life belts on board or discharging sewage in port, or whatever, even to stop him at sea. Except for his known record, without convictions, alas, Rudolph could probably sue if we don't find that drawing—meaning, if you don't!" Wisely, he didn't wait for a reply but hurried out.

Grey chuckled, cocked his massive head, and began to study the papers and photos, using a lift-up sort of easel pivoted on one arm of the chair. A boat is a small world of its own, very limited as to space, and the plans showed every cubic inch. The Rembrandt drawing, he learned from the accompanying notes, written in Trask's neat, printlike hand, measured only thirty-six by nineteen inches. What that implied about a hiding place was by no means clear. For one thing, it might be rolled up, thus fitting into a cylindrical opening about three inches in diameter and no more than nineteen inches deep. On the other hand, if kept flat—surely Rudolph would not be vandal enough to fold the priceless thing!—the drawing would need a sizable rectangular, if shallow, spot. No, he wouldn't fold it, except very loosely; a damaged Rembrandt would sell for less. But one couldn't rule out a careful, noncreasing arrangement taking up a rather small square, for example. Altogether, a lot of angles; too many for comfort, Grey mused wryly.

For almost three hours, he went over the data, pleased, as always, with their completeness, testifying to Trask's competence and care, but he still had no glimmer of an idea.

Pressing a stud in the right arm of his chair, he got a crystal flask of brandy. Taking minute sips, tiny caresses of the palate, he went into deep thought, but the theater of his mind had nothing to show him; the stage was empty. . . .

Sighing, he put the dossier aside, knowing the importance of a fresh start when a problem proved intractable. The small FM radio behind his head came on; he found a Brandenburg Concerto and relaxed, listening.

Thirty minutes later, he tried again, this time using an excellent magnifying glass on photos of the ship. He started with the very bilges and worked up. One blank after another; no hiding place missed by Trask revealed itself to his inner—or outer—eye.

Then the deck, the fittings, the mast—it was hollow probably, but the detective had found no openings whatever, so no Rembrandt inside. His eye moved up the mast; the achromatic triplet lens brought out every minute detail in the sharp photo. At the very top, his gaze stayed fixed. He reflected a moment as if in doubt, then riffled among the pictures for another shot of the thing that held his attention; left side, right side. He moved the lens in and out, counting . . . little fires glowed in his eyes . . . most odd, unless . . . a matter once again of the plausible inference . . . ten minutes later he was on the phone to Trask.

"It was right there!" the detective told him the next morning. "Inside the flag. Who the devil would guess a flag had two thicknesses? They're not made that way."

"Right," Grey agreed. "Rudolph must have done this job himself while ducking and dodging through the fog—as you guessed."

"Sure, I did fine there," Trask said ruefully, "but I missed the flag. What made you pick it?"

"First, it was just a wild thought. Like you, I assumed one layer of cloth, so if he'd just pinned or stapled the drawing to it, anybody could have spotted that, even from the deck. Then I thought of two flags fastened together, and studied both sides. That's what cooked Max's goose. In his haste, he didn't realize he'd bungled things. You see, one flag was up-to-date, with fifty stars, but the other side of the same flag, presumably, in a different photo angle, had only forty-eight. That told me I was almost certainly right about a two-ply cloth."

"He sewed them in a hurry, all right. When we lowered Old Glory, it became very obvious." Trask shook his head wonderingly. "It *was* a purloined letter thing in a way, after all, wasn't it?"

"I'd say so," the scientist agreed. "Not many things on a ship are more obvious than a flag whipping in the wind."

"Yes," the detective said, grinning. "And a double flag should be twice as obvious—but only to you!"

MURDER ON THE HONEYMOON

by C. B. Gilford

She could have killed him—Tony, her husband—and they'd been married scarcely more than a week.

"Look, Carol," he had said, "these three guys asked me to golf with them. You know how crazy I am about the game, and I know you don't play. Would you mind very much?"

Every day there'd been some kind of excuse—something to take him away for two or three hours—till it became a matter of pride with her not to object anymore, not to beg for his continuous company. But a girl would think, on her honeymoon . . .

"I'll be home by seven at least," he'd said. "Our usual table. You can wander over to the lodge and get a head start on the cocktails if I'm late . . ."

If he were late! It was eight now, or past. The sun was dissolving into the ocean, its red dyeing the purple. The Japanese lanterns strung over the dining deck had flickered on like early fireflies. She'd had three cocktails, and she was angry and reckless.

Now, finally, she'd endured the curious stares of the other diners just long enough and the pitying glances of that waiter: *Oh-oh, Mrs. Linvale is being stood up tonight. The honeymoon didn't last long.*

She left the dining deck and went down to the

beach. It was growing darker every moment. Already
there was a slight chill in the air, but it was welcome
after that hot blush of embarrassment she'd felt making her departure. She unbuckled her sandals and
took them off so she could walk barefooted in the
cool, wet sand. She headed north, away from the
lodge, not knowing where or how far she intended to
go.

She was walking fast, taking long strides to work
off her anger, when she first saw the stranger. He
seemed to come from the cottages or may be down
from one of the hiking trails on the wooded mountain-
side. He was cutting in front of her, heading for the
water, but then when he saw her approaching, he
halted directly in her path and waited for her.

She was too surprised to stop, or detour, or retreat,
so she kept walking straight toward him. He was a
young man, not as tall as her husband and not as
heavy. His hair was sandy, not dark like Tony's. He
wore swimming trunks, as if he'd come down for a dip
in the ocean.

He stayed right where he was, letting her come
closer. Then, just before she could walk past him, he
said softly, "Have a light?"

It stopped her somehow, despite her intentions to
the contrary. She looked up at him, seeing for the first
time the white cigarette dangling from his lips. It was
all she could see of his face because the darkness
seemed to have descended swiftly, and he had turned
away from her a little.

She was alone on the empty beach with this
stranger. They were more than a hundred yards from
the lodge. Lights from the cottages blinked here and
there amid the trees, none very close, yet she had a
vague awareness that this man, though not big, was
well built, muscular.

"No, I'm sorry," she told him, and started to walk
past.

It happened then very quickly. He stepped behind

her, and before she could turn to ward him off, he had her. His right hand clapped solidly over her mouth, prevented her from screaming, almost from breathing. His left arm encircled her waist, catching both her arms at the elbows, and he was half carrying, half dragging her down the slope of the beach toward the water.

She fought him with her feet and legs, the only parts of her body which could move, but it was only flesh pounding against flesh, and hers was softer than his. Her heels hammered his shins, slowing him a little, almost tripping him once but failing to stop him. Then they were in the surf. She felt the water swirling about her legs, rising, receding.

The man was trying to drown her!

That was when he stopped. He stood there, still holding her helpless but not taking her any farther. A breaker, a little bigger than the others, washed past them, waist-high. She felt his body straining against the ebb. She kept still for the moment, ceasing her struggles, waiting for his decision. When he was ready to start dragging her again, she was ready to resist again. That was her only thought.

Then he did the unexpected. He put his lips to her ear and spoke loudly so she could hear him above the surf. "Mrs. Linvale, I'm going to let go of you now. Please don't scream and don't run away because I have something important to tell you. I'm your friend."

He didn't let go suddenly. She felt the tension relaxing in his body very, very slowly. He still had her, and if she chose to fight or to scream, he could put the strength back into his hold on her.

"I could have killed you. Drowned you. Do you understand that? But I didn't, and I won't. I'm your friend. Promise you won't scream when I let go of you."

She nodded her head, promising. She would promise anything.

His hand released her mouth then, but his left arm still held her waist lightly. She turned inside the circle of it so that she could look up at him. She found his face smiling and not at all the face of a murderous fiend.

"Let's go up on the sand and sit down and talk," he said.

His arm didn't leave her waist. It stayed there, piloting her through the surf, holding her steady when another breaker came in. It was incredible how different the pressure of that arm was now.

"Right here," he said finally, when they'd reached dry sand. "That dress of yours is a little messed up now, anyway, so a little sand won't hurt it. I'll bet you're tired. You put up a pretty good fight."

She was tired. She sank full-length onto the sand. There didn't seem to be another ounce of strength left in her entire body. If he wanted to kill her up here instead of down in the water, she could offer not the slightest resistance.

All he did, however, was stretch himself beside her, propping up on one elbow. "Shall I start from the beginning, Mrs. Linvale?" he asked after several minutes. "Or may I call you Carol?"

She was too weak to object.

"All right," he said. "You're here on your honeymoon with your husband, Tony Linvale. Before your marriage a couple of weeks ago, you were Carol Richmond, the heiress, just turned twenty-one. Am I right so far?"

She didn't answer.

"You didn't know much about Tony Linvale, but he was handsome and charming. It probably occurred to you he might be a fortune hunter, but you were infatuated."

No, she wanted to say. She loved Tony.

"That brings us to your arrival here at this honeymoon paradise with the ever-loving Tony, who, almost as soon as he gets here, starts acting funny."

The shame returned, burning in her cheeks. "What do you mean by that?" she challenged him.

"You know what I mean, Carol. You had the old-fashioned notion that on their honeymoon the bride and groom hang around together pretty much. Only Tony starts to skip off a couple of hours every day, and you don't know exactly where."

She had her breath back now, and her wits. "Just tell me why you dragged me into the water and tried to kill me."

"I'm getting to that."

"What has Tony got to do with it?"

"Everything."

She sat up, and when she did, the stranger sat up, too. "All right, tell me."

"Have you ever heard your husband mention Diane Keith?"

"No, never."

"Well, she's the person he's been seeing when he sneaks away from you."

"I don't believe it!"

"You're right on cue, Carol. Every wife says that when she first gets the bad news. But you'd better believe it, honey, if you want to stay alive."

She answered him slowly this time; slowly, coolly. "All right, tell me about Diane Keith."

"Diane Keith is Tony Linvale's girl friend, mistress, or wife, I'm not sure which. Right now she's living at the next lodge up the beach, the Mar-del-Sud, but he meets her at all sorts of places. When your husband tells you he's going to play golf, or whatever he tells you, he goes to see her." He paused, his face close to hers. "Why don't you say you don't believe me?"

She tried not to believe or disbelieve but only to listen and learn. "What's the rest of the story?" she asked him.

"That's where I come in," he said. "My name's Gil Hannon, by the way."

She just went on looking at him.

"I won't try to pretend to be anything more than I am. I've had my ups and downs, and right now I'm down—but no police record. Somehow, though, your husband imagined I was just the boy for him. He hired me to kill you."

Having survived the experience of thinking she was going to die, this wasn't the climactic shock. She didn't believe him, but she could be calm about it. "That's a lie," she said.

He shrugged. "I just went to all the trouble of showing you how it was planned, but I guess you're so gone on Tony Linvale that not even seeing is believing, huh?"

"Of course I love Tony."

"Still? Listen, Tony didn't want to do the job himself because he realized that the husband would be suspected in the sudden death of the rich young wife. So he really did play golf this afternoon, and he's sticking with those golfing chums of his as long as he can this evening because they're his alibi. Tony figured you had the habit of walking it off when you got angry, even that you'd walk in this direction. I was to grab you, drown you in the ocean. You'd be missing for a day or two; then your body would be washed up on the beach somewhere. Either you would have gone swimming alone and were drowned, or maybe you'd committed suicide because you'd imagined your husband didn't love you. The one thing it wouldn't look like would be murder."

Her brain whirled. It was logical, and yet it wasn't because it made Tony a murderer, and he wasn't that. "No," she said. "No . . ."

"If I'd simply knocked at your door and told you this, you naturally wouldn't have believed me. I chose this way to show you how it had been planned."

"Why didn't you go to the police?"

"Would they have believed me any more than you would? When your husband made me this proposition, my first reaction was just to turn him down cold, but then it intrigued me somehow. Then I got a look at you, and I got intrigued still more. By you, let's say."

"By me?" She felt a new uneasiness now, skeptical of Hannon.

"That's right. I couldn't help wondering why somebody with such a gorgeous wife should want her dead. This Diane Keith isn't bad looking, but she's not you and is quite a bit older."

There was nothing inherently repelling about this Gil Hannon, and yet she couldn't help being afraid of him. She shivered, suddenly aware that she was soaking wet. "I'm going now," she told him.

He jumped up ahead of her and helped her to stand. He even roamed the beach and gathered up her purse and shoes. "You still don't believe me, do you?" he said, handing them to her.

"I don't know . . . but I've got to go now. . . ."

"I'll walk with you." He took her arm, led her back halfway toward the lodge, then up to the first stone path. He seemed to know where she lived. They stopped finally before the door of cottage number eight.

"Here's the bridal suite," he announced, "and nobody's home. Tony's going to stay plenty late tonight, till midnight, anyway. Then he's going to bring his pals home with him for a nightcap so they can be witnesses to the fact that the bride is missing. If that doesn't convince you, baby, just wait till you see his face when he sees you're still alive, very much alive."

She was putting the key into the lock. "Good night, Mr. Hannon."

She had the door open when he grabbed her shoulders. It took her by surprise, but she didn't struggle with him. She knew how strong he was, but she could scream, and she would if she had to. The next cottage was only fifty feet away. "Let me go," she told him, "or I'll—"

"Look here," he said, unimpressed, "you're too damned stubborn. But be careful, will you? Don't tell him about tonight. Say you stayed here all evening. That'll stall him, anyway, and maybe give me a chance to prove this to you in some other way. Will you promise to do that?"

His face was only inches from hers, and he was standing directly under the little light over the door. Rather untended hair, a well-tanned face, maybe rugged but certainly not handsome, with eyes probably gray. She considered him for a moment. "All right," she said finally.

"Good. I'll get in touch with you again."

He let her go with somewhat obvious reluctance. She made her escape while she had the chance, went inside, and shut and locked the door behind her. From the window she saw him retreat down the flagstone path. Only then did she turn on the lights. She looked everywhere, living room, bedroom, and bath. Tony wasn't there, and it was past nine o'clock.

She got rid of her wet clothes, showered the sand out of her hair, put on pajamas and a robe. But she still hadn't come to any conclusions. Tony's continued absence worried her.

At ten-thirty she turned off all the lights and lay down on the bed in the darkness. Somehow she found herself accepting Gil Hannon's prediction that Tony wouldn't be home till midnight. Beyond that, however, she refused to believe.

It was just past midnight when Tony did arrive. She checked the time by the luminous hands of her little alarm clock. She heard several male voices on the path outside, then Tony's key working in the lock, finally the door opening.

"Come on in for one drink," Tony said.

"No, no, it's too late," somebody answered. "Man, we've kept you long enough. You're on your honeymoon."

"That's just why I want you to come in," Tony insisted. "I want you guys to back up my story. Come on, now. I'll see if Carol's awake. . . ."

She heard him crossing the living room, then the bedroom door opened, and his big shoulders almost filled the doorway. His hand groped for the switch, and then the lights came on.

"Carol . . ."

There he was, tall, dark-eyed, curly-haired, his chest and his muscular arms startlingly bronzed against his white, open-throated polo shirt. She sat up in bed and looked at him. Their eyes met, and she tried to see in his the answers to her questions.

Was he surprised to find her there alive? He was smiling, somewhat sheepishly, ashamedly, it seemed. Which was appropriate, wasn't it?

Then, after a long silence, without saying anything at all, he backed out of the room and shut the door. She heard him speaking to his companions in the living room.

"Look, guys, Carol's asleep, and maybe I'd better not wake her up. Why don't we have that drink some other time?"

"Sure, Tony . . ."

Murmuring muted good nights, the voices faded away. The front door was closed, locked. Tony's footsteps crossed the room, and again he opened the bedroom door.

The look on his face was completely different now, all abject humility and contrition. He walked slowly over to the bed.

"Are you still speaking to me?" he asked her.

"I'm not sure," she told him frankly.

He sat down on the bed, close to her but not touching her. "I suppose I could think up some fancy excuse," he began, "but I don't want to lie to you, Carol."

He bent toward her slowly. She didn't move. His mouth came into contact with hers. This was the language he spoke best of all, she thought. He kissed her, and she let him.

* * *

They slept late the next morning. Carol's first awareness was of Tony's lips brushing gently against her cheek. Without opening her eyes, she turned to meet his kiss. It was so easy to forget with Tony . . . but what he said brought it all instantly to the front of her mind again.

"Darling, we've got a date for some deep-sea fishing this morning."

Yes, he had said "we." She opened her eyes and looked at him. He was grinning enthusiastically. *Like a big kid,* she thought. "But I told you," she said, "that I'm afraid of riding in a small boat on the ocean."

His face clouded. The boyish enthusiasm had changed to boyish disappointment. "That's right, you did tell me that."

The idea came into her mind. The traitorous, disloyal idea. She would cooperate with him . . . if that was what he wanted. "Darling," she said, "I don't want to spoil your fun. I know I married the sportsman type. I know I'll have to give you up sometimes."

"But this is our honeymoon, Carol, and I've left you alone enough already."

"Tony, I insist. Deep-sea fishing ought to be great fun for you."

In the end, seeming at last to succumb to her insistence rather than deciding for himself, he consented to go. He didn't know how long the trip would take, but he guaranteed he'd be back long before dinner—in time for a swim, in fact. There'd be no repetition of last night. He seemed to forget they'd had no breakfast.

She watched him go down the path, all in white, shirt, trousers, shoes. Then, without waiting to get dressed herself, she phoned the Mar-del-Sud and asked for Gil Hannon.

"This is Carol Linvale," she said when his sleepy voice answered.

He woke up right away. "Well, we're still on speaking terms, I see. That means friend husband acted according to prediction last night."

She ignored the thrust. "Tony has just left here. Says he's going deep-sea fishing. You could do me a favor, Mr. Hannon."

"You name it. Keep you company, maybe?"

"I was thinking maybe he's gone to meet this Diane Keith. . . ."

"I'll bet he has. He'll be looking for me, too, asking what went wrong last night. You didn't tell him anything, did you?"

"No, I didn't tell him. If you find out where he's meeting Diane Keith today, I wish you'd let me know."

"Now *you're* hiring me, is that it?"

"All right, I'll hire you if it's necessary."

"It isn't necessary. I'm in this for the fun of it. You want to see Tony and Diane actually together, huh? Well, there's nothing I'd like better to show you. Will you be at your cottage?"

"Yes, I'll be here."

"I'll be seeing you, then."

She wondered after she'd hung up if she'd done the right thing. She was acting as if she trusted Gil Hannon, and she didn't. But there was something to be gained from finding out whether Diane Keith really existed. That would be worth trusting even Gil Hannon for.

She dressed in white shorts and green blouse and tied back her black hair firmly with a green ribbon. She surveyed herself in the mirror during the process, trying to be critical, asking herself whether Tony wanted only her money or her. She had looks, didn't she? Good eyes, good features, well-cared-for skin, nice figure. Gil Hannon liked her, didn't he? Or did he?

For a little while she sunned herself in front of the cottage. Later, she returned inside and paced. She was angry now. Gil Hannon had said she was "infatuated" with Tony. Perhaps that was the explanation. Even if she didn't believe he wanted to kill her, she was still allowing him to make a fool of her.

A sharp knock on the door interrupted her dark thoughts. It was Gil Hannon, dressed in slacks and open-throated shirt, but he looked rugged in clothes, too.

"Want to check on Tony?" he asked her.

"I said I did."

"Okay, let's go."

He led the way up to the road where he'd parked his car, a three-year-old convertible, dusty with travel. They headed south.

"I talked with Tony a few minutes ago," Hannon confided. "I told him I waited for you last night but that you never showed up. He seemed pretty disappointed, but he told me to wait around for future instructions, and I said I would."

They drove for about five minutes, then the road climbed sharply, hugging the cliffside. Trees momentarily cut off their view of the ocean. Hannon found the place he was looking for, swung the car onto the gravel shoulder, and stopped.

"Ten to one they've met here," he said. "I eavesdropped on his phone conversation, and this is a place I met him once."

He led the way through trees and underbrush, helping Carol over the difficult places. Finally, he stopped and pointed down for her to look.

Fifty feet almost directly below them was the ocean, its waves pounding in against inhospitable rocks and throwing up geysers of white foam. Nestled in among the rocks and just out of the reach of the surf was a small, level plot of pink sand. It was occupied by a man and a woman.

Carol recognized Tony instantly, but it was the woman she looked at. It was difficult to decide from this vantage point whether she was pretty or not. She wore a two-piece white swimming suit, and her legs were deeply tanned. Her face and her hair were completely hidden by a wide-brimmed straw.

They were talking, Tony and the woman. They sat together side by side in the same position, their knees drawn up under their chins, close to each other but not touching, both gazing out to sea.

"The lady's name," Hannon said, "is Diane Keith."

Carol stared. She couldn't take her eyes off them. Tony had lied to her, he hadn't gone deep-sea fishing. He'd kept a secret rendezvous with a woman.

"They're not making love," she said aloud.

Hannon laughed softly. "No, I don't think they make love every second they're together."

She suddenly felt furious with him. "Mr. Hannon, tell me the exact truth. Have you ever *seen* my husband making love to that woman?"

He shrugged. "No, I've never seen it."

They climbed back up to the car. Hannon made a sharp U-turn and headed back the way they had come. He was grimly silent all the way. Carol knew he was angry at her stubbornness, but she didn't care. She'd have to see more than she had seen in order to believe him.

When they got back, she leaped out of the car before he could open the door for her. "Thank you, Mr. Hannon," she told him.

"What are you going to do now?" he asked.

"I don't know."

"You're neither jealous nor afraid?"

"I'm a little of both," she confessed, "but I refuse to panic."

"You can call me if you need me," he said, and the convertible roared off, leaving her desolate.

Tony returned to the cottage at four in the afternoon. He was superficially gay, but underneath there was a sourness. The day had not gone well with him, Carol knew.

"Let's take a swim," he hailed her.

She shook her head. She was wearing a simple little print dress, rather formal for this place at this time of day. "How was the fishing?" she asked.

"No luck."

"You did go out?"

"Oh, sure."

He told the lie easily, but then he was accustomed to lying. He came to her, took her shoulders, and bent to kiss her. She turned away.

"What's the matter?"

"That's a silly question, isn't it?"

"You're mad because I left you alone today."

"My problem isn't as simple as that, Tony. The fact is, I don't believe you went fishing."

He stepped back, staring at her suspiciously. "No? What do you think I did, then?"

"You tell me." She wasn't as calm as she sounded. She wanted him to confess his lie, to confess Diane Keith, to explain her. There could be an explanation. Diane Keith could be an old flame who was black-mailing Tony now that he had married wealth. There might be a hundred explanations. She would understand.

He looked at her for a long time, not saying anything, and perhaps she felt a tiny ripple of fear go through her. He wasn't even pretending to love her now. He seemed angry, frustrated, impatient. Finally, he turned and without a word walked out the door.

She was left not knowing what to do or think. Her accusation had startled him, but he wasn't certain how much she knew. Perhaps he was rushing back to Diane Keith. Perhaps she would never see him again. No, he'd come back . . . if he loved her . . . or if he wanted to kill her. She waited, wondering whether she should stay or run.

It was almost six when Gil Hannon called. "Carol, are you alone?"

"Yes."

"Mind if I drop in for a minute? There's been a new development."

"I'll be here," she promised.

He came quickly. He looked furtive and troubled, but he stopped for a moment to admire her. "Your husband's a fool," he said. "Why should a man dream of getting rid of a wife as beautiful as you?"

"What's the new development?" she interrupted him.

He sat in a chair and lit a cigarette. "What have you two been talking about?" he asked. "Did you tell him you knew about Diane Keith?"

"No, I only told him I didn't believe he went fishing today."

"What did he say to that?"

"Nothing. He just walked out on me."

"If he figured it wasn't worthwhile lying anymore, he must think you know something. So that's why he's in such a hurry." Hannon leaned back, took a long drag. "He talked to me again just now. Same proposition—he wants me to kill you."

She buried her face in her hands, hoping to shut out the awful pictures—Tony with that woman on the beach . . . Tony returning and looking at her, suspicious, distant, strange. Surely not her Tony . . . surely she couldn't have been that blind when she married him.

"I stalled him off," Hannon was saying, "but I can't do that indefinitely. And *you* can't keep on stalling, Carol. You've got to understand that your life is in danger. If Tony can't get me to do the job for him, he'll find someone else. Look, has it been arranged legally that Tony inherits your estate if you die?"

She nodded without looking up. Yes, they'd both written wills. Tony had some property back in New York. He wanted her to have it, he'd said, if anything happened to him. She'd signed a matching will. Everything she had, her father's fortune, would go to Tony.

"Then you're not safe," Gil Hannon said, "till you get that changed."

She nodded again.

"I'll drive you back home," Hannon went on. "We'll go straight to your lawyer."

She looked up. He'd come across the room, and now he went down on one knee directly in front of her. "You file for divorce," he continued, "and then there'll be no profit in Tony's murdering you. Afterward, you can take your time to think all this over. Come on, we'll go in my car."

She found herself crying. "You're very kind, Gil."

"It's simple," he answered. "I love you."

Then, before she realized what was happening, he leaned forward and put his lips on hers. Automatically, instinctively, she recoiled.

"I'm sorry," he said quickly.

Then, suddenly, it was she who was sorry. Gil Hannon was trying to help her. He was good and kind. She reached out and touched his hand briefly. "You're wonderful, Gil," she said.

"But I'm going a little too fast," he argued. "You're married. I guess it still hasn't sunk in with me that a guy could be married to you and want to get rid of you. Let me take care of you, and the first thing I want to do is to get you away from Tony."

She shook her head.

"What do you mean? Do you still love the guy?"

"I married him."

"Don't you believe your eyes? Don't you believe me?"

She thought for a long time, and finally she said, "It's hard for a woman to admit she's been wrong. You see, I still don't *know*."

Gil Hannon got to his feet, not bothering to conceal his anger. "Then I guess I'd better have it out with Tony myself."

He left without explaining what he meant.

When Gil came back, it was long past dark, long past dinner time, almost ten-thirty. She had scarcely moved during his absence. Tony had not returned. She had switched on a single lamp, had tried to think, to sort out all the terrible, confused emotions.

Gil walked in without knocking. He stood in the middle of the room, his face twisted, gleaming with sweat. She could see his chest heaving under his thin, damp shirt. "I've been with your husband," he said. "We had quite a few drinks and quite a lot of talk. He offered me a wad of money if I'd dispose of you. I wish you could have heard the conversation, Carol, but I told him no sale." He came a step closer. "I'm going into town and make a statement to the police."

She nodded. "All right. Maybe that's the best thing."

He knelt in front of her once again. "Now listen to me, sweetheart. Your husband's up at the Mar-del-Sud with Diane Keith. He's had a lot to drink. He may get ideas, like wanting to do the job himself, so I brought you this."

He pulled the gun out of his hip pocket and laid it in her lap. It was small, black, deadly-looking.

"Your husband gave it to me. Don't ask me when he got it. He said I could even use a gun to kill you if I wanted, as long as he had his alibi. So you see, he's pretty desperate. I told him I wouldn't use it, but I refused to give it back to him. I figured you're the one who needed it."

She was terrified. "What am I supposed to do with it?"

"Use it on Tony Linvale if he comes back here to-night in the state he's in."

"But I don't know how to use a gun. . . ."

"Flip up this safety, and pull the trigger."

"But I could never hit anything, I know . . ."

"Just keep shooting. Nobody's going to hang around with a hail of bullets flying everywhere."

Rather than allow her to argue further, he kissed her—forcefully, authoritatively this time, and she was too numb to resist.

"Lock the door behind me," he said, and was gone.

She followed him to the door and did as she'd been told. Standing there then, she found the gun in her right hand.

It was the gun that suddenly made her afraid now and made her realize that she did believe Gil Hannon. She'd struggled against that belief for two hours, but now she knew. The gun was real. The gun had convinced her. Her life was in danger. Tony Linvale, the man she had loved, the man she had married, wanted to kill her—for her money and for the sake of another woman.

In her terror, she found herself acting. She turned off the lights. Darkness was safer. She sat in the easy chair which faced the door, and she kept the gun in her right hand. Flip the safety up, Gil had said.

Oh, why hadn't she believed Gil a little sooner? Why hadn't she gone with him to the police? Gil had called her stubborn, but she was worse than that. She was stupid.

That was when she began to hear the sound. A small sound, scarcely distinguishable at first above the distant surf, but then louder. Someone approaching on the path outside, slowly, stealthily. She held the gun in a tight grip, tried to gear herself mentally to the idea of using it because the sound was definitely now at the door of her cottage—and there it stayed, like someone leaning or rubbing heavily against the door. Trying to push it open? Then the sound of the knob turning. No good, of course, with the door locked. Then finally a sound which terrified her—a key in the lock.

She searched for the safety catch on the gun, pushed it as Gil had shown her. Shoot . . . keep shooting. It was the only thing she could do.

The key had turned now, the door was unlocked. Slowly, with the tiniest squeak, it was pushed ajar. In the doorway, silhouetted by the dim light out on the path, was the figure of a man. Big, muscular-looking, sort of leaning against the door frame, peering into the dark interior of the cottage. Right at her.

"Don't come in, Tony. I've got a gun, and I'll use it." Her own voice, hoarse, betraying fear.

There was no answer from the doorway, but the man leaned farther in. Seemed to be crouching. To spring at her? Yes. She fired.

She didn't count the shots. She only knew that she kept firing till the gun was empty and pulling the trigger produced only a hollow click.

It was enough, though. The figure in the doorway tottered, then fell forward, hit the floor with the sickening thud of a lifeless thing.

She stared at the shadowy heap for a long moment. Finally, she managed to stand. The gun, useless now, dropped out of her hand. She groped for the lamp switch. When she found it, her nerveless fingers had difficulty turning it in the required direction. It was more seconds before the light came on, and by that time there were voices out on the path.

People had heard the shots. Faces crowded into the doorway. Eyes which looked at her, at the body on the floor, and then at her again.

"She shot her husband," somebody said.

Gil Hannon handled the case for the defense when the police came. He had been on his way into town to talk to them when the thing happened. Heard about it there at state police headquarters when he got there, turned right around and came back, and arrived not long after the ambulance. He spoke for Carol during the investigation.

It was a long night. Lieutenant Wagner was in charge of the routine. Photographs were taken of Tony Linvale's body as it lay on the floor. A doctor ascertained that Tony had died of a bullet wound in the heart. Once the corpse was taken away, Lieutenant Wagner tried to straighten out the facts.

Diane Keith was a reluctant witness. She refused to

verify Gil Hannon's story of Tony's wanting his wife killed, but she was so broken up over Tony's death that it was obvious that Tony Linvale had been involved with her.

Seeing Diane Keith at close range calmed Carol considerably. Tony had never loved her, Carol. He'd wanted her dead, wanted only her money. She regretted that she had killed him, but he'd wanted to kill her. He had deserved to die.

Gil spoke frankly to Lieutenant Wagner. He had never for a moment considered hiring out to Tony Linvale, but the fact that a man on his honeymoon wanted his wife killed had intrigued him. Then, when he'd met Carol, he'd fallen in love with her. He'd wanted first to take her away, out of Tony Linvale's reach, but, well . . . he didn't blame Carol for being skeptical. He still loved her.

Lieutenant Wagner listened attentively to all of them. He was a small man with a terrier look about him, inquisitive, friendly, and suspicious, all at the same time.

"Things seem to fit together pretty well," he said finally.

"You agree," Gil said, "that Mrs. Linvale did shoot in self-defense."

"Yes. There seems to be no other motive."

"Then we can wrap this up, can't we, Lieutenant? Carol's been under quite a strain. . . ."

But the lieutenant was pacing about the room. "There's just one thing that bothers me," he remarked softly. "Mrs. Linvale claims never to have used a gun before. In her excitement, she shoots and doesn't stop shooting till the gun is empty. She shoots wildly. We've found bullets everywhere, floor, ceiling, walls. But then one bullet—just one—hits Mr. Linvale right in the heart."

Carol looked desperately at Gil.

"Accident," Gil said. "One of those freaks."

"Could be," the lieutenant admitted.

"What are you thinking?" Gil demanded. "That the bullet in Tony's heart came from another gun?"

Wagner shook his head. "Probably not. We'll get the bullet out and check it, but probably not."

"Well, what, then?" Gil asked angrily.

"I don't know." Wagner was shaking his head in puzzlement. "I just don't know. There's something that is missing somewhere. . . ."

It was Carol who found the something. She spoke without thinking, out of concern, perhaps even out of affection. "Gil," she cried out, "you're hurt! You're bleeding!"

Lieutenant Wagner saw it then, too—blood seeping down from inside Gil Hannon's trouser leg, making a red stain on his gray sock. Gil ran for the door, but the lieutenant was there ahead of him.

It was hard for Carol to believe, but Lieutenant Wagner was quite certain. She sat in Wagner's office at headquarters and tried to understand and accept.

"We've got the evidence," Wagner assured her. "Hannon met your husband at the Mar-del-Sud, and they drove back toward your cottage in Hannon's car. Somewhere along that lonely road, Hannon shot him. He left the body in the car, came to you, handed you the gun, tried to scare you, and succeeded. Then he lugged the body down to the cottage, opened the door with your husband's key, and propped the body in your doorway. You shot wildly and winged Hannon in the leg, right through the cottage wall. But he got back to his car, bandaged his leg, changed his trousers, and drove here to our headquarters as he'd told you he was going to do."

She was in a daze. "Tony never wanted me killed?"

"Oh, I think he did. There's Diane Keith, you know."

"Then what did Gil Hannon hope to gain?"

"You."

"Me?"

"First, he tried to pry you away from your husband. That didn't work. Then he set up the shooting. You'd be safe—self-defense—and he'd be the hero. He took the risk of committing murder on the assumption that you'd marry him."

She rose from her chair quickly. "I'm going now," she said. "Is it all right if I go?" She felt faint. "I never would have married Gil Hannon, you know."

The lieutenant nodded agreeably. "Of course you wouldn't have," he said.

A GALLON OF GAS

by William Brittain

The legs of Sy Cottle's chair scraped on the rough-hewn plank floor as he got up, walked to the iron stove in the center of the room, and rammed another piece of wood into the blazing fire. It was going to be a cold, stormy night. Already he could hear the north wind sighing through the mountain pines and wet, heavy snowflakes spattering against the front window.

It'd be a hellish night for anyone caught outside. In spite of the heat from the stove, Sy felt a shiver run along his spine as he returned to his perusal of the mail-order catalogue by the light of the kerosene lamp.

He didn't hear the first gentle tapping on the building's front door; it was masked by the keening wind. The second time, the knocking was louder and more urgent. Sy looked up in surprise from a two-page spread of hunting shirts. What kind of tomfool would come to such a deserted part of the mountains on a night like this?

It took some time to undo the rusty latch of the front door, and meanwhile, the knocking grew to a loud pounding. Finally, he was able to swing the door

open on protesting hinges, and a figure rushed inside
in a flurry of snow.

The man wore a gray snap-brim hat and a light
raincoat. His shoes, once fashionably stitched and
highly polished, were now two lumps of mud and wet
leather. He went to the glowing stove and began rubbing his hands, soaking up the heat gratefully.

City feller, thought Sy.

"It's c-cold out there," said the man through chatter-
ing teeth.

"Yeah," answered Sy, and then was silent. No sense
wasting words till he found out what the man wanted.

The man began peeling off his sodden coat. "My
name's John Da . . ." There was a long pause. "John
Dace," he said finally.

"Uh huh. I'm Sy Cottle. Somethin' I can do for
you?" he asked.

"Gas. I need gas for my car. It ran dry about eight
miles back." Dace waved a hand to indicate the direction from which he'd come. "I had to walk."

"I see. Lucky you came this way. The nearest place
in the other direction is Cedar Village, and that's
twenty-five miles from here. You could have froze to
death before you got there."

"I know," said Dace. "We stopped in Cedar Village
on the way. But about the gas . . ."

"What makes you think I've got any gas around
here?"

"Why, I saw the pumps outside, and I thought . . ."

"Too bad you couldn't have seen 'em in daylight,"
said Sy, shaking his head. "Rusted solid, both of 'em. I
haven't pumped a gallon of gas in the last seven years.
When the state put in that new six-lane highway over
in the next valley, it about put me out of business.
Sometimes two, three weeks go by without my even
seeing a car on this road, especially in the winter. It's
all a body can do to earn enough money to stay alive."

"But . . ." Dace's face was a study in panic. "But
I've got to get some gas."

Sy scratched the stubble on his face and took a battered cigar from his shirt pocket. "That's the trouble with you city fellers," he said, scratching a wooden match on the table and lighting the cigar. "Always in a hurry. Now, the highway boys'll be around by this road in another week or so. They'll give you a tow."

"No! You don't understand. I've got to have the gas now. Tonight!"

"I see." Sy eyed his visitor shrewdly. "How come it's so all-fired important for you to get your car movin' tonight?"

"My wife—she's waiting for me in the car. She could freeze to death before morning."

"Um." Sy considered this for several seconds. "That does put a new face on the matter," he said.

"Look, old-timer," snapped Dace. "If you've got gas here, I need a couple of gallons. If not . . ." He reached for his coat.

"Won't do you no good to leave here," said Sy. "Especially with the snow pickin' up the way it is. Like I told you, Cedar Village is twenty-five miles back the way you come."

"Then I'll go on."

"The nearest place on up the road belongs to Steve Sweeney," said Sy complacently. "He runs a small airport, so he'd probably have some gas you could buy." He sucked slowly on the glowing cigar. "Course, it is seventeen miles from here. . . ."

Dace looked about him like a trapped animal. "I'll— I'll walk back and get Helen," he said in a shaking voice, "and bring here here."

Sy got up from the chair and sauntered to the window. "That's sixteen miles you'd be walkin', round trip," he said softly. "You'd probably make it to the car all right. But comin' back? I dunno. Especially with a woman. Ever see anybody that was froze to death, mister?"

"But I've got to do something!" moaned Dace.

"That's true," said Sy. "Well, maybe—just maybe I

got some gas in a drum out back. I might be willin' to sell you a little, seein' as my truck's up on blocks for the winter with the tires off and the radiator drained."

"You've got gas?" Dace breathed a long sigh, and his tense body relaxed. "I'll buy some. Two gallons ought to be enough." He reached into a hip pocket and drew out a wallet.

"Just a minute, mister."

"What's the matter?"

"Have you given any thought to how you're going to carry this gas? You can't just pour it in your pocket, you know."

"Why, can't I just borrow a jug or something?"

"I don't set much store by havin' my stuff borrowed," said Sy. "But I might be willing to sell you a jug. This one right here, for instance." He reached down and pulled a glass container from underneath the table.

Dace smiled wryly. "Okay, old-timer," he said. "I suppose you've got to make a little on this, too. How much for the jug?"

"Five dollars."

"Well, that's kind of expensive, a gallon of gas for five dollars. Especially since I'll be needing two of them. But I guess when you're out here in the middle of nowhere, you have to fleece the tourists while the getting is good. Here, you old robber," Dace took a ten-dollar bill from the wallet and extended it toward Sy.

Sy ignored the money and looked Dace straight in the eye. "I don't think you got the drift of what I told you," he said flatly. "The five dollars—that's for the jug. It don't include the gas."

"What! Five dollars for that thing—and no gas? Why, I could pick one up in any store in the world for a quarter."

"That's true. What store you plannin' on visitin' tonight?"

Dace stared at the window, where a crust of snow

had formed over the glass. He clenched his fists in impotent fury. "How—how much for the gas?" he asked finally.

Sy flicked a glance at Dace's wallet. "Oh, seein' as you've been so pleasant about the whole thing, and bein' in distress and all . . . Let's say fifty dollars a gallon."

"Fifty dollars! Hell, that's highway robbery!"

"The price of gas is goin' up," Sy said calmly.

"That's not funny," replied Dace.

"Wasn't meant to be. Just a statement of fact."

Desperately, Dace flipped through the bills in his wallet. "Damn!" he muttered finally. "I've only got sixty dollars here."

"Well, that'll buy you a gallon, and—figuring the cost of the jug—you'll have five dollars to keep," smiled Sy. "I won't charge you nothin' for warmin' yourself at the stove."

"That's real decent of you," snarled Dace. "But I've got to have two gallons."

"But it don't look like you can pay for 'em," said Sy. "Unless your wife's got some money on her. Speakin' of that, she must be gettin' mighty cold out in that car."

"Look, two gallons. Please. I—I'll give you my watch." Dace began tearing at the strap on his wrist.

"Don't need a watch. Time don't mean much in these parts. But if I was you, I'd be gettin' back to the car with that gas. The snow seems to be gettin' worse. Then on your way back here, you decide whether you want to buy more gas or stay on here until somebody passes by. I can give you a good deal on a room with grub thrown in. Daily or weekly rates."

Without waiting for a reply, Sy took the empty jug into the rear of the building and filled it from a large gasoline drum. When he returned, Dace had already put on his coat.

"Here's your money," Dace snarled, extending a fist-ful of bills. "I hope you choke on it."

"That ain't no way to talk to a man who saved your life," grinned Sy. He took the money and counted it carefully. "Fifty-five dollars. It's been a pleasure doin' business with you. I wish I could give you a lift, but like I said, my truck's laid up for the winter. I guess I can expect you back in about two, three hours. That right, Mr. Dace?"

With a shouted oath, Dace threw open the door and walked out into the howling storm.

It was nearly midnight, and the wind and snow had stopped when Sy heard the crunching of automobile tires outside the building. He opened the door and watched Dace get out of the car and approach, followed by a slender woman dressed in light clothing which was almost no protection against the frosty air. As they entered the building and huddled near the stove, Sy could see that their lips were blue with cold.

"This is Helen—my wife," said Dace by way of introduction. "I told her about the gas you were—eh—kind enough to sell me."

"Always glad to be of service," Sy said with a smile. "You two decide whether you want to buy another gallon?"

"I've got some money," said Helen in a soft voice. "We'll take the gas."

"Good, good. Only thing is, the price went up again. A gallon costs sixty-five dollars now. Course, you can use the jug you already bought, so that's saving right there."

Helen opened her purse. "This ought to pay for the gas," she said, tossing a small bundle toward Sy. It fell to the floor with a faint thump.

Sy bent to examine the packet, and Dace heard him gasp with surprise. "Why, all the money in here!"

"That's what you wanted, isn't it?" asked Helen.

"Yeah, but . . . Wait a minute. On this paper strap it says . . ."

Sy looked up in surprise and straight into the muzzle of the revolver which Dace had pointed at him.

"It says 'Bank of Cedar Village,' doesn't it, old-timer?" said Dace. "And we've got a lot more bundles like that out in the trunk of the car. I told you we'd been in Cedar Village, but I didn't tell you why."

"You—you robbed the bank up there." Sy gasped in sudden realization. "But you said you didn't have no more money when you was here before," he accused them.

"You don't think I'd be crazy enough to carry it on me while I was walking, did you?" grinned Dace. "No telling what kind of characters I'd meet on these back roads."

"Look, Mr. Dace," Sy said, looking wide-eyed at the gun. "There don't nobody have to know you was here. I—I can keep my mouth shut for—for—"

"For how much, old-timer? I'm sorry, but your prices are kind of high. I've got a better way of handling you. Helen, get some of that wire that's hanging on the wall there and tie him up."

"Should I gag him?"

Dace shook his head. "Let him shout. From what he's told me, there won't be anybody along this way for at least a couple of days. We'll have plenty of time to get away from here."

In moments, Sy was tied securely to the chair. He could feel the copper wire biting into his wrists, and he knew it would be impossible to free himself without assistance. His feet were wired off the floor to the rungs of the chair, effectively preventing him from shifting his position.

"We'll take the gas now," said Dace, looking down at him. "All we need."

Sy remained silent.

"Two gallons," mused Dace. "That's all it would have taken."

"What do you mean by that?" asked Sy.

"We knew all about that airport you mentioned when we planned this job," explained Dace. "Just seventeen miles up the road from here. We figured to take this back road while the police were looking for us on the highway. A pilot who's a friend of mine was going to land a small plane at the airport, and we'd be out of these hills before anyone could come near us."

"But you had to forget to gas up the car before the heist," taunted Helen.

"That's right. So we ran out of gas. If you'd sold me only two gallons, old-timer, we could have made it to the airport without stopping here again. But you got greedy, so we had to bring the car back here or risk running dry farther up the road. And in the meantime, how were we to know you hadn't heard about the robbery on the radio or something?"

"But I swear I didn't hear anything," gasped Sy. "I don't even own a radio, that's the truth."

"Sorry, old-timer, but we had no way of knowing that. And it's a little late now for it to make any difference."

The car was quickly filled with gas, and Helen went outside. Dace took an extra moment to examine the wires that bound his captive.

"Mr. Dace?" said Sy in a hoarse whisper.

"Yeah?"

"It usually gets awful cold after a snowstorm in these hills."

"So I've heard."

"Sometimes it goes below zero. And the fire in that stove is good for only a few more hours."

"You're probably right about that."

"I'll freeze to death, Mr. Dace."

"You didn't seem too worried when it was my wife out in the cold."

"Dying is a pretty high price to pay just for gypping you out of an extra gallon of gasoline."

"Well, it's like you said, old-timer."

"What do you mean by that?"

"The price of gas is going up."

THE DEADLY TELEPHONE

by Henry Slesar

Mrs. Parch was labeling preserve jars in the dining room when the telephone rang, and she paused in her labors to count the identifying rings. *One*, Mrs. Nubbin, *two*, Mrs. Giles, *three*, Mrs. Kalkbrenner; *four* . . . It was her own and Mrs. Parch, sighing with a reaction close to disappointment, wiped her sticky fingers on the generous folds of the apron and walked into the living room. It was only a thirty-foot distance, but she was panting by the time she unhooked the receiver. Mrs. Parch was stout, her figure bell-shaped in the formless gray dress she wore every weekday. "Hello?" she said loudly into the mouthpiece.

"Is this Mrs. Helen Parch?" It was a man's voice, not familiar to her. Her answer was almost resentful.

"Yes, this is Mrs. Parch. Who's this?"

"My name is Atkins, Mrs. Parch, and I'm with the county sheriff's office. I wonder if it would be convenient for me to drop in and see you this afternoon? There's something rather important I have to talk to you about."

"Important? Are you sure you have the right party?"

"I'm sure Mrs. Parch. It won't take very long. I'm in Milford at the moment, and it'll only take me five minutes to drive out to your house."

"Well, I don't know." She was plainly flustered. Even familiar visitors were few in the rural stretches of the county, and thought of a stranger . . . "Can't you tell me over the phone, Mr. Atkins? I'm kind of busy today."

"I'm afraid not, Mrs. Parch. I'm sorry. . . ."

"Well, all right, then. Now's as good a time as any, so I'll wait for you."

"Thank you," Mr. Atkins said gravely, and waited politely for the woman to break the connection. She did, and then looked at the silent instrument with wonder. It was no use going back to her preserving chores because Mrs. Parch knew that the phone would be ringing again in another few minutes, just as soon as her eavesdroppers thought a decent interval had passed. She was right, of course; eight minutes later, it gave four short rings, and she heard the flat, nasal voice of Mrs. Giles.

"Helen? How are you? Just thought I'd call and see how things are."

"Uh-huh," Mrs. Parch said knowingly but without cynicism. She had shared this party line for almost fifteen years, and it was common knowledge that its members participated in all calls. The open accusation would have shocked all of them, but it was true nevertheless. "How's Jacob?" Mrs. Parch said casually, preserving the rules of etiquette. "I understand he's been re-siding the barn last couple of days."

"Yes, he's been busy," Mrs. Giles said vaguely. "Well, what's new with you, Helen? Anything interesting happen?"

Mrs. Parch pursed her lips, feeling a sudden defiance. She knew that Mrs. Giles was burning with curiosity about Mr. Atkins, but she wouldn't give her the satisfaction of talking about it. "No, nothing new," she said smugly. "Just finishing up my preserves is all. Part I hate worst of all is making labels. I can hardly hold a pencil with this arthritis of mine."

"You sure that's all?" Mrs. Giles said. "I heard your phone ring a minute ago. . . ."

"It was just Mr. Hastings," the woman said coldly. "Calling about my mower. Took it in the other day for sharpening."

"Oh," Mrs. Giles said, and Mrs. Parch chuckled silently somewhere in the vastness of her bosom. She knew that Mrs. Giles recognized the lie, and she also knew she could never be accused of it. Mrs. Giles sniffed into the receiver, said a few more polite words to give the conversation an air of normality, and hung up.

When Mrs. Parch went back to the dining room, she was grinning broadly with satisfaction. Five minutes later, there were three rings, and she scurried across the floor on her tiny feet and noiselessly lifted the receiver, covering the mouthpiece with her hand. It was Mrs. Giles, of course, telling Mrs. Kalkbrenner about the strange man who was paying a call on Mrs. Parch that very afternoon. They speculated as to its meaning, and neither seemed able to satisfy their curiosity.

Mrs. Parch hung up before they did and went into the bedroom to make herself somewhat more presentable for her expected visitor. He arrived a few minutes later, a lean man with bony ribs that showed through his sweated shirt. He carried his jacket over his arm, and he was mopping at his high balding forehead with a crumpled handkerchief. "Mrs. Parch?" he said. "I'm Daryl Atkins of the district attorney's office."

"Come on in, Mr. Atkins. Well, you certainly made good time."

"Got here as fast as I could. This kind of thing, well, even a couple of minutes can make a difference." He looked around the small, cozy parlor, its shade drawn against the sunlight. "Certainly a lot cooler in here," he said. "Must be ninety on the road."

"Maybe you'd like a cold drink."

"I would, ma'am, but not until we have a talk."

He took a seat on the sofa, sitting tentatively on the cushion without putting his damp shirt against the antimacassared back. Mrs. Parch sat in the rocker and folded her plump hands in her lap, waiting patiently.

"Mrs. Parch," he said, "do you remember a man named Heyward Miller?"

"Miller?" She screwed her face up reflectively. "No, the name doesn't sound familiar. Course there's Mrs. Miller at the post office; I don't suppose there's any connection."

"No, no connection." He frowned and looked at the tasseled rug at his feet. "Heyward Miller and his wife lived out at the old Yunker place maybe eight, nine years ago. They were only here six months when his wife died and he sold the place to the Kalkbrenners. Does that help you to remember, Mrs. Parch?"

She scratched her cheek lightly. "I do remember *something* about him. Yes, now I do." Her breath became shorter, and she put one hand on her bosom. "Oh, yes, Miller. That awful man! How could I forget about *that*?"

"I thought you'd remember, Mrs. Parch, I mean, after those things he said about you. He was a mighty disturbed fellow, the way I heard the story. Of course, I don't really know the whole truth; so it's not my place to pass along any opinion. . . ."

Mrs. Parch drew herself up stiffly. "The man was a fool," she said harshly. "You ask anybody about him. He just didn't *belong* out here."

"Well, just for my own sake, Mrs. Parch, could we talk about what happened? Just for the record?"

"I've got nothing to say about it."

Atkins sighed. "The way I was told the story, this man Miller and his wife were married about a year when they bought the Yunker's place. She was going to have a baby in three months. Only something happened one night; she got sick, very sick, and he tried to put through a call to the doctor. . . ."

Mrs. Parch closed her eyes and clenched her fists on her lap.

"Now, I wasn't in the county at the time, you understand, so all I can do is report what I was told. But as I understand it, Miller got on the phone, and you and another lady were talking. Swapping recipes or something like that."

"It was Mrs. Anderson," the woman said quietly. "I was talking to Mrs. Anderson."

"She still live in the neighborhood?"

"No. Her and her husband moved to California five years ago, and she died."

"Anyway," Mr. Atkins said, mopping his face, "this man Miller asked if you'd get off the line so he could call the doctor for his wife. The story I hear is that you both refused."

"He was rude," Mrs. Parch said. "He was downright insulting to us."

"Yes. Nevertheless, you wouldn't get off the line, and Miller couldn't get through. Matter of fact, he claims you stayed on deliberately so's he couldn't get through."

"That's a lie!" Mrs. Parch said passionately. "We talked just as long as we had to and no longer."

"But he didn't get the doctor in time, that was the whole point, wasn't it? And his wife died."

"Now look here, Mr. Atkins—"

The thin man raised a bony hand. "Please, Mrs. Parch, I didn't come out to rehash the past. All that is your business and none of mine. Except that something happened this morning, and it sort of *makes* it the business of the county sheriff's office."

"What do you mean?"

"Well, I don't reckon you know what happened to Miller after he sold his place to the Kalkbrenners. He was pretty broken up about losing his wife and all; he moved to New York City. Six months later, he got in trouble for breaking into a hardware store. Didn't take anything but a few boxes of nails and stuff like that, and he was sent to prison for about six months. It was in prison that they decided he was mentally incompetent, and he was remanded to a state institution. He's been there ever since, almost eight years. Only now he's got away, Mrs. Parch, and that's why we're a little concerned."

"Got away?" The woman crumpled the hem of her apron into her hand. "How do you mean, got away?"

"Escaped. We got the news late last night, but it's over a week since it happened. Somebody at the institution thought of notifying us since Miller used to do a lot of raving about . . . well, what happened. Kind of made us uneasy, Mrs. Parch. I guess you can understand that. Now we don't know for *sure* that he wants to make trouble for you, but it didn't seem right to take any chances. You see what I mean?"

Mrs. Parch stood up, the bell of her dress swaying slightly. Her voice quivered when she said: "You mean you think this Miller is after *me?* For what happened eight years ago?"

"The man's not to be trusted," Atkins said quietly. "That's the whole point. The institution was maybe two hundred miles from here, but if he was really out for—well, I guess you'd call it revenge—that's not such a distance to travel. I wanted to warn you about the possibility, that's all."

She put her hands to her face. "But I'm all alone out here!" she said. "He could murder me in my sleep!"

"We're really not *sure* of anything, Mrs. Parch. I don't want you to get that idea. But if you could get a neighbor or somebody to stay with you for a few days or else visit a relative or something, it just might be a good idea."

"Can't the sheriff protect me?" She caught a sob in her throat.

"I'm afraid that's not possible right now, Mrs. Parch. Not unless we had more positive information that Miller was in the vicinity. The way things are now, this is just a wild surmise. You understand?"

"Yes, yes," she said numbly. "Maybe I could go to my sister's place. In Cedar Falls. . . ."

"That might be a good idea."

"I haven't seen her in ten years. We never got along, my sister and me."

Mr. Atkins smiled. "There's always a good time for a reconciliation, eh, Mrs. Parch?" He stood up. "Listen, I didn't come here just to alarm you. There's nothing definite about this, nothing at all. If we learn anything further, we'll call you up just as soon as we do. And if you have any reason to get in touch with us, just ask for the county sheriff's office. Speak to me personally. You remember the name?"

"Atkins," Mrs. Parch whispered.

"Daryl Atkins," the man said. Then he smiled broadly and stood up. "I sure wouldn't mind that cold drink now, Mrs. Parch."

Atkins's automobile wasn't five minutes out of her driveway when the telephone jangled four times. She answered it and heard Mrs. Giles say: "Helen? Did I see a car stop at your place?"

"No," she said raspingly. "You didn't see any car."

"But I thought *sure* I—"

"Mind your own business!" the woman said angrily. "Can't you ever learn to mind your own business?"

"Well!" Mrs. Giles said. She hung up, and Mrs. Parch cursed the fact that she hadn't done it first. A few minutes later, the telephone rang three times, but she ignored it. Instead, she went upstairs as rapidly as her weight and failing breath allowed and began rummaging through the bureau drawers for the telephone number of her sister in Cedar Falls. She found it at last among an album of yellowed snapshots and brought the scrap of paper downstairs. She picked up the phone receiver without any attempt at surreptitiousness, but Mrs. Giles and Mrs. Kalkbrenner had already concluded their conversation concerning her bad manners. She dialed the operator and had to wait almost ten minutes before they had a line cleared to

Cedar Falls. Even then it did no good because the Cedar Falls operator reported that her sister's telephone had been discontinued for the summer. It was just like Margaret, who had probably gone to the beach house, to save a few dollars by cutting off the phone service. She grunted angrily when she heard the news, and the unkind thoughts about her sister drove out all her fears about Miller for a while. She was even sufficiently recovered to complete the labeling of her preserves and spent a busy afternoon hauling them down to the cellar. She was so preoccupied that when the phone rang five times (it was for Mrs. Ammons, a new neighbor), she didn't care enough to listen in despite her natural curiosity. By evening, she hadn't forgotten about Atkins's warning, but her nerves had been soothed considerably.

It had been a long day. The sun had stayed high and hot, and it was almost eight-thirty when it finally dipped behind the brown hills and let the cool night air take over. She made herself a simple supper of yesterday's leftovers, did a little sewing, and then settled down with a rental-library novel to conclude the evening. The telephone rang twice, but she ignored it. A moment later, she heard a dog barking near the house. It was the Giles' dog, an aging collie, not given to outbursts of canine temper. She wondered at it mildly and put down the book. When the barking continued, she took off her glasses, got up, and went to the window. The sudden recollection of her possible peril sent a shock of fear through her body. She went to the front door, unlatched it, and looked outside, into the uninformative darkness. She closed it again, bolted it, and went to turn on an additional lamp in the parlor. The Giles' dog stopped barking and began to howl until someone applied the end of a rolled newspaper to its bottom. There was a clumping noise below, in her cellar, as if something had fallen to the stone floor, and she knew that she was no longer the sole occupant of the house.

She almost stumbled on her way to the telephone. When she picked up the receiver and heard Mrs. Giles nasal voice, she gasped. "Please! Get off the phone!"

"Who's that?" Mrs. Giles said.

"Helen," Mrs. Parch said. "It's Helen! For God's sake, Emma, get off the line. I have to call the police—"

"The police? Whatever for?"

"I don't have time to explain! I have to call the sheriff's office! Get off the phone! Get off the phone, or I'll be killed!"

Mrs. Kalkbrenner laughed. "Now who'd want to kill you, Helen? You must be having nightmares."

"I thought you said it was *preserves* you were putting up," Mrs. Giles tittered. "Sure it wasn't a little cider, Helen?"

"For heaven's sake!" Mrs. Parch shrieked. "Get off the phone!"

"You see what I mean," Mrs. Giles said significantly to Mrs. Kalkbrenner. "You see what I was telling you?"

"Umph," Mrs. Kalkbrenner said. "I certainly do."

"Some people just don't know what courtesy means," Mrs. Giles said. "It's a good thing to really *know* your neighbors, isn't it, June?"

"It sure is, Emma."

"Please, please," Mrs. Parch sobbed. "I've *got* to get through. I've *got* to use the phone—"

She dropped the receiver when she heard the sound of creaking stairs in the cellar. She ran into the kitchen and slammed the cellar door shut. The latch didn't hold, so she put a chair against it and ran back to the dangling receiver. She heard Mrs. Giles' voice again and screamed in hatred and terror at her. She was still screaming when the hand took the receiver from her and replaced it on the hook. It was a thick, hairy hand and possessed of terrible strength.

EGO BOOST

by Richard O. Lewis

One's ability to shape his own destiny is usually conditioned by self-confidence—but occasionally by self-restraint.

Police Lieutenant DeWitt called me shortly after 8:00 p.m. "Dr. Harper," he said, "I have a customer for you. Picked him off the bridge about a half hour ago. Are you interested?"

Bridge? Then I suddenly remembered one of the things we had been discussing when we had last met. "Oh, sure!" I said. "Of course I'm interested! Tonight?"

"Either that," came the lieutenant's voice, "or I'll have to book him and lock him up till morning. That could make matters worse, you know."

"Definitely!" I agreed. "Better bring him right over."

"I haven't been able to find out much about him," the lieutenant continued, "but I'll give you what I learned so you'll have something to go on. Thirty-five years of age, an accountant, married, no children, lives in the suburbs, won't give us any reason for his attempt to jump from the bridge. Guess that's it."

"Good enough," I said. "I'll be waiting."

After replacing the telephone, I leaned back in my chair for a moment of reflection. The rate of suicides and attempted suicides had been climbing steadily during the past year. For some reason, a leap from the railing of the high bridge seemed to be the favorite method for ending it all, perhaps because once the leap was made, the point of no return would be reached immediately, and if the person changed his mind on the way down, there was nothing he could do about it. Also, it wasn't messy.

During the past couple of years, Lieutenant DeWitt and I had met at a few social gatherings and had become friends. At our last little get-together, the subject of increasing suicidal attempts had come up, and we had both agreed that the present method of treating such cases was wholly inadequate. If a man were emotionally depressed enough to attempt to take his own life, a reprimand from police officers and a threat to deny him his personal freedom could only aggravate the condition, and a jail or station house was certainly not a desirable place to conduct therapy of a psychological nature, as it were.

As a practicing psychologist, I felt certain that a man-to-man talk with the distressed person in a pleasing environment offered a possible solution for the problem. By utilizing my years of formal training concerning the vagaries of the human mind, it should not be a too difficult task for me to ferret out the underlying cause for the suicidal attempt—bring it out into the light of day, as it were—and lay it by the heels for all time. At least it was better than anything else at hand.

So, with the lieutenant's rather skeptical assent, I had volunteered my services—on a purely experimental basis, of course.

By the time Lieutenant DeWitt arrived and was ushered into my study, along with the man who was destined to be the first experimental case, I had everything in readiness: soft lighting that scarcely reached the book-lined shelves of the walls, a tiny but comforting glow from the gas logs in the fireplace, subdued music—an atmosphere designed to induce relaxation.

Lieutenant DeWitt introduced the man as Bertram

Brunell, and as I gave a friendly shake to his unre-
sponsive hand, I noted that his posture was one of ut-
ter dejection. His eyes were downcast and restless,
and his lean face, pale from lack of sunshine or out-
door activity, sagged as if holding it together were too
much effort.

"I am pleased to know you," I said, and indicated
an overstuffed chair facing the davenport. "Make
yourself comfortable while I show Lieutenant DeWitt
out. I'll be right back."

At the door, the lieutenant paused a moment. "Call
me as soon as you've finished," he suggested. "I may
have to send someone after him, you know."

"Right."

Back in the study, I rubbed my hands warmly together, sat down, and smiled companionably at the
man across the low coffee table from me. "Well, Mr.
Brunell," I began, deciding to take the direct approach,
"it seems that we have a bit of a problem."

Brunell gazed unseeingly at the hands in his lap,
the fingers of which were tensely twining and untwin-
ing about each other, and said nothing.

"Sometimes when we bring the problem into the
open and discuss it, it has a tendency to diminish in
stature," I said. "Do you care to tell me about it?"

Brunell's gaze left his nervous fingers, his eyes
darting right and left as if searching for some avenue
of escape.

An introvert? Undoubtedly; a man who kept his
problems locked up secretly and forever within himself, denying them an outlet, letting the increasing
pressure of them mount to the point of final explosion.
He had reached that point earlier in the evening, and
although he had been restrained from leaping from
the bridge, the pressure was still there and running
dangerously high.

I got up quickly, went to my liquor cabinet, and
poured two martinis from the supply I had prepared
for the occasion, just in case the necessity arose.

"Here," I said, proffering him one of the long-stemmed glasses. "You'll no doubt find it quite relaxing."

He unlaced his fingers, took the glass in hand, eyed it hesitantly for a moment, then took a sip. Evidently finding the liquor to his liking, he took a long swallow. "I—I don't drink much," he said, his hand trembling slightly as he put the half-emptied glass on the coffee table. "Never have."

It figured. Some men could resort to alcohol in times of stress, go on a binge, flip their lid, and relieve the pressure—for a while, at least—but not Brunell. He just was not the type.

I took a sip from my own drink and resumed my place opposite him. "Sometimes," I said, "we let our problems pile up within us, keep them locked inside, permit them to magnify themselves until they assume such gigantic proportions that they seem insurmountable."

Brunell stared absently at his glass. I hoped he was paying some heed to what I was telling him.

"If we discuss our major difficulty with someone else, bring it out into the open, as it were, we can then view it in an abstract rather than an emotional manner."

Brunell picked up his glass, drained it, and replaced it on the table. He nodded slightly, as if in agreement, but remained silent.

I knew from past endeavors that some people experienced great reluctance when it came to baring their souls to others, even to friends. Yet I had to reach him in some way if I were to save him from himself.

"Sometimes a problem is so personal in nature that it is almost impossible to discuss it openly with a stranger," I said, refilling his glass from the martini supply. "Even so, mere conversation—sympathetic understanding, as it were—can often help one view his difficulties in a more rational environment."

Although Brunell continued to remain silent, I

could see by the way he had twisted his head to one side, his brow creased into thoughtful lines, that I had begun to reach him and that he was trying to get things sorted out in his mind.

Finally, he began nodding his head slowly as if he had reached at least a partial understanding of his inner self. "I—I guess I'm just a coward," he breathed.

It was not exactly the response for which I had hoped, but it was better than nothing. I could see now that a major part of his trouble was a deep-seated inferiority complex. He lacked self-confidence, was in desperate need of an ego boost.

"We are all cowards in one way or another," I said. "We all have one or more fears of various kinds—claustrophobia, cardiophobia, air phobia, felinophobia, to name a few—and if we let them dominate our lives, we are in for trouble."

I then proceeded to give him a ten-minute lecture of a therapeutic nature, stressing the importance of human dignity, belief in one's self, and the ability to shape one's destiny. I finished by citing several cases wherein some of my patients had achieved remarkable success under my guidance.

When I had finished, he nodded his head and took a sip from his glass. "I guess you're right," he said.

He was obviously more relaxed now, maybe because he had begun to get things straightened out in his head or because of the liquor, or due to a combination of both. Anyway, I felt that my efforts were beginning to bear fruit.

"I made the mistake of letting things pile up for the past couple of years," he continued, "until tonight when they reached a climax. . . ."

"Right," I said. "The final straw that broke the camel's back, as it were. Then, afraid that you did not have the ability to eliminate your difficulty, you chose to eliminate yourself instead."

Brunell focused his gaze on his glass, eyes narrowing.

I decided that now was the time to do more probing. "If you have a definite problem that you would care to discuss with me," I suggested, "something you would like to bring out into the open perhaps . . ."

He shook his head slowly. "N-no," he said. "You have already helped me see things in a different light. I guess it won't hurt to tell you that I drew out all my savings, cashed in all the assets I could, and was preparing to fly away to parts unknown. Then I realized that I would still have the problem that would hound me into sleepless nights wherever I went. In desperation, I finally decided to take the easy and final way of complete escape by—well, you know . . ."

"Above all else," I reminded him, "a man must believe in himself!"

Suddenly, Brunell tossed off the rest of his liquor and got to his feet, his long, pale face molded into determined lines and his eyes meeting mine for the first time since he had entered the room. "You have done a lot for me," he said, extending his hand, "and I want to thank you. I feel certain that I can shape my own destiny from now on."

"If I have helped you," I said, enjoying the firm clasp of his hand, "that in itself is my reward. And no more bridge jumping. Right?"

"Right."

I phoned Lieutenant DeWitt immediately after Brunell's departure. "Dr. Harper here," I said. "I am happy to report that our first experimental case has been concluded in a highly satisfactory manner."

"Do you want me to pick him up?"

"Not at all. I sent him on his way in a cab just a few minutes ago after relaxing him with some drinks and giving him a much-needed ego boost, a strong dose of self-confidence, as it were."

"I see. I must admit that I was a bit skeptical at first." He paused a moment. "You sure he'll be all right?"

"I personally guarantee it. No more bridge jumping. He left here a changed man!"

After cradling the phone, I picked up my book and resumed reading where I had left off earlier. I must have read for a full two hours and was considering going to bed when the phone came suddenly to life. I scooped it up. "Dr. Harper here," I said.

"You may have given your patient too much of an ego boost." It was the voice of Lieutenant DeWitt. "Or too much liquor. Or both."

"Why?" I gasped. "Surely Brunell didn't go back to the bridge and jump?"

"We don't know yet. We can't find him. We've been searching for him everywhere, including the river, for the past hour."

"I don't understand. . . ."

"The manager of a motel at the edge of town reported hearing shots in one of his units a little more than an hour ago. When we investigated, we found the bullet-riddled body of Mrs. Brunell, along with the mutilated body of what had obviously been her boy friend. Naturally, we're looking for Brunell."

That revelation left me stunned for a moment. Then I suddenly remembered what Brunell had said about having cashed in all his assets, and the answer became crystal clear. "Well, you needn't search in the river anymore," I said. "Right now, Brunell is undoubtedly on his way to parts unknown with his life's savings in his pocket."

"Thanks a lot!" There was a sharp click as DeWitt broke the connection.

I gazed thoughtfully at the silent telephone for a moment or two. Well, my psychological approach to the patient's difficulties had not been a *total* failure, I reasoned. Brunell, it seemed, had at least solved a couple of his problems in a very direct and decisive manner, as it were.

MARTHA: IN MEMORIAM

by Richard Hardwick

It started in July at the Dunbars' cocktail party. I had planned to pass it up and take in an early movie, but Martha called me at six and asked me to take her.

"I was going with Tommy," she said, frank as always, "but a business meeting came up, and he's stuck. I do want to go, Norman. Be an angel?"

I told her I'd be an angel or anything else she wanted me to be. I was in love with Martha, faithfully, slavishly, completely, hopelessly. Martha knew it—in fact, everyone knew it. But to Martha, I was simply the nodding head and sympathetic eyes she told her troubles to, the spare when Tommy or Joey or Bill fell through. I didn't like the role, but it was better than not being with Martha at all.

It was after seven when I rang the bell of her apartment. She opened the door, and I stood there and looked at her. She was beautiful. The most beautiful woman I had ever seen, and each time it was like seeing her for the first time, so lovely she took my breath away, so unattainable my heart felt like a rock inside me.

"You are an angel," she said, kissing me on the cheek.

"Marry me. We'll fly away and have a dozen kids, all as beautiful as you and angelic as me."

She laughed. "I'm almost ready," she said. She leaned to straighten her stocking. I smiled. Good old Norman. Just one of the girls.

The Dunbars' party was a carbon copy of every other cocktail party that summer. Or any other summer. The same faces, the same jaded conversation growing louder as the empties piled up beneath the bar. There was one exception that night. Ed Pollard was there.

Carl Dunbar, the host, steered Martha and me across the room as soon as we arrived. "Norm, a fella here claims to be an old pal of yours," Carl said. We stopped at a group that was laughing over someone's joke. I recognized Ed immediately, standing at the other side of the knot of laughing guests. The same tall, handsome, self-assured Ed I'd known fifteen years before, a little gray at the temples now, but no paunch, no sag beneath the chin.

"Norm!" He moved around the group, his hand out, teeth flashing in a smile. "Norm Grundy, you old son-ofagun!" His hand grabbed mine, squeezed, but his eyes were on Martha.

"Hello, Ed. It's been a long time." I turned to Martha. "I'd like you to meet Martha Young. Martha, this is Ed Pollard."

"Fraternity brother, roommate, and old friend," Ed added. "I'm very happy to know you, Martha."

It must have started at that very minute, though I wasn't aware of it because everyone looked at Martha the same way. You couldn't help yourself.

After the party, we joined Ed and several others for dinner. Ed sat on one side of Martha and told us about himself. He was in town to start the ball rolling on his company's new Southern plant, and when the plant was done, he was staying on as regional manager. I recalled that Ed had married the daughter of B. J. Ashwell, Ashwell Pharmaceuticals, which cut a large slice of the country's patent medicine melon. Ed, who would have met up with success under almost any circumstance, rose rapidly with the company.

He said he was staying at the Imperial and asked me to have lunch with him one day soon. It occurred to me later that Ed made no mention of his wife that night.

I might never have learned of Martha's affair with Ed Pollard if she hadn't told me herself. Martha used me as a sort of sounding board, an echo of herself. We were having cocktails at Joe's, a little bar off Broad Street, one afternoon a couple of weeks later. Martha had phoned me at the office and asked me to meet her, and now she looked at me over the table, a smile on her lips and dreamy happiness in her eyes.

"You're not feeling that way just because you're having a drink with me," I said. "What is it?"

She gave a little laugh and put her hand over mine on the table. Then she drew it back and slowly turned her cocktail glass on the table. "I'm in love, Norman. I'm in love with the most wonderful man in the world."

I listened to anything and everything Martha wanted to say, but I was frank in everything I said to her. "I'm sorry to hear that because I know I'm not quite the most wonderful man in the world. Who is the undeserving dog?"

"Norman!" she said sternly, then her face softened. "I'm sorry, Norm. I know how you feel. . . ."

"No hearts and flowers. Who is he?" I picked up my drink and saw that my hands shook. I was always afraid of losing Martha, and that was crazy, too, because I never had her. She wasn't mine to lose. Martha was twenty-eight and single by choice. It would have been a fairly safe bet to say that almost every male who ever knew her had proposed—one way or another—to Martha. I knew a woman as irresistible as she was could not remain single forever. Someone was bound to come along sometime.

The dreamy look came back to her face. "Ed," she said. "Ed Pollard."

My mouth dropped open. I put my glass down, turning it over, spilling my half-finished drink over the table and myself. "Ed . . . *Pollard?* He's—he's married, Martha. Surely you know that much about him! What on earth have you got yourself into?"

Suddenly, she was angry. "You're not my—my guardian, Norman! You needn't be so righteous!"

Martha was no starry-eyed, innocent little girl, but I'd thought she had better sense than this. "I'm not being righteous, just realistic. What do you think he's going to do, get a divorce?"

"That's exactly what he's going to do. As soon as the time is right."

"*Ha!*" I motioned for the waitress to bring me another drink. "Ed Pollard hasn't changed a damned bit. The same old master."

Martha rose quickly, picked up her handbag. "I've heard enough, Norman. Good-bye."

I took hold of her wrist. "No—don't go. I'm sorry. It's just that . . ." She sat down again, and we were both silent as the waitress cleaned away the mess I'd made and set the fresh drink before me. The waitress went away, and I took Martha's hand. "I'm serious. I *know* Ed! He's vain, selfish. He's insincere—"

"I think we'd better change the subject. I shouldn't have said anything about this to you. I thought you'd understand."

"You'll get hurt. You'll get hurt bad, and I don't want to see that happen to you."

"You think you know him," Martha said almost patronizingly, "because you and he were in college together. Are you the same as you were then? Of course not! And neither is Ed. You don't know him at all."

"I know he married the Ashwell money, and he's not going to turn it loose. No, not even for you."

She took her lipstick from her handbag and carefully began to apply it. It was a habit with Martha when she wasn't satisfied with something.

"Do you have any idea," I said, "how much dough the Ashwells have?"

She looked at me angrily. "I misjudged you. You're—you're jealous!"

That stung, and I suppose I showed it.

Martha bit her lip. "Please forgive me, Norman. I—I shouldn't have said that."

"Oh, but you should because you're right. I *am* jealous! I'm jealous of every man who looks at you, but I also know Ed Pollard!"

This time she got up, and I couldn't stop her. She picked up her bag and said good-bye. I watched her go across the room, making her way among the tables. I saw the heads at the bar turn as she went past and out the door into the sunlit street.

Martha had made a mistake this time, I was sure. A bad one.

I didn't see her for some time after that. It wasn't because I didn't try. I called her every day at the department store where she worked as an ad illustrator and at her apartment in the evenings. She was angry about the way I'd acted; either that, or she was discovering I had been right about Pollard.

It was almost unbearable being treated as I was. The cocktail hours I spent with Martha, the shows or parties I took her to, were all I had, and even so, they were simply a form of self-torture. Maybe there's a streak of masochism in all of us; this was the way mine operated.

I saw Ed Pollard occasionally at the golf club or some civic function or other. As the Ashwell plant progressed, Ed's influence became greater. He was bringing money and employment to a town that wanted to grow. I discovered through a mutual acquaintance (Ed did not cultivate me once he found that I was simply a fringe character without position or influence) that Ed had bought a large house on Valley Road and that his wife and children, who were vacationing abroad, were joining him in six or eight weeks. I wondered how Martha fit into this picture. It was certainly not the action of a man contemplating divorce.

At last, Martha agreed to meet me one afternoon. I knew by her voice she was upset. She was quiet as we took a booth at Joe's, and I ordered the drinks. The drinks came. Martha drank almost half hers and then looked over at me.

"Have you seen him lately? Have you talked to him?" she said.

"I see him occasionally at the club. He's a little out of my class, you know."

"But—but you have talked to him. What does he talk about?"

"Not you, if that's what's worrying you."

She was annoyed. "You know what I mean. What are his plans?"

"I thought you knew what his plans were," I said. "You told me he was going to get a divorce." I toyed with my drink. "The place he bought on Valley Road isn't exactly a honeymoon cottage, Martha. His family's joining him here in a few weeks."

"Why, he told me!" she said.

"He *told* you? What are you, Martha, some simpering high-school kid? He told you what? That he was crazy for you, and sneaking around wasn't enough for either of you, and he was going to divorce her and throw away God knows how many millions?" I stopped and took a gulp of my drink. "I think you've lost your senses."

She was crying softly, soundlessly, her head down and both hands clutching her glass as though it were a stanchion to keep her from falling.

"I didn't want to see you get hurt," I went on, "but you are, you already are hurt." I reached out and put my hands over hers. "Why don't you break off? My last dozen proposals are still open."

"I love him, Norman. I can't help that."

"Then have it out with him. If he's promised these things, tell him to get busy."

"He says it would ruin him now if anyone found out about—us. No one knows, no one, that is, but you. I had to tell you."

"How do you know it's such a secret?" I said.

She looked at me in alarm. "Have you heard anything?"

I shook my head. "No."

"We never meet here in town," she said. "Always away from here, at a motel or hotel in some other city."

"It's not like you."

She smiled. "Don't be Victorian, Norman. And there's nothing sordid about it. We love each other; that's the difference."

"Ed Pollard loves Ed Pollard—and money."

She was thinking of something else and paid no attention to what I'd said. After a moment, she looked at her watch, ran her lipstick over her lips, and got up. "I'll talk to him. You'll see. I'm right. I *know* I am."

The phone beside my bed rang that night after midnight. It was Martha. "Norman . . . Norman, I've got to talk to someone. . . ."

I sat up on the edge of the bed, tapping a cigarette out of the pack, spilling half the pack on the floor. "What is it? What's wrong?"

"Can I—can I come to your apartment?"

I could tell by her voice that she had been crying. "I'll pick you up," I said. "Where are you?"

"No . . . I'll take a cab. You don't mind . . . ?"

"I'll be here. I'll be waiting. And, Martha, whatever it is, don't worry. Okay?"

She said something unintelligible, and the line went dead. I sat there for several seconds, listening to the buzzing of the telephone, my cigarette unlit in my hand.

Her face was streaked when I met her at the door.

"I'll get you a drink. Meantime, get in there and wash your face. You're a mess."

She tried to smile, and I kissed her on the forehead and went to the portable bar. I mixed two stiff drinks.

Martha sat on the sofa, on the very edge, primly, the drink revolving nervously in her hands. "You were right, Norman. You were right about everything. He had no intention of getting a divorce. He never did, not from the very first." She looked up at me, her eyes almost blank, as though from shock. "He said—he said he'd kill me if I didn't stop bothering him."

I stiffened. "He said—*what!*"

She nodded rapidly, then smiled weakly and ran her hand through her hair. "The funny part, the very hilarious part, is that I still love him. Maybe even more now."

She finished her drink and got up to make herself another. I watched her until she sat down again.

"You're a threat to him now," I said. "You represent something that could upset his very carefully balanced apple cart. The thing for you to do is forget him, forget him completely. Go away somewhere if you have to, but get Ed Pollard out of your system."

"I don't understand it," she said quietly. "I know he's just what you said he was, and yet I can't help loving him. How do you explain it?"

"I *don't* explain it! I simply say you've reached the end of a damn poorly conceived interlude in your life."

We talked on in the same vein for more than an hour, Martha drinking more than usual. Nothing was accomplished, at least as far as I could see. She had simply come to me as she always did, not as to an adviser but to someone who would just listen, a tape recorder that talked back. She kept pouring her own drinks, and at last she passed out on the sofa. I took her in the bedroom and spent the balance of the night on the sofa myself.

When I awakened the next morning, Martha was gone. There was a hurried little note apologizing and a postscript that told me she'd get in touch with me later.

But I left the city that afternoon on a business trip and was gone for a week. The minute I returned, I phoned Martha. I learned that she hadn't been to her office in four days, nor had she called in. I dialed her apartment but got no answer, and then I called the superintendent of the apartment house, who knew me, and he told me he hadn't seen her for several days. After that, I phoned several of our mutual friends, and they all said they hadn't seen her for a number of days.

I wondered. Maybe Martha and Pollard had gone away. Maybe she had been right all along. I picked up the telephone and slowly dialed the temporary offices Ed had taken during the construction of the plant. A secretary answered. Yes, she said, Mr. Pollard was in, who was calling? Gently I placed the receiver down. A hollow feeling of fear gnawed at me. I knew Martha—perhaps as well as anyone knew her—and it was not at all in her character to go away without explanation. Something was wrong, badly wrong. I remembered the threat Pollard had made, but I put it from my mind.

I drove to her apartment and had the superintendent let me in. Her clothes seemed to be all there, though I couldn't be certain. The apartment gave the impression of its occupant's having merely stepped out for a pack of cigarettes or a movie.

"If she comes back," I said to the superintendent, "please call me right away."

I was seriously worried now. I went home and telephoned the hospitals, even the jail and the city morgue, but there was no trace of Martha.

I was on the verge of calling the missing persons

bureau when I again remembered the threat Ed Pollard had made. Martha's determination not to break off with Pollard, the last time I'd seen her, had certainly not lessened. I supposed it had a great deal to do with her pride, for Martha was not familiar with being rejected. Very likely she had gone back to him, threatening him with exposure, and Pollard could easily have panicked and done exactly what he had threatened to do.

But I waited another week. I had to be sure. By this time I was finding sleep difficult. My weight had dropped five or six pounds. I made the decision one night as I lay in bed staring into the darkness, seeing Martha's face, hearing her voice. I'd go to Pollard, and I'd demand to know what he had done.

The following day, while on a business trip in another city, I—on impulse—bought a gun. It was a small target pistol, a .22 caliber revolver. I had never so much as fired a gun of any sort in my entire life. I purchased several boxes of cartridges and practiced shooting in a woods along the highway as I returned home.

I planned to use the gun to persuade Pollard I meant business. I wanted him alone, of course, and I wanted him off guard. Pollard, I knew, walked the four blocks from his office to his hotel every day after work. I'd heard that he was moving to the house he had bought on Valley Road as soon as the decorators were finished, probably in a week or so, and my best chance would be before he made the move.

He left his office at five each afternoon, and I stationed myself in my car outside the office building. The first day, someone was with him. The second day, he came out alone and turned in the direction of his hotel.

My heart pounded as I pulled to the curb abreast of him. I smiled at him through the open car window.

"Hi, Ed! Hop in, and I'll give you a lift!"

He seemed to hesitate for a moment, then crossed

the sidewalk to the curb. "Hello, Norm. Haven't seen you in a while." He got in and slammed the door. I pulled away from the curb.

"Hear your family's joining you soon," I said, wondering if my voice sounded as strange to Ed as it did to me.

"That's right."

"I'm looking forward to meeting them." I moved my hand casually inside my coat and felt the gun tucked there under my belt.

"Fine," he said. He was quite obviously not in a talkative mood.

"By the way, Ed," I said, feeling the tremor in my voice as I spoke. "Have you—seen anything of Martha lately?"

I turned my head slightly to get his reaction. He had a cigarette in his mouth. His hand paused—just for the briefest instant—as he reached to punch the dash lighter. His recovery was quick. He smiled at me with that man-to-man charm he could command so well when the occasion arose.

"Martha?" he said. "Martha who?"

I turned down a side street, one that led out of town. "Martha Young. You're not trying to tell me you don't know her?" I could hardly squeeze the words out. The gall of the man! Martha *who!*

He turned directly toward me. There was no smile now on his face, but a look of shrewd appraisal. "Is that the girl you introduced me to at some cocktail party a few months back? No, I haven't seen her, Norm. And it puzzles me that you should ask me—"

"Puzzles you! Come off it, you rotten—"

He must have noticed my hand inside my coat, or I imagined he did. Anyhow, in my completely wound-up condition, I jerked the gun out. Ed put his hand up in a gesture of shielding himself the instant I fired. The bullet went through the hand, through the fleshy part between the thumb and forefinger, and struck him in the chest.

"Norm . . . ?" He lifted the hand, looked at it incredulously. I squeezed the trigger again, with the muzzle almost touching him, and as I did this, those big-little-boy eyes looked at me so pathetically, so questioningly, that I was momentarily filled with sudden regret for what I had done.

But he had murdered Martha, of that I was certain, and this was for Martha, *in memoriam,* so to speak. And so I emptied the gun into Ed Pollard.

When the killing was discovered, it went completely unexplained. By some miracle, no one saw me with Ed, and I dumped his body on a quiet dirt road outside of town and then came back to my apartment. I washed the plastic seat covers where Pollard had bled, and I threw the gun in the river. No one could come up with any motive for the killing of a man like Ed Pollard. The newspapers praised him for his civic-mindedness and for the industry he represented. By the end of the week, the opinion was that he'd been held up and killed by a person or persons unknown.

What actually happened remained only in my memory, and in time, I was sure, even that would fade because I had done what had to be done. I had done what was right. In the meantime, Martha's employers put in a missing persons report on Martha.

I was in my office, unpacking my briefcase from a short trip upstate. I heard the door open. I looked up, and there she was. Martha. Tall, deeply tanned, ineffably beautiful. A contrite smile played about her lips.

"Hello, Norman. I'm back."

I couldn't speak. I could only stare.

Her smile faded. "What's wrong? You look very strange. I thought you'd be glad to see me."

"You . . . where . . ." I had to sit down; I couldn't go on. Martha came and sat on the corner of the desk. I said at last, "No one knew where you were . . . Ed . . . I thought he . . ."

"I'm sorry, Norman. I didn't mean to worry you, I

really didn't, but I had to go away and think it through. I took your advice, Norman. I suppose I always will. I went to a little place in Mexico, a little fishing village. I painted, and I read." She smiled. "I got over him. I was a fool, but I did get over him."

"But I . . . I thought he . . ."

"What is it? What's wrong?" Martha said.

"Did you know—that he's dead?"

She slowly stood up. "Ed?"

I nodded, watching her face closely. She moved to the window and looked down into the streets below. Finally, she said, "How did he die?"

"He was shot. He was shot seven times with a pistol."

"Ed—shot? Who on earth would shoot Ed?"

I stood up and straightened some papers on my desk. "The police . . . nobody seems to know."

Her back was still to me as she stared out the window. The street sounds suddenly seemed louder. High above the city, I heard a flight of jets. Martha's head straightened, and she said, "You started to say something about him when I came in."

A prickly feeling came over me. There was something in her voice that hadn't been there before, a change of tone. Her hands were stiffly by her sides.

"Did I? It was—I was just so surprised to see you. I thought—well, you did say he threatened you. . . ."

She turned quickly, her gaze intent on my face. I'd never seen her look that way before, aloof—and, somehow, cold. "Yes," she said. "Yes, that's right, isn't it?"

She walked slowly toward me, and quite suddenly she seemed like another person, a complete stranger. I couldn't take my eyes away from her; there was something compelling, hypnotic about the way she looked at me, coming closer, still closer. Then, with her face inches from mine, she raised her hand, and with the tips of her fingers, she traced the outline of my jaw, my mouth.

"I did tell you he'd threatened me," she said softly, "didn't I?"

She stepped back then, turned away from me. She took her lipstick from her purse and applied it carefully, expertly. She turned and smiled at me.

"Buy me a drink? I've missed Joe's—and I've missed you, Norman."

I hesitated. I knew I should have said, "I've missed you, too," but I couldn't say it.

"Poor Norman." She took my arm. "That whole thing's past now. Now it'll be just like old times, won't it?"

She stood there smiling up at me. There was no question as to what she had done. She couldn't have spelled it out any clearer for me.

"Sure," I heard myself say, "like old times."